LOOKING AT THE WORDS OF OUR PEOPLE

**First Nations
Analysis of Literature**

Collected by Jeannette Armstrong

LOOKING AT THE WORDS OF OUR PEOPLE

**First Nations
Analysis of Literature**

Collected by Jeannette Armstrong

THEYTUS BOOKS LTD.
Penticton, British Columbia
1993

THEYTUS BOOKS LTD.
Copyright 1993 remains with artist and/or author

We would like to thank the *Canada Council* for their financial support.

Theytus Books Ltd.
Paperback - ISBN : 0-919441-52-1

Canadian Cataloging in Publication Data

Main entry under title:

Looking at the Words of Our People:

ISBN : 0-919441-52-1

1.   Canadian literature (English)—Indian authors—History and criticism.* 2. Canadian literature (English)—20th century—History and criticism.* 3. Canadian literature (English)—Metis authors—History and criticism,* I. Armstrong, Jeannette C.
PS8089.5.I6L66 1993   C810.9'897   C94-910081-1
PR9188.2.I6L66 1993

Cover Design : Richard Gray
Cover Art : Rose Spahan
Book Design : Forrest A. Funmaker

THEYTUS BOOKS LTD.
257 Brunswick Street
Penticton, V2A 5P9, British Columbia

Printed and bound in Canada

Contents

Editor's Note

In the past two years I have been invited to address conferences convened by English departments, participate on panels about Native Literature in Native Studies programs and attend forums on Post Colonialist Literature and Women's Studies. I accepted such invitations with a certain amount of trepidation. My concern arose from my need in such circumstances to clearly express the fact that I am not an authority on First Nations Literature, that I depend upon native critical thought and draw on it in order to contribute in a valuable way to such dialogue.

It was with this concern that I addressed a panel called "Reading First Nations" at a Conference on Post-Colonial and Commonwealth Literatures hosted by Queens University in 1992. My concern was with reading First Nations Literature and its subsequent pedagogy. In that presentation I suggested that the questioning which forms the critical pedagogical voice, might belong to the internal questioning that is first a reading and a sense-making of, by the culture from within which it arises.

I suggest that First Nations cultures, in their various contemporary forms, whether an urban-modern, pan-Indian experience or clearly a tribal specific (traditional or contemporary), whether it is Eastern, Arctic, Plains, Southwest or West Coastal in region, have unique sensibilities which shape the voices coming forward into written English Literature.

In that sense, I suggest that First Nations Literature will be defined by First Nations Writers, readers, academics and critics and perhaps only by writers and critics from within those varieties of First Nations contemporary practise and past practise of culture and the knowledge of it.

I suggest that in reading First Nations Literature the questioning must first be an acknowledgment and recognition that the voices are culture-specific voices and that there are experts within those cultures who are essential to be drawn from and drawn out in order to incorporate into the reinterpretation through pedagogy, the context of English Literature coming from Native Americans.

7

I suggest that the pedagogical insistence of such practise is integral to the process. In doing so I suggest that First Nations literature, as a facet of cultural practise, contains symbolic significance and relevance that is an integral part of the deconstruction-construction of colonialism and the reconstruction of a new order of culturalism and relationship beyond colonial thought and practise.

It was with these concerns in mind that I decided to edit a collection of Native academic voices on First Nations Literature and include views on the relevance of First Nations literary analysis itself. This collection is an example of the diversity of voice and opinion from various regions and various cultural experience. This collection includes essays which will be helpful in identifying contemporary issues related to literature as well as a very useful coverage of the first Native American gathering of writer's in Oklahoma in 1992. I felt that gathering a collection of Native academic voices on First Nations Literature is one way I can insist on listening to First Nations analysis and the best way to contribute to the dialogue on English Literature and First Nations Voice within literature itself.

Jeannette Armstrong
November 1993

SAYS WHO:

COLONIALISM, IDENTITY AND DEFINING INDIGENOUS LITERATURE

by

Kateri Damm

Kateri Damm

Kateri is a band member of the
Chippewas of Nawash, Cape Croker
Band on Georgian Bay, Ontario and of
mixed Ojibway/Polish Canadian/
Pottawotami/English descent. She was
born in Toronto where she lived for several years before her family moved to the
Cape Croker area in 1976. She received
her Honour's B.A. in English literature
at York University in 1987 and is currently completing her Master's degree in
English Literature in Ottawa, Ontario,
before moving to the Cape Croker reserve with her two dogs; Otis and A.J.
my heart is a stray bullet was her first
collection of Poetry.

As the debate over the issue of 'appropriation of Native voice' in literature continues to be refined, argued and explored, it brings to the fore questions about definitions of 'Nativeness' or 'Aboriginality' as well as the sources, validations and problematics associated with these definitions. The question of who has the right to speak of, about, for Indigenous peoples quickly leads to the question of who or what is "Indigenous" and in what ways is "Indigenous" literature distinct from other world literatures. In his "Introduction" to *All My Relations: An Anthology of Contemporary Canadian Native Fiction*, Thomas King notes that "when we talk about contemporary Native literature, we talk as though we already have a definition for this body of literature when, in fact, we do not. And when we talk about Native writers, we talk as though we have a process for determining who is a Native writer and who is not, when, in fact, we don't." (King, p. x).

Definitions of who we are affect not only First Nations peoples in North America but Indigenous peoples around the world who have been subjected to "the White Man's burden" of authority and control through the domination and assimilationist tactics of colonizing governments. "Who we are" has been constructed and defined by Others to the extent that at times we too no longer know who we are. The resulting confusion, uncertainty, low self-esteem and/or need to assert control over identity are just some of the damaging effects of colonization.

In Canada, Australia, New Zealand and the United States, successive colonizing governments have used language and the power of words backed by military fire-power to subjugate and control the Indigenous peoples of the land. Language has been used not only to control what we do but how we are defined. For example, the names by which First Nations people are known in Canada are often not the names by which the people refer to themselves but the (sometimes bastardized) names by which other First Nations referred to them. Thus, the Anishnabek are known as Ojibway and for years the Inuit were known as Eskimo. To further complicate matters, the colonizing governments constructed and imposed labels and definitions of "Indian" identity in an effort to limit and control treaty and aboriginal rights and to promote assimilation and the elimination of the "Indian problem." As a result, in Canada the *Indian Act* regulates who is and is not entitled to government recognition of "Indian status." This has led to a rather complicated and confusing number of definitions of Native identity, all of which have political, geographic, social, emotional, and legal implications. There are status Indians, non-status Indians, Metis, Inuit, Dene, Treaty Indians, urban Indians, on reserve Indians, off-reserve Indians; there are Indians who are Band members and Indians who are not Band members. There are First Nations peoples, descendants of First Nations, Natives, Indigenous peoples, Aboriginal peoples, mixed-bloods, mixed-breeds, half-breeds, enfranchised Indians, Bill C-31 Indians. There are even women without any First Nations ancestry who gained "Indian status" by marriage. And these are just some of the labels we must consider in identifying ourselves. There are also definitions based on Tribal/First Nations affiliations, on language, on blood quantum....But what does this have to do with a discussion of literature? Well, it forces us to consider some of the assumptions at the basis of our readings and criticism of Indigenous writing and orality. It forces us to examine our own positions vis a vis the text or story and the writer or speaker as well as to consider the context in which both the story composition and telling are done. King says that;

> In our discussions of Native literature, we try to imagine that there is a racial denominator which full-bloods raised in cities, half-bloods raised on farms, quarter-bloods raised on reservations, Indians adopted and raised by white families, Indians who speak their tribal language, Indians who speak only English, traditionally educated Indians, university-trained Indians, Indians with little education, and the like all share. We know, of course, that there is not. We know that this is a romantic, mystical, and, in many instances, a self-serving notion that the sheer number of cultural groups in North America, the variety of Native languages, and the varied conditions of the various tribes should immediately belie. (King, p.xi).

As King suggests, one of the difficulties in applying a rubric which encompasses such a wide diversity of writers, experiences and histories as well as the art and literature which arises from them, is that any one, solitary label distorts the multiplicity by suggesting that there is a cohesive, unitary basis of commonality among those so labelled. This is an obvious danger of any generalization but in this case the danger is exacerbated because the definition of these commonalities is left to the readers' imaginations, which, because of the ways in which Indigenous peoples have been characterized and defined as "bloodthirsty," "savages," "cannibals," or "noble," simple "children of nature" throughout contact and into the present day, have been informed by stereotypes and misrepresentations. Stereotypes such as the Drunken/ Lazy/Promiscuous Indian, or the Noble Savage, or the 19th Century Plains Indian as Prototype, continue to pervade the consciousness of those, both Native and non-Native, who have been "educated" through Western institutions. Historically, these institutions have acted as tools of the State, often in concert with the Church, to civilize and control Indigenous peoples while nurturing and preserving the righteousness of imperialist attitudes. Consequently, stereotypes, maintained through the education system, are the points of reference for many readers who make numerous faulty and at times damaging assumptions about "Native" writers and the types of literature we produce or ought to produce.

Too often, the image of the Indigenous writer which comes to mind will be one of a "storyteller," "traditional" in appearance and dress, dark skinned, raven haired, who uses "legends" or "myths" to teach the audience about his or her culture. This highly romanticized image discounts those who do not fit easily within it. Many Indigenous writers have had the unpleasant experience of not meeting someone's stereotype. Metis writer and professor Emma LaRocque tells of her experience with a CBC radio journalist who after an hour long interview during which she regaled him with "cultural sorts of information" suddenly realizes that she is a professor and ends the interview asking, "Could you tell me where I could find a *real* Metis storyteller?" (LaRocque in *Writing the Circle,* p. xxiii). She is not alone. Janice Gould, in her essay "The Problem of Being 'Indian': One Mixed-Blood's Dilemma" tells of mixed-blood Mohawk writer Beth Brant's experience with this sort of cultural ignorance:

> After her reading a white woman came up to her and said, "I don't see why you go on about being a half-breed. You look white enough!" This was another way of saying Brant did not look Indian enough. Her Indianness was erased (Gould in *De/Colonizing the Subject*, p. 84).

Indianness can be erased when the reality of Indigenous life confronts the fiction of Indigenous stereotypes. As Carol Lee Sanchez notes in her essay "Sex, Class and Race Intersections: Visions of Women of Colour" in *A Gathering of Spirit: A Collection by North American Indian Women*;

> To be Indian is to be considered "colourful," spiritual, connected to the earth, simplistic, and disappointing if not dressed in buckskin and feathers; shocking if a city-dweller and even more shocking if an educator or other type of professional (Sanchez in Green, p. 163).

Unfortunately, the erasure of another's identity can be a very damaging and oppressive action based on ignorance, racism and racial power relations which create an environment in which non-Natives feel justified in questioning another's identity. In reality, most Native writers do not fit easily into the construction of the "White Man's Indian" although most of us will share some of the attributes. While it is true that First Nations people across Canada, and around the world, share certain values which arise out of our connections to the land and out of our common histories and experiences with colonizing governments, in some ways pan-Indianism and other such simplistic generalizations become self-fulfilling prophecy: some of what we share is the result of having been treated in similar fashion, as if we were one people. However, along with this cautionary note we should not underestimate the power of the bonds of shared experience. As the recent international Indigenous writers, performing and visual artists conference, "Beyond Survival," demonstrated, these bonds are powerful and can unite people from Greenland to Zimbabwe to Brazil to Hawaii in a way that treaties and government negotiations never have. Perhaps this is because Indigenous peoples share an understanding that we have been and still are forced to conform to other peoples' images of us. That in our own countries we are expected to agree, to reach consensus on a variety of complex issues such as constitutional amendments, self-government, Aboriginal rights, and 'freedom of expression,' even though we are distinct peoples spread over large, vastly different territories. That systems comprised of many voices constantly and consistently demand we speak with one voice and then chastise and deride us when we cannot or will not. Perhaps it is because together we do not constantly have to explain, we do not constantly have to face opposition or doubt or disbelief. Perhaps it is because (more often than not) we allow each other to change, experiment and grow without calling each other's identity into question. Although within our cultural groups we can be very rigid in the expectations placed on our members, we seldom lock each other in to romanticized images that are impossible to maintain.

In Canada, First Nations writers are often expected to write about certain issues, to share certain values, to use certain symbols and icons, to speak in certain ways. We are expected to know everything about our own cultures and histories from land claims to spiritual practices to traditional dress. More than that, we are expected to know this for all 52 First Nations in Canada and, where applicable, in the United States. And when we write, we are often expected to draw on this knowledge in writing poetic "tales" about shamans and tricksters and mighty chiefs. Perhaps this is why so many of the non-Native writers who write about us, write this way. Or perhaps it is because of them that these expectations have been placed on us.

So, who are we and what are we writing about if not that? Rayna Green in the "Introduction" to the anthology *That's What She Said: Contemporary Poetry and Fiction by Native American Women* says that

> [The writers in this anthology] can be looking for something Indians call "Indianness" — what sociologists call "identity" and Bicentennial patriots called "heritage." Because most of them — with few exceptions — are "breeds," "mixed-bloods," not

reserve-raised, they aren't "traditional," whatever that might mean now (Green, p. 7).

Part of what it means now is that we remember the past and carry it with us. It means that because of our ancestry and our connections to the land we are distinct peoples within our societies, but that 500 years of contact have not left us unaffected. We are affected by the world around us, albeit some more than others, and we are less and less likely to conform to the definitions of a non-Native imagination. What it means is that the reality is that we have not faded into the earth like snow before the summer sun of 'progress' nor have we stagnated in some sort of retrograde time capsule. We have survived and will continue to survive because of, and in spite of, the changes.

One of the most important changes may well be that there are increasing numbers of First Nations peoples who are mixed-blood and whose identity as 'Indian' or 'Native' or 'Indigenous' or 'Aboriginal' or 'Organic' (as Zimbabwe writer Freedom Nyamubaya prefers) will continue to disrupt and influence commonly held perceptions of what this means. As we continue to refine these definitions, to redefine ourselves, the question of what Native or Indigenous literature is, will necessarily be refined as well. Janice Gould in her essay, "The Problem of Being 'Indian': One Mixed-Blood's Dilemma" asserts that.

> we must bear in mind that there are in this country enormous numbers of mixed-bloods, not only of Native American ancestry. There are varieties of mixed-blood experience lived by the students we have now and by the students we will have in the future. Mixed-bloodness will be an issue of profound interest to many of them. They will look for ways to explore their complexity through literature. So the voices of mixed-blood Asian, African American, Hispanic and Indian writers must be elicited, listened to consulted, and considered in a global perspective. We will be prodded to challenge concepts of acculturation and assimilation, of race and ethnicity. We will be asked to examine in a

more thorough, radical, and frightening way this legacy of racism. We may not even be able to consider issues of gender and class before we explore this troubling thing we call race. I believe that facing these issues is some of the most vital work ahead for feminist educators and scholars (Gould in *De/Colonizing the Subject*, p. 87).

These issues will continue to demand the attention of writers, scholars, readers as the concept of mixed-bloodness continues to be defined and asserted. Already the voices of mixed-bloods play an important role in the breaking of silences, the telling of Indigenous perspectives, the dispelling of lies and stereotypes, the creation of Indigenous literature.

In examining Indigenous literature to date, one finds that many of the earliest published Indigenous writers from various colonized countries in the world deal with issues of cultural/racial identity and mixed ancestry in their works. The idea that mixed-bloods have a dual perspective and can bridge the gap between Indigenous and white societies through writing is one which recurs and echoes in the work of many Indigenous writers around the world. For example, one needs only to look at the work of Indigenous literature 'pioneers' such as E. Pauline Johnson and Beatrice Culleton in Canada, Patricia Grace and Keri Hulme in New Zealand, Sally Morgan in Australia and Leslie Marmon Silko and N. Scott Momaday in the United States to see how prevalent these issues have been all along and how important the voices of mixed-bloods still are in the development of Indigenous literature. Rayna Green says that:

> Some [mixed breeds] might say that writing is just their role. That's what breeds do. They stand in the middle and interpret for everyone else, and maybe that's so. That's what they are. (Green, p. 7).

Certainly this is part of who mixed-blood Maori writer, Keri Hulme is. In her novel *The Bone People*, she examines issues of identity and 'Maori-ness' through the interrelationships of her three main characters: Kerewin Holmes, a part Maori, part European writer and painter; Simon Peter, a mute, fair-haired boy of undetermined ancestry; and Joe, Simon's Maori foster father. For Hulme, being of mixed Maori/Pakeha blood places her in a position which necessarily impacts on her writing: not simply on how she writes but that she chooses to. She says that as a mixed-blood

> ...you can never truly belong to one side or the other - as a person who is intrinsically a mongrel you can never be fully committed to one way alone. Now I'll throw again and again to my Maori side, but there is no way honestly I can say that I will totally ignore or exclude, or even want to exclude, all the joys and benefits of the Pakeha side of things. But I envy those people who are one-sided. I also, and not with any sense of superiority or contempt, think that they are limited because again the advantage and the joy is being able to be on both sides of the fence (and there is one), to have more than one set of ears, to have more than one set of eyes. (Peek, p. 3).

Having more than one set of ears and eyes, having the ability to see and understand and speak of what lies on both sides of the fence is one of the benefits espoused by writers and characters of mixed ancestry. In her first collection of short stories (the first collection of stories by a Maori woman writer) Patricia Grace also addresses issues of Maori-ness, self-identity and mixed ancestry. She does so most explicitly through her story "And so I go." In this story the narrator/ speaker/ writer is preparing to leave his Maori community:

> And so I go ahead for those who come. To stand midstream and hold a hand to either side. It is in me. Am I not at once dark and fair, fair and dark? A mingling. Since our blue-eyed father held our dark-eyed mother's hand and let her lead him here. (Grace, p. 43)

The narrator is leaving his community and family to "learn new ways," to assume his role as an interpreter standing in two worlds. Aware of his cross-cultural positioning he speaks of his ability to create understanding between his mother's and his father's peoples and of the need to recognize a future of more cross-cultural 'minglings':

> And so I go because of love. For our mother and her people and for our father. For you and for our children whose mingling will be greater than our own. I make a way. Learn new ways. So I can take up that which is our father's and hold it to the light. Then the people of our mother may come to me and say, 'How is this?' And I will hold the new thing to the light for them to see. Then take up that which is our mother's and say to those of our father, 'You see? See there, that is why'... Let me do this and do not weep for my going. I have this power in me. (Grace, pp. 43-44)

The power of the mixed-blood, some would argue, is to be able to see and speak the strengths and weakness of both Indigenous and non-Native cultures. Often the mixed-bloods, if they can avoid becoming what Lee Maracle calls "crippled two-tongues," become 'bilingual' interpreters, able to speak in the idiom of both 'White' and 'Indigenous' groups. Mixed-bloods see with two sets of eyes, hear with two sets of ears and those who write find the ability to assimilate and process all of this into a kind of tertium liquid: a blending or 'mingling' that cannot be completely ignored or discounted by either side.

On her dual position as a person of mixed-blood, the main character in Beatrice Culleton's novel *In Search of April Raintree* says half-jokingly that "maybe that's what being a half-breed was all about, being a critic-at-large" (Culleton, p. 125). However, April Raintree initially learns from the system to see and hear only the negative aspects of her two cultures, especially the Metis culture which is attacked and oppressed by a system which portrays them as "dirty," "stupid," "lazy" "savages."

The search for self-identity and for acceptance of who she is arises, in part, from April Raintree's ability to use her fair-skin to deny her Metis heritage. Unable to accept the identity for Native 'girls' inculcated in her through the stereotypes forwarded by her foster 'mother' and child welfare worker and embarrassed by the portrayal of Native peoples in the school system and by her own limited contact with them, April learns to be "ashamed of being a half-breed" (Culleton, p. 110). Brainwashed into hating that side of herself, April tells herself that "if I could assimilate myself into white society, I wouldn't have to live like this for the rest of my life" (Culleton, p. 85). She tries through most of the book to hide her Metis heritage, to reject her Native ancestry. Finally though, April regains the power to see both sides and, significantly, it is then that she realizes she can and should write her story.

In Search of April Raintree, a fictionalized 'autobiographical' novel, based on Culleton's own life and experiences, follows a woman's search for her true, hidden, identity. It follows her search for acceptance of who she is as a woman of mixed Native/European ancestry. For Culleton this search, and the writing of it, had to include both sides of her background. It had to allow her to write as a person of mixed ancestry, standing midstream, looking at the positive and negative on each side. For her, that is the only way she can be truthful; that is her role as a writer. She says

> I've been fair and honest in the book and that's the way I want to keep writing. I want to look for good sides, too, both parties, so to speak. (Culleton in *Contemporary Challenges*, p. 103)

Aboriginal Australian writer Sally Morgan's autobiographical family history addresses issues similar to those addressed by Culleton's novel. Although the two books are quite different, both Morgan and Culleton write about the problematics of defining Aboriginal identity, especially for peoples of mixed-blood, particularly those who are fair-skinned and do not fit the public image of who and what an Aboriginal woman ought to be. Both books also raise the issue of how the denial of Aboriginal ancestry has been encouraged by colonizing governments and how ultimately damaging this is to individuals, their families and their communities. In Morgan's book, it is her grandmother and mother who have learned to deny their Aboriginality out of fear of racism and oppression by the colonial government. Through their experiences with White society, the two women have learned to fear the government and its ability to dis-empower Aboriginal people. Afraid that the system will apprehend their children and take their house, the two women resolve to maintain their family by denying their ancestry. Morgan's book is about the process of overcoming that fear, understanding it and accepting the family's Aboriginal identity.

Early in her search Morgan questions what it means to be Aboriginal and for her to identify as an Aboriginal:

> Had I been dishonest with myself? What did it really mean to be Aboriginal? I'd never lived off the land and been a hunter and a gatherer. I'd never participated in corroborees or heard stories of the Dreamtime. I'd lived all my life in suburbia and told everyone I was Indian. I hardly knew any Aboriginal people. What did it mean for someone like me?

Later Morgan realizes that if she denies her "tentative identification" with her Aboriginal ancestry she would be denying her grandmother as well. She decides to "hold on to the fact that, some day, it might all mean something" (Morgan, p. 141). Some time later she decides to write a book about her family's history so that she can uncover the truth about who she is and why she had been denied her identity as an Aboriginal woman. In trying to answer this, Morgan must also uncover and understand the ways in which Aboriginal people had been colonized and disempowered by the government. However, as a woman of mixed blood who had been assimilated into 'White' society, she is empowered by her access to information. She is able to write the book because she employs the advantages of her dual position.

Native American writer Leslie Marmon Silko is also keenly aware of her positioning as a writer of mixed descent. For her, being of mixed ancestry opens the boundaries and disrupts the rules that

normally bind racial and cultural groups. In a 1992 interview, Silko
said

> It helped reinforce this attitude that I've always had of
> "don't tell me about limits or boundaries or rules. Don't
> tell me because they don't apply to me" and that partly,
> again is going back to this mixed ancestry that I
> have...at the same time I always had this sense that
> these things were having to be, that these rules were
> explained to me but even as either side of the family
> was explaining them, I always had this sense "but of
> course.".[I could see] the other side too... (Silko on
> *Imprint,* 1992)

In her first novel *Ceremony* Silko suggests that ceremonies must
be revitalized and maintained through continual change to reflect the
changing conditions of Native American peoples. Her main character,
Tayo, is a mixed breed who struggles to retain and accept his identity
as a Pueblo after returning home from the war. Through most of the
novel, Tayo suffers from a dissolution of self, fully aware of his
fragmentation: "he inhabited a gray winter fog on a distant elk mountain
where hunters are lost indefinitely and their own bones mark the
boundaries" (Silko, p. 14). It is only through the creation of new
ceremonies which reflect the total reality of who he is, that Tayo is
able to heal spiritually and emotionally. It is by opening the boundaries
of what is" traditional" and "ceremonial" that Tayo survives.

> He cried the relief he felt at finally seeing the pattern,
> the way all the stories fit together - the old stories, the
> war stories, their stories - to become the story that
> was being told. He was not crazy; he had never been
> crazy. He had only seen and heard the world as it always
> was: no boundaries, only transitions through all
> distance and time. (Silko, p. 258)

Tayo assimilates the fragments of his life, the stories, the cultures,
the traditions and becomes whole again: by integrating all aspects of
his being and resisting the falsely rigid bounds of culture within which

he could not be whole. Only then can he survive.

Silko's novel is similar in many ways to the 1966 Pulitzer Prize winning novel *House Made of Dawn* by Kiowa/Cherokee writer N. Scott Momaday. Momaday's main character, like Silko's, is a young American Indian who returns home from a foreign war, his sense of identity torn apart, searching to recover his "Indianness." Living in two worlds, the Pueblo and Navaho worlds of his father's people, and the larger modern world that surrounds them, Abel's sense of identity dissolves. He is man caught between two cultures, striving to be whole and he finds healing in his reenactment of the Navajo healing ceremony from which the title of the novel is taken. Abel turns to the ceremonies to make himself whole, and through his revision and reclaiming of them he sings a chant to the sun, to celebrate his healing, his survival: "He was running, and under his breath he began to sing. There was no sound, and he had no voice; he had only the words of a song. And he went on running to the rise of the song. *House made of pollen, house made of dawn.*" (Momaday, p. 191).

That Abel's journey, like Tayo's and April Raintree's ends, with his survival, the beginning of a new life, is significant. Survival, after all, has been the focus of our energies as Indigenous peoples since contact. However, in terms of our roles as Indigenous writers, part of our cultural survival in the future depends on our ability to re-focus our attentions creatively and artistically. To step outside of the reactive mode into which our peoples have been placed so consistently. Through our writing we can continue to break the conventions which have strived to render us voiceless and 'illiterate.' In fact, we are not and never were wordless:

> In Canada, as elsewhere much of Native writing, whether blunt or subtle, is protest literature in that it speaks to the process of our colonization: dispossession, objectification, marginalization, and that constant struggle for cultural survival expressed in the movement for structural and psychological self-determination (LaRocque in Writing the Circle, p. xviii).

Kateri Damm

Standing midstream, the minglings can bridge the gap, open the borders, tear down the walls of the colony. So, do the definitions and labels really matter? Yes. Although we may never come to a consensus on them, we must continue to assert our own definitions of who we are and to reject the imposed definitions of a colonizing system which would reduce us to nothingness with misrepresentative, overly-broad or trivializing labels of identification. When we express ourselves and when we listen to the creative and cultural expressions of others, we must do so from an informed position so that we do not contribute to the confusion and oppression but instead, bring into sharper focus who we are. By freeing ourselves of the constricting bounds of stereotypes and imposed labels of identity, we empower ourselves and our communities and break free of the yoke of colonial power that has not only controlled what we do and where we live but who we are. In this way, Indigenous literatures will shape themselves on their own terms.

Through the power of words we can counteract the negative images of Indigenous peoples. We can fight words with words. Then, with the weakening of colonial attitudes we can move together towards greater cultural, artistic and creative forms of expression that reflect the changing faces of who we are. Along the way, our identity as Indigenous writers, whether mixed-blood or fullblood, will continue to inform our work and strengthen us spiritually and politically. We will look with two sets of eyes and hear with two sets of ears and we will speak from the place where we stand with full confidence in the power of our voices. Indigenous literatures will resist the boundaries and boxes. In reality, more of our varied voices will be raised in art, literature and music and the definitions of who we are will be forced to change. Our different voices will create a new harmony. More importantly we will open the borders to each other.

In her preface to *Writing the Circle*, Emma LaRocque asks "These are our voices - who will hear?" Perhaps the time has come when non-Natives will stop negating our identities and silencing our voices. Perhaps with the border crossings of the mixed-bloods they will finally hear us. If not, the time has come for Indigenous peoples around the world to open our hearts and minds to each other. We can become the best audience for our arts and literature. We can write our

24

own stories and determine for ourselves who and what we are. For today, as Green says,

> ..."identity" is never simply a matter of genetic make-up or natural birthright. Perhaps once, long ago, it was both. But not now. For people out on the edge, out on the road, identity is a matter of will, a matter of choice, a face to be shaped in a ceremonial act.
> (Green, p. 7).

Ho-wuh!

Bibliography

Brant, Beth. editor. *A Gathering of Spirit: A Collection by North American Indian Women*. Toronto: The Women's Press, 1988.
Culleton, Beatrice. *In Search of April Raintree*. Winnipeg: Pemmican Publications, 1983.
Green, Rayna. editor. *That's What She Said: Contemporary Poetry and Fiction by Native American Women*. Bloomington: Indiana University Press, 1984.
Gould, Janice. "The Problem of Being Indian - One Mixed-blood's Dilemma" in *De/Colonizing the Subject: The Politics of Gender in Women's Autobiography*. Minneapolis: University of Minnesota Press: 1992.
Grace, Patricia. *Waiariki and other Stories*. Markham: Penguin Books Canada, 1986.
Hulme, Keri. *The Bone People*. Markham: Penguin Books Canada, 1986.
Imprint, "Interview with Leslie Marmon Silko" T.V. Ontario, August, 1992.
King, Thomas, editor. *All My Relations: An Anthology of Contemporary Canadian Native Fiction*. Toronto: McClelland and Stewart Inc., 1991.
LaRocque, Emma. "Preface of These Are Our Voices - Who Will Hear?" in *Writing the Circle*. Jeanne Perreault and Sylvia Vance, editors. Edmonton: NeWest Publishers Limited, 1991.
Morgan, Sally. *My Place*. South Freemantle: Freemantle Arts Centre Press, 1987.
Momaday, N. Scott. *House Made of Dawn*. New York: Harper & Row, 1989.
Peek, Andrew, "An Interview With Keri Hulme" in *New Literatures in Review*, number 20, Winter South 1990, New Literatures Research Centre, University of Wollongong.
Silko, Leslie Marmon. *Ceremony*. New York: Signet, 1977.

POST HALFBREED:

INDIGENOUS WRITERS AS AUTHORS OF THEIR OWN REALITIES

by

Janice Acoose

Janice Acoose

Janice graduated with a Double Honours Degree in both Native Studies and English. She has also received a Master's Degree in English from the University of Saskatchewan. As a writer, she has had several poems, some short stories, and has been published in an array of journals and anthologies. She also writes for the *Saskatoon Star Phoenix* as well as *Saskatchewan Indian* and *New Breed*, with an upcoming guest editorial column for *Windspeaker* out of Alberta. A mother of two, she enjoys being with her special partner, and spending time with her children. She is currently on leave from her lecturing position with the Saskatchewan Indian Federated College (S.I.F.C.) as an English Professor. Janice is co-producing and scriptwriting for a 13 part T.V. series focused on Indian artists.

...fenced in and forced to give up everything that had meaning to (our) life....But under the long snows of despair the little spark of our ancient beliefs and pride kept glowing, just barely sometimes, waiting for a warm wind to blow that spark into a flame again.

- Mary Crow Dog

Maria Campbell's *Halfbreed* (1973) encouraged many Indigenous people to begin writing, and her text initiated the process of representing Indigenous women both positively and knowledgably. Many contemporary Indigenous writers like Jeannette Armstrong, Beth Cuthand, Lenore Keeshig-Tobias, Daniel David Moses, Jordan Wheeler, Emma LaRocque, Beatrice Culleton, Thomas King, Lee Maracle, Tomson Highway, Basil Johnson, Ruby Slipperjack and Marie Annharte Baker write from culturally distinct positions that challenge non-Indigenous writers' stereotypical images of Indigenous women. Thus, *Halfbreed* both established a new literary trend that encouraged Indigenous writers to create more realistic images of Indigenous women and forced Euro-Canadian readers of literature to re-examine their former beliefs.

In *Contemporary Challenges: Conversations with Canadian Native Authors,* Lutz writes "Native writing in Canada, especially in the last year,...is so vital, there's so much coming out! It's almost exploding. It's so powerful and it's so multidimensional" (175). By way of introductory remarks, in the preface to Maria Campbell's interview, Lutz describes *Halfbreed* as "a best seller and still...the most important and seminal book authored by a Native person from Canada" (41). In conversation with Ms. Campbell, Lutz insists that although she may not see herself as a writer, "with *Halfbreed*...she really started something" (42). The majority of the writers interviewed by Lutz agree. Jeannette Armstrong describes *Halfbreed* as "an important book in terms of Native literature" (25). Beth Cuthand insists that "*Halfbreed* is a classic. If people are studying Canadian Native literature, they have to read it. *Halfbreed* is a standard" (35). Lenore Keeshig-Tobias, citing the importance of Campbell's contribution to other Indigenous writers, uses Daniel David Moses's words to describe her as "The Mother Of Us All" (83). One of the most recently published young Indigenous authors, Jordan Wheeler, maintains that *Halfbreed* "still has a record as the best selling first book by anybody in Canadian history" (74). In the preface to *Writing the Circle*, Emma LaRocque describes both Beatrice Culleton's autobiographical *In Search of April Raintree* and *Halfbreed* as "powerful mirrors to Canadian society" (xviii).

While *Halfbreed* is often cited as one of "Native" literature's earliest accomplishments, according to Lutz, "Native" literature is not new. In the preface to Contemporary Challenges, Lutz summarizes approximately 30 years of literary accomplishments by Indigenous writers.

Citing Emily Pauline Johnson as one of the first Native writers, Lutz locates the roots of Native literature early in the 20th century. He maintains that although there was no written literature by Native people, the oral tradition enriched the literature in the century between "treaty making and the present" (2). According to Lutz, Native people's voices were absent from the written literature until the 1960s. However, he insists that even those early attempts by Native writers were "heavily edited by non-native missionaries, anthropologists, and hobbyists...(who) tended to represent Native 'tales' from the igloo, the smokehouse, or the campfire as 'quaint' or 'exotic,' fit for ethnological inquiry but not for serious literary studying" (2). Lutz refers to the accomplishments of Native writers in the early 1970s like Harold Cardinal's 1969 *Unjust Society*, Maria Campbell's 1973 *Halfbreed*, and Howard Adams' 1975 *Prisoner of Grass*, and suggests that those books were dismissed as protest literature so they were "not really considered part of Canadian 'literature' as defined by English departments and literary scholars in the mainstream" (2).

By contrast, Lutz insists that currently there are exciting additions to Canadian literature because more Native people are writing and articulating their own realities. As examples, he cites the 1987 special Native volume of *Canadian Fiction Magazine 60*, edited by Thomas King; *The Native in Literature: Canadian and Comparative Perspectives* anthology, edited by Thomas King, Helen Hoy, and Cheryl Calver; the University of British Columbia's 1990 Canadian Literature;

and Penny Petrone's survey of Native literature in *Native Literature in Canada*.

In terms of drama, Lutz calls attention to Tomson Highway (*Rez Sisters*), Daniel David Moses, and Drew Taylor. Specifically, in regards to Indigenous women writer, he cites Beatrice Culleton's 1983 *In Search of April Raintree*; Jeannette Armstrong's 1985 *Slash*; Ruby Slipperjack's 1987 *Honour the Sun*; and Joan Crate's 1989 *Breathing Water*; Lee Maracle's 1988 *I Am Woman*, 1990 reprint of *Bobbi Lee: Indian Rebel*, and *Sojourner's Truth*; Lenore Keeshig-Tobias's 1988 magazine *Trickster*; and Maria Campbell's (and co-author Linda Griffith's) 1989 *Book of Jessica*. Lutz also refers to Marie Annharte Baker and Sue Deranger who "campaigned against Jeanne Perreault and Sylvia Vance's anthology *Writing the Circle*" (3).

In comparison to Vance and Perrault's book, he cites books published by Native presses such as Theytus Books which collaborated with En'owkin Centre in Penticton to produce such anthologies as *Seventh Generation* (1989) and *Gatherings*, and Pemmican Press which produced the anthology *Our Bit of Truth* (1990). Lutz also calls attention to Thomas King's *All My Relations* (1990), and his first novel *Medicine River* (1990). He describes King as "the most successful Native promoter/writer of First Nations literature in Canada to date" (4).

As for more recent writers to come into Native literature, Lutz refers to Jordan Wheeler and his "first monograph, the three novellas in *Brothers in Arms*," poets Bruce Chester (*Paper Radio*, 1986), Daniel David Moses (*The White Line*, 1990), Joan Crate (*Pale as Real Ladies*, 1989), Marie Annharte Baker (*Being on the Moon*, 1990), Beth Cuthand (*Horsedance to Emerald Mountain*, 1987 and *Voices in the Waterfall*, 1989), and Wayne Keon (*Sweetgrass* II, 1990).

Many of these contemporary Indigenous writers challenge Non-Indigenous writers' way of seeing and subsequently writing about Indigenous women. Contemporary Indigenous writers positively and knowledgeably construct aspects of their cultures that have been previously misrepresented by outsiders who knew little about the cultures about which they wrote.' [1. *See end note*] In this way, Indigenous writers following the example of Maria Campbell's *Halfbreed* significantly challenge literary trends. Writing from places

31

of strength — their own specific cultures — these writers provide an abundance of new ways to see and thus understand Indigenous peoples. Emma LaRocque strongly emphasizes that:

> ...there are just a thousand angles from which to see Native people — our vastness, our diversity, our different personalities, never mind, just plainly, our humanity. White North America, not to mention white European peoples, haven't even begun to see us. (198)

LaRocque's calling attention to the "thousand angles from which to see Native people" challenges the former monolithic "Indian" so prevalent in Euro-Canadian literature. However, while there are numerous cultural differences among Indigenous peoples, there are also some very basic similarities.

As indicated in Chapter One, Indigenous peoples share a common ideology premised on autochthony. This Indigenous ideology significantly challenges many Euro-Canadians' formerly held beliefs about Indigenous peoples, who were prior to Maria Campbell's *Halfbreed*, depicted in Canadian literature as pagans with no moral base, no rules, no values, and no developed political, social, or economic systems. In the interview with Hartmut Lutz, Jeannette Armstrong explains that "with Native people...it's difficult for us to look at things in a separate way. Everything is part of something else. Everything is part of a continuum of other things: a whole" (16). Thomas King concurs; he suggests, with:

> Native society there is the sense that everything is part of a living chain and you have to pay attention to what happens with the animals, with the environment. The world as an organic flow...we have a particular sense of the physical world that is so much a part of culture and so much a part of the ceremonies and everything else. They are connected. (116)

This connectedness, for most Indigenous people, influences our

way of seeing, being, and doing. It also challenges the traditionally-held notions in Canadian literature about Indigenous peoples being a dying race, the suffering victims with no hope of survival, or the "Native" bound and determined to assimilate and make it in the White world. Lee Maracle maintains:

> For us, thinking is a complete and total process. In a sweat, or the Big House or wherever, around the pipe you harness all your energy, physical, spiritual, emotional, and intellectual, and you retreat into solitude to work out the nature of your particular solidarity with creation. And you retreat into lineage, as well, because the farther backward in time you travel, the more grandmothers you have, the farther forward, the more grandchildren! You actually represent an infinite number of people, and the only physical manifestation is yourself. Also, you own your own "house" and that's all you own. It's this "house" that I live in. The "I" that lives in here is the thinking "I," the being "I," the "I" that understands creation, understands that the object of life is solidarity, understands that there are consequences for every action. (172)

This peculiar way of relating to the environment, of seeing, being and doing has significantly influenced Indigenous writers. Tomson Highway insists that Indigenous peoples have a mythology thousands of years old. Even though it has been severely eroded by Christian missionaries and their religion, Highway insists that the spirit of it has survived and is becoming even stronger (91). In "Tides, Towns, and Trains" Emma Larocque explains that Native cultures are "inextricably related to lands and resources" while she insists that Euro-Canadian culture "continues to invade these lands and resources, pulling the ground from under Native cultures, (and) creating a power/powerless relationship" (79).

For many Indigenous writers, the act of writing thus becomes an act of resistance, an act of re-empowerment. Lee Maracle maintains that when Indigenous people write, we are "reclaiming our house, our lineage house, our selves" (Lutz, 176). Emma LaRocque reinforces this idea. She insists that she took up writing in grade eight out of a need to "self-express because there was so much about our history and about our lives that...has been disregarded, infantilized, and falsified" (Lutz, 181).

LaRocque maintains, consequently, that "I think I had this missionary zeal to tell about our humanity because Indian-ness was so dehumanized and Metis-ness didn't even exist" (181). Speaking with Lutz, LaRocque calls attention to her particular source of power, her strength. She explains that she comes "from a background of beautiful oral literature. Both my grandmother and my mother were fantastic storytellers and I think that influenced me" (183).

Tomson Highway refers to his source of strength and influence in the preface to Geoffrey York's summary of the events at Oka in *The Dispossessed*. He writes:

> ...my parents are strong, beautiful people, as are my numerous brothers and sisters. And they all, except for three, speak nothing but Cree and, in the case of my parents, Chipweyan. The white people whom I happened to meet and associate with along the way were, almost without exception, tremendously supportive and encouraging. With their help, I am now, like many Indians of my generation, able to go back to help my people--equipped, this time, with the wisdom of Homer and Faulkner and Shakespeare and Bach and Beethoven and Rembrandt and McLuhan and many other thinkers, artists, and philosophers of the white world. But equipped, as well, with the wisdom and the vision of Big Bear and Black Elk and Chief Seattle and Tom Fiddler and Joe Highway and the medicine people, the visionaries of my ancestry - and the Cree language in all its power and beauty. At all times I have had the Trickster sitting beside me. In Cree we call him/her Weesaueechak...it is just unfortunate that his/her first meeting, seven lifetimes ago, with the central hero figure from that other

mythology—Christian mythology—was so shocking
and resulted in so many unpleasant occurrences (ix).

As Tomson Highway's writing demonstrates, Indigenous peoples
in Canada tenaciously clung to our cultures, our way of seeing, being,
and doing. Despite 400 years of cultural invasions, Indigenous cultures
have survived and are very much alive, in one way, through the
mythology. During those invasions, however, the mythology went
underground and consequently contemporary Indigenous peoples'
spirits are infused with it. Indeed, Highway insists that, "There is a
spirituality that still is so powerful and beautiful and passionate!" (Lutz,
91).

Indigenous cultures and languages have survived, according to
Maria Campbell, because of our relationship to the land, "the Mother"
(Lutz, 163). This maternal language base distinguishes Indigenous
peoples' languages and cultures, and therefore the writing, from non-
Indigenous peoples' language and writings which are rooted in a
patriarchal hierarchy. Campbell maintains that for about four or five
years she was very frustrated with her writing, or lack of it. She says:

> I blamed the English language, because I felt that the
> language was manipulating me.
>
> So I went to the old man who's been my mentor,
> my teacher, my grandfather,...I had talked to him about
> storytelling, but I never talked to him about what I
> felt the language was doing to me; going to him as a
> writer to another writer. And he just laughed, probably
> thinking, "Why didn't she come here a long time ago!"
> "It's really simple," he said, "why you have trouble
> with the English language, it's because the language
> has no Mother. This language lost its Mother a long
> time ago, and what you have to do is, put the Mother
> back in the language!" And then I went away, and I
> thought, "Now, how am I going to put the Mother
> back in the language?" Because, in our language and
> our culture, as well as Indian people's culture, Mother
> is the land (Lutz, 49).

While a number of Indigenous peoples, in their writing, proclaim their re-connection to the Mother, many writers engage themselves in the struggle against systemic and institutional racism. In *Writing the Circle*'s preface, Emma LaRocque calls attention to the various types of "power politics in literature" that for too many years disempowered Indigenous peoples by dismissing, romanticizing, censoring, and labelling us" (xvi-xvii). She insists that Indigenous peoples were not rendered voiceless despite very deliberate and institutionally sanctioned attempts to silence us. Indeed, Indigenous peoples continue to write albeit often from the "margins" or from a position of "resistance." [2. *See end note*]

Basil Johnson, a writer from the Anishnabe nation, describes the process which led to his various texts. He explains:

> I was asked to start an Indian program in a museum which I carried out by teaching in the galleries and going out to the communities. I realized that neither students nor teachers were prepared to study, or to listen to a presentation, because the books available to them were poor in quality and in content. I...look(ed) at this display that was mounted by a group of grade five/six students,...which they mounted after studying an Indian unit in depth for six weeks. It was a marvellous display. Over in one corner...a young chief wearing a paper headdress, with arms folded in the "traditional" manner of a Blackfoot chief and he had on his lapel with a cardboard label with the word "Blackfoot." So I went over to this little guy because he was all by himself....Then I observed that he looked morose. "How come you look so sad, chief?" And he looked around to see that there were no teachers within the vicinity, and he explained, "Sir,...I always thought Indians were neat, always wanted to be an Indian. But, sir, after six weeks of studying teepees that my team and I selected from these six aspects," he said, "is that all there is, sir?" That is when I started to write! I

wasn't even thinking about categories, I simply
thought, there is a need for Ojibway Heritage. After
that was finished, there was a need for Ojibway
Ceremonies, and that became fiction simply because
there was a fictional character in the thing that is based
on ceremonies and rituals. Then it was Moose Meat
and Wild Rice because Native people like humour, not
subtle humour like Canadians want. (233)

Contrary to the "Natives" in White-Canadian writers' fiction, a
good majority of Indigenous peoples' texts thematically deal with
survival of individuals, communities, and nations, just as Johnson's
texts do. Thomas King, in his introduction to *Canadian Fiction
Magazine 60*, argues that images constructed by "Native" writers are
"quite unlike the historical and contemporary Native characters in
white fiction" (8). He maintains that:

Rather than create characters who are inferior and
dying, Native writers have consciously created Native
characters who are resourceful, vibrant, and tenacious.
Like traditional trickster figures, contemporary Native
characters are frequently tricked, beaten up, robbed,
deserted, wounded, and ridiculed, but, unlike the
historical and contemporary Native characters in white
fiction, these characters survive and persevere, and, in
many cases, prosper. Contemporary Native literature
abounds with characters who are crushed and broken
by circumstances and disasters, but very few of them
perish. Whatever the damage, contemporary
characters, like their traditional trickster relations, rise
from their own wreckage to begin again. (8)

Putting the Trickster back among Indigenous peoples re-
establishes harmony and balance to Indigenous peoples' way of being,
seeing, and doing. The Trickster, according to Tomson Highway, is
an "extraordinary figure" without whom "the core of Indian culture
would be gone forever" (*Dry Lips*, 13). Indeed, Highway writes:

> The dream world of North American Indian mythology
> is inhabited by the most fantastic creatures, beings and
> events. Foremost among these beings is the "Trickster,"
> as pivotal and important a figure in our world as Christ
> is in the realm of Christian mythology. "Weesegeechak"
> in Cree, "Nanabush" in Ojibway, "Raven" in others,
> "Coyote" in still others, this Trickster goes by many
> names and many guises. In˙fact, he can assume any
> guise he chooses. Essentially a comic, clownish sort
> of character, his role is to teach us about the nature
> and the meaning of existence on the planet Earth; he
> straddles the consciousness of man and that of God,
> the Great Spirit. (12)

Lenore Keeshig-Tobias explains that the Trickster is also a "Teacher...a paradox; Christ-like in a way. Except that from our Teacher, we learn through the Teacher's mistakes as well as the teacher's virtues" (Lutz, 85). As both Keeshig-Tobias and Highway suggest, Trickster, as the central culture hero for "Native" people, is comparable to Christ, the central cultural hero of Christianity's first book, the Bible.

This very basic difference distinguishes Indigenous peoples' writing from non-Indigenous peoples' writing: Indigenous peoples' writing primarily grows out of a gynocratic-circular-harmonious way of life while non-Indigenous peoples' writing in Canada has primarily grown out of a Christian-patriarchal hierarchy. Contemporary Indigenous writers who write from this ideological base thus challenge Canadian literary traditions by creating more knowledgeable and positive images that grow out of this ideology. Also, contemporary writers are constructing characters and plots based on Trickster, who can adopt any guise and is not confined to a specific gender. In addition, unlike the Trickster's Christian counterpart, her/his/its motivation is neither solely altruistic nor virtuous: Trickster manifestations function just as easily doing unkindly, suspicious, and sometimes cruel deeds as she/he/it does doing kind and virtuous deeds. Perhaps the most important aspect of contemporary Indigenous peoples' writing that distinguishes our writing from non-Indigenous peoples is the Trickster who endures all: the survivor.

Not surprisingly, a group of concerned Indigenous writers (Lenore Keeshig-Tobias, Daniel David Moses, Tomson Highway) are diligently working to re-establish the Trickster in their stories, drama, and poetry. In Contemporary Challenges Lenore Keeshig-Tobias explains that those writers organized the Committee to Re-establish the Trickster. Keeshig-Tobias suggests that prior to the establishment of that Committee many of those writers were frustrated because they were unable to find issues, forms, symbols, or structures in their work they could understand. She also insists that the Committee was necessary for Indigenous writers to continue writing because it encouraged them to believe in their work and support one another. Indeed, Tomson Highway, in *The Dispossessed*, maintains that we of this generation, of contemporary Indigenous writers are

> Ever so little by little,...picking the Trickster, that ancient clown, up from under that legendary beer table on Main Street in Winnipeg or Hastings Street in Vancouver, and will soon have her standing firmly up on his own two feet so she can make us laugh and dance again. Because, contrary to the viewpoint presented by that other hero figure, what she says foremost is that we are here to have one hell of a good time. (ix)

Many Indigenous writers maintain Trickster survives incredibly challenging experiences only to live and begin again. Just as the traditional Trickster culture hero/fixer-upper survived great odds, contemporary Indigenous writers are writing their cultures back into stability and thereby assuring survival.

Maria Campbell's own incredible survival journey -- from a healthy and whole child to an unhealthy and unwhole woman and finally to recovered woman -- is in some ways, reminiscent of that of the Trickster. Also, as one of the first Indigenous women who successfully utilized the colonizer's language to articulate her oppression, she significantly altered the way that non-Indigenous peoples looked upon Indigenous people. Canadians forever thereafter were forced to rethink their former beliefs because as Penny Petrone writes of *Halfbreed* in Native Literature in Canada, "it is a disturbing testimony to the ugliness of racism in Canada's social history" (120).

Campbell's story, albeit woven with both tremendous pain and suffering, is one of survival and subsequent liberation. Appropriately, she follows Louis Riel, who prophesied at the time of his execution in 1885 that one hundred years later his people would rise up, and the artists, musicians, and visionaries would lead the way. Similarly, among the original peoples, numerous spiritual and medicine people in the past have spoken of a revival of Indigenous cultures through the efforts of the artists, musicians, poets, and visionaries of the seventh generation. As this chapter has clearly shown, the movement initiated by Maria Campbell's Halfbreed is growing ever stronger. Indeed, as Tomson Highway writes in *The Dispossessed* "it's an exciting time to be alive, seven lifetimes after that first meeting (European contact). I look forward to every minute of it" (ix).

End Notes

[1]   See for example: W.P. Kinsella's *Dance Me Outside*, Margaret Laurence's "The Loons" in *A Bird in the House*, Wallace Stegner's *Wolf Willow*, W.O. Mitchell's *Jake and the Kid*, Martha Ostenso's *Wild Geese*.

[2]   For a more informed discussion of resistance or margin writing see Agnes Grant's "Contemporary Native Women's Voices in L:iterature," Noel Elizabeth Currie's "Jeannette Armstrong & the Colonial Legacy" and Barbara Godard's "The Politics of Representation: Some Native Canadian Writers" in *Native Writers and Canadian Writing*

Bibliography (For POST HALFBREED and HALFBREED)

Adams, Howard. *Prison of Grass: Canada from a Native Point of View*. Saskatoon: Fifth House Publishers, Rpt.,1989.

Albers, Patricia. "Introduction: New Perspectives on Plains Indian Women." *The Hidden Half: Studies of Plains Indian Women*. Lanham, MD: UP of America, Inc., 1983. 1-15.

Allen, Paula Gunn. *The Sacred Hoop*. Boston: Beacon Press, 1986.

Althusser, Louis. "Ideology and Ideological State Apparatuses." *Contemporary Critical Theory*. Ed. Dan Latimer. Toronto: Harcourt Brace Jovanovich, Publishers, 1989.

Armstrong, Jeannette. *Slash*. Penticton, B.C.: Theytus Books, 1988.

Axtell, James. *The European and the Indian: Essays in the Ethnohistorv of Colonial North America*. Oxford: Oxford UP, 1981.

Baker, Marie Annharte. *Being on the Moon*. Winlaw, B.C. Polester Press Ltd., 1990.

Bataille, Gretchen. "Transformation of Tradition: Autobiographical Works by American Indian Women." *Studies in American Literature*. New York: The Modern Language Association of America, 1983. 85-99.

Berkhoffer, Robert F. *The Whiteman's Indian: Images of the American Indian from Columbus to Present*. New York: Vintage Books, 1979.

Bourgeault, Ronald. "Women in Egalitarian Society." *New Breed Journal*. Excerpts January-April 1983: 3-8.

Buffalohead, Priscilla. "Farmers Warriors Traders: A Fresh Look At Ojibway Women." *Minnesota History 48*, 1983. 236- 244.

Cameron, Deborah, ed. *The Feminist Critique of Language: A Reader*. London: Routledge, 1990.

Campbell, Maria. *Halfbreed*. Toronto: McClelland and Stewart Limited, 1973.

Cappon, Paul, ed. *In Our Own House: Social Perspectives on Canadian Literature*. Toronto: McCleiland and Stewart Limited: 1978.

Charnley, Kerrie. "Concepts of Anger, Identity and Power and the Voices of First Nations Women." *Gatherings: The En'Owkin Journal of First North American Peoples*. 1, 1990. 11-22.

Cornillon-Koppelman, Susan, ed. *Images of Women in Fiction: Feminist Perspectives*. Bowling Green, Ohio: Popular Press 1972.

Culleton, Beatrice. *In Search of April Raintree*. Winnipeg: Pemmican Publications, 1983.

Crow Dog, Mary and Richard Erdoes. *Lakota Woman*. New York: Harper Collins Publishers, 1990.

Cuthand, Beth. *Voices in the Waterfall*. Vancouver: Lazara Press, 1989.

Erdich, Louise. *The Beet Queen*. Toronto: Bantam Books, 1986.

——*Love Medicine*. Toronto: Bantam Books, 1984.

——*Tracks*. New York: Harper & Row Publishers, 1988.

Fanon, Frantz. *Black Skin, White Masks*. New York: Grove Press, Inc., 1967.

——*The Wretched of the Earth*. New York: Grove Press, Inc., 1963.

Fonow, Mary Margaret and Judith A.Cook. *Beyond Methodology: Feminist Scholarship as Lived Research*. Bloomington: Indiana UP, 1991.

Fulton, Keith Louise. "Feminism and Humanism: Margaret Laurence and the Crises of Imagination." *Crossing the River: Essays in Honour of Margaret Laurence*. Ed. Kristjana Gunnars. Winnipeg: Turnstone Press, 1988.

Gaber-Katz, Elaine and Jenny Horsman. "Is It Her Voice If She Speaks Their Words?" *Canadian Woman Studies*. #9, 1988. 117-120.

Godard, Barbara Thomson. *Talking About Ourselves: The Literary Productions of Native Women in Canada*. CRIAW Paper no.ii., 1983.

Grant, Agnes, ed. *Our Bit of Truth: An Anthology of Canadian Native Literature*. Winnipeg: Pemmican Publications Inc., 1990.

Green, Rayna. "The Pocahontas Perplex: The Image of Indian Women in American Culture." *Sweetgrass*. 1984. 17-23.

Highway, Tomson. *Dry Lips Oughta Move to Kapuskasing*. Saskatoon: Fifth House Publishers, 1990.

Hooks, Bell. *Talking Back: Thinking Feminist. Thinking Black*. Toronto: Between the Lines, 1988.

——*Yearning: Race. Gender. and Cultural Politics*. Toronto: Between the Lines, 1990.

Hryniuk, Margaret. "They Have Taken Our Land, Now Want Our Words," *Leader Post*. Apr.19, 1990. 6.

Hughes, Kenneth James. *Signs of Literature: Language, Ideology and the Literary Text*. Vancouver: Talonbooks. 1986.

Independent Commission on International Humanitarian Issues *Indigenous Peoples: A Global Quest for Justice*. London: Zed Books Ltd., 1987.

Johnston, Gordon. "An Intolerable Burden of Meaning: Native People in White Fiction." *The Native in Literature: Canadian and Comparative Perspectives*. Ed. Thomas King, Cheryl Calver, and Helen Hoy. Toronto: ECW Press, 1987. 50-65.

Keeshig-Tobias, Lenore. "Stop Stealing Native Stories," *Globe & Mail.*, Jan.26, 1990. 7.

King, Thomas, ed. *All My Relations: An Anthology of Contemporary Canadian Fiction*. Toronto: McClelland and Stewart Inc.,1990.

——ed. *Canadian Fiction Magazine 60*. Toronto, The Coach House Press, 1987.

——Cheryl Calver, and Helen Hoy, ed. *The Native in Literature*. Toronto: ECW Press, 1987

Kinsella, William Patrick. "Linda Star." *Dance Me Outside*. Ottawa: Oberon Press, 1977.

Kroetsch, Robert. *The Studhorse Man*. Toronto: General Publishing Ltd., 1970.

Krupat, Arnold. *The Voice in the Margin: Native American Literature and the Canon*. Berkeley: University of California Press, 1989.

Lachapelle, Caroline. "Beyond Barriers: Native Women and the Women's Movement." *Still Ain't Satisfied: Canadian Feminism Today*. Toronto: The Women's Press, 1982. 257-264.

Laurence, Margaret. *A Bird in the House*. Toronto: McClelland & Stewart, 1985.

LaRocque, Emma. *Defeathering the Indian*. Agincourt, Canada: The Book Society of Canada Ltd., 1975.

——"Tides, Towns and Trains." *Living the Chances*. Ed. Joan Turner. Winnipeg: University of Manitoba Press, 1990. 76-90.

——Preface. *Writing the Circle: Native Women of Western Canada*. Eds. Jeanne and Sylvia Vance. Edmonton. NeWest Publishers Limited, 1990.

Leacock, Eleanor. "Montagnais Women and the Jesuit Program for Colonization." *Myths of Male Dominance: Collected Articles on Women Cross-Culturally*. New York: Monthly Review Press, 1981. 43-62.

Littlefield, Lorraine. "Women Traders in the Maritime Fur Trade." *Native People Native Lands: Canadian Indians, Inuit and Metis*. Ottawa: Carleton UP, 1987. 173-183.

Lutz, Hartmut. "The Circle as Philosophical and Structural Concept in Native American Fiction Today." *Native American Literature*. Pisa, Italy: Servizio Editoriale Universitario, 1989. 85-99.

——ed. *Contemporary Challenges: Conversations with Contemporary Canadian Native Writers*. Saskatoon: Fifth House Publishers, 1991.

——"'Indians' and Native Americans in the Movies: A History of Stereotypes, Distortions, and Displacements," *Visual Anthropology. 3*, United States: Harwood Academic Publishers, 1990. 31-46.

Mandel, Zli. "Imagining Natives: White Perspectives on Native Peoples." *The Native in Literature: Canadian and Comparative Perspectives*. ed. Thomas King, Cheryl Calver, and Helen Hoy. Toronto: ECW Press, 1987. 34-47.

Maeser-Lemieux, Angelika. "The Metis in the Fiction of Margaret Laurence: From Outcast to Consort." *The Native in Literature: Canadian and Comparative Perspectives*. Ed. Thomas King, Cheryi Calver, and Helen Hoy. Winnipeg: ECW Press, 1987. 115-129.

Maracle, Lee. *I Am Woman*. North Vancouver, British Columbia: Write-on Press Publishers Ltd., 1988.

——*Bobbi Lee: Indian Rebel*. Toronto: Women's Press, 1990.

——*Sojourner's Truth & Other Stories*. Vancouver: Press Gang Publishers, 1990.

Medicine, Beatrice. "'Warrior Women' - Sex Role Alternatives for Plains Indian Women." *The Hidden Half: Studies of Plains Indian Women*. Lanhem: UP of America, Inc., 1983. 267-277.

Mitchell, W.0. *Jake and the Kid*. Toronto: McClelland & Stewart. 1985.

Monkman, Leslie. *A Native Heritage: Images of the Indian in English-Canadian Literature*. Toronto: University of Toronto Press, 1981.

——"The Tonnerre Family: Mirrors of Suffering." *Journal of Canadian Fiction*, 27, 1980.

New, W.H. *A History of Canadian Literature*. London: Macmillan Education, 1989.

——*Native Writers and Canadian Writing: Canadian Literature Special Issue*. Vancouver: UBC Press, 1990.

Newman, Peter. *Company of Adventurers*. Ontario: Penguin Books Canada Limited, 1985.

Osennontion and Skonaganleh: ra. "Our World: According to Osennontion and Skonaganleh:ra." *Canadian Woman studies/ les cahiers de la femme*. Downsview, Ont.: York University. 7-19.

Philip, Marlene Nourbese. "The Disappearing Debate: Racism and Censorship." *Language in Her Eye: Views on Writing and Gender by Canadian Women*

Janice Acoose

Writing in English. Toronto: Coach House Press, 1990.

Smits, David D. "The 'Squaw Drudge': A Prime Index of Savagism." *Ethnohistory, 29*. 1982. 281-301.

Stedman, Raymond William. *Shadows of the Indian: Stereotypes in American Culture*. London: UP of Oklahoma, 1989.

Sutherland, Ronald. *Second Image: Comparative Studies in Quebec/Canadian Literature*. Toronto: New Press, 1971.

Swann, Brian and Arnold Krupat, eds. *Recovering the Word: Essays in Native American Literature*. Berkeley: University of California Press, 1983.

Stegner, Wallace. *Wolf Willow*. London: UP of Nebraska, 1980.

Thomas, Clara. "'Planted firmly in some soil': Margaret Laurence and the Canadian Tradition in Fiction." *Critical Approaches to the Fiction of Margaret Laurence*. Ed. Colin Nicholson. Vancouver: UBC, 1990. 1-14.

Thwaites, R.G. *The Jesuit Relations and Allied Documents*. 73 vols., New York: Pageant Books, 1959.

Ussher, Jane. *The Psychology of the Female Body*. London: Routledge, 1989.

Vangen, Kate. "Making Faces: Defiance and Humour in Campbell's Halfbreed and Welch's Winter in the Blood." *The Native in Literature: Canadian and Comparative Perspectives*. Toronto: ECW Press, 1987. 188-203.

Van Kirk, Sylvia. *Many Tender Ties: Women in Fur Trade Society. 1670-1870*. Winnipeg: Watson And Dwyer Publishing Ltd., 1980.

— "'Women In Between': Indian Women in Fur Trade Society in Western Canada". *Out of the Background: Readings in Canadian Native History*. Toronto: Copp Clark Pitman Ltd, 1988. 150-163.

Waubageshig, ed. *The Only Good Indian*. Toronto: New Press, 1970.

Wa Thiong'o, Ngugi. *Writers in Politics*. London: Heinemann Educational Books, 1981.

Weedon, Chris. *Feminist Practice & Poststructuralist Theory*. Basil Blackwell Ltd., 1988.

Wiebe, Rudy. "Proud Cree Nation Deserves Much More Than Funny Stories" *Globe & Mail*. Feb.17, 1990. 3.

Wilkinson, Gerald. "Colonialism in the Media." *The Indian Historian*. 7, 1974. 29-32.

Wolff, Janet. "Art as Ideology," *The Social Production of Art*. London: Macmillan Education Ltd., 1981.

Woodcock, George. "Prairie Writers and the Metis: Rudy Wiebe and Margaret Laurence." *Northern Spring*. Canada: D.W. Freisen & Sons, 1987. 94-109.

York, Geoffrey. *The Dispossessed*. London: Vintage U.K., 1990.

Popular Images of Nativeness

by

Marilyn Dumont

Marilyn Dumont

I am Metis. Dislocated from the Alberta Metis Settlements and my extended family I grew up, first, in logging camps where my parents worked and, second, in a small southern Alberta farming community.

I have been writing for an audience for twelve years and publishing for eight years in literary journals such as: *Blue Buffalo, CV II, A Room of One's Own, Other Voices, Newest Review* and in two anthologies: *Writing the Circle* and *The Road Home*. A first collection of poetry is soon to be published.

I presently make my living from freelance writing and video & film production in Edmonton, Alberta.

If you are old, you are supposed to write legends, that is, stories that were passed down to you from your elders. If you are young, you are expected to relate stories about foster homes, street life and loss of culture and if you are in the middle, you are supposed to write about alcoholism or residential school. And somehow throughout this, you are to infuse everything you write with symbols of the native world view, that is: the circle, mother earth, the number four or the trickster figure. In other words, positive images of nativeness.

But what if you are an urban Indian, have always been, or have now spent the greater part of your life living an urban lifestyle? Do you feign the significance of the circle, the number four, the trickster in your life? Do you just disregard these things? Or do you reconstruct these elements of culture in your life so you can write about them in "the authentic voice," so you can be identified (read 'marketed') as a native Artist?

This is not to argue that an authentic voice does not exist, nor that the artists who do write about/from the "traditional" experience write without the integrity of having that experience. Nor am I arguing that native culture is dying and that these symbols do not exist within the full integrity of the living culture. However, what I am arguing, is that there is a continuum of exposure to traditional experience in native culture, some of us have been more exposed to it than others, but this does not mean that those who have been more exposed to it are somehow more Indian, as if we are searching for the last surviving Indian. Because this notion of *Indians vanishing* is the effect of 19th Century ideas about culture as static, this notion of culture as something immutable compounded by the Indian Act affects images of ourselves as either *too Indian or not Indian enough*. You're too Indian if you are not articulate in the english language (if a native language is your first language) and you're not native enough if by way of growing up in an urban center you became articulate in english instead of your own native language. Because if you are articulate in english, then you may be seen as coming from a privileged class and are scrutinized to determine how native you really are, scrutinized for your authenticity (by both Indian and white sides).

This prevalent 19th Century notion of culture as static which is founded on the belief that there exists in the evolution of cultures, a pristine culture which if it responds to change is no longer pure, and therefore, eroding and vanishing affects our collective 'self-images' as either: pure - *too Indian* or diluted - *not Indian enough.*

These colonial images we have of ourselves informs me that internalized colonialism is alive and well in the art we generate and which gets transferred by media into the popular images which are supported by the art buying public (read: white patrons).

But what is the experience of the urban native? Indians who grew up in urban centres, one or more generations removed from the subsistence economy that characterizes predominant images of "Native." The urban native who participates in all the trappings of a wage economy as best he/she is able to. The urban native who is increasingly becoming the majority. Why do popular images of us lag behind our reality? Images that portray us as rural, living a subsistence economy, traditional, when more and more natives are living the experience of an urban wage economy? Sixty percent of Alberta's native population now lives in urban centres. What force drives this perception, this tenacious image of us as traditional, rural, living a subsistence economy?

I would argue that there is a connection between domination and representation (1). Which prompts me to ask the question, "If the representation of me is inaccurate, how does this impact on my art?" But more importantly, "How does this representation affect my self-image?" I would argue that the misrepresentation of me makes me doubt my experience, devalue my reality and tempts me to collude in an image which in the end disempowers me. As film maker Pratibha Parmar states:

> "Images play a crucial role in defining and controlling the political and social power to which both individuals and marginalized groups have access. The deeply ideological nature of imagery determines not only how other people think about us but how we think about ourselves" (2).

In short, I think the pervasive images of natives as rural (*North of 60*), traditional (*Dances with Wolves*) and living a predominately subsistence economy affect how native people participate and are perceived as participating in the Canadian economy and political arenas.

The upshot is that I am increasingly writing from my experience as an urban native. To write what I experience as an urban native writes against what is believed to be popularly true, but which is the reality for increasing numbers of native people. To write what I experience is to write against a tenacious 19th Century myth and an image-making machine which misrepresents me.

Granted some natives in isolated communities are still connected to the land in meaningful ways, and this argument is not intended to diminish the value and existence of that experience. However, this is one experience of nativeness and there is a multiplicity of experiences out there that go on being ignored because they do not fit a popular understanding of culture, but which have to be expressed because their denial by the image making machine is another kind of colonialism. And if I, as a native person, engage in the denial of my own image then I am participating in just another variety of internalized colonialism which blinds me and fosters my disempowerment.

So, in short, I now see myself increasingly committed to writing out of my own urban experience and using images in my art which counter these monolithic, singular images of "nativeness" that are popularly seductive but ultimately oppressive.

End Notes

1. Bell Hooks, *Black Looks: race and representation* Toronto: Between the Lines, 1992, 3.
2. Ibid., 5.

Native Literature:

SEEKING
A CRITICAL CENTER

by

Kimberly M. Blaeser

Kimberly M. Blaeser

Kimberly is currently an assistant professor in the English and Comparative Literature Department at the University of Wisconsin-Milwaukee. A mixed-blood of Ojibway and German ancestry from White Earth Reservation in Minnesota, she teaches 20th century American literature, including courses in Native American Literatures and American Nature Writing. Her essays, poetry, journalism, short fiction, reviews and scholarly articles have appeared in various journals and collections including *World Literature Today, American Indian Quarterly, Akwe:kon, Earth Song, Sky Spirit*, and *Narrative Chance: Postmodern Discourse on Native American Indian Literatures*. Her book *Gerald Vizenor - Writing in the Oral Tradition* will be published by the University of Oklahoma Press and a collection of her poetry, *Trailing You*, by Greenfield Review Press.

Uncle Luther, a character in Louis Owen's *The Sharpest Sight,* offers some advice Indian intellectuals should take to heart. In Owen's novel, the old man gives his own reading of Herman Melville's *Moby Dick* and identifies the central failing of Melville's protagonist, claiming that the "storyteller in the book forgot his own story" (91). The antidote to this failing involves a balance: "You see, a man's got to know the stories of his people, and then he's got to make his own story too" (91). But the stakes get higher and the tasks more difficult for Native Americans and mixed-bloods; not only must we "know the stories of our people" and "make our own story," but, Luther warns, "We got to be aware of the stories they're making about us, and the way they change the stories we already know" (91). We must know the stories of other people -- stories from the American and world canons -- especially the stories told about Indian people; and we must be aware of the way our own stories are being changed: "re-expressed" or "re-interpreted" to become a part of their story or their canon because, as Luther warns, stories have political power: "They're always making up stories, and that's how they make the world the way they want it" (91). As I see it, the lesson for Indian intellectuals involves contemporary criticism and literary interpretation, because literary theory and analysis, even "canonization," can become a way of changing or remaking Native American stories.

This essay extends Luther's (or Owens') warning and challenge to contemporary scholars: it is a call and, as its title suggests, a search for a way to approach Native Literature from an indigenous cultural context, a way to frame and enact a tribal-centered criticism. It seeks a critical voice and method which moves from the culturally-centered text outward toward the frontier of "border" studies, rather than an external critical voice and method which seeks to penetrate, appropriate, colonize or conquer the cultural center, and thereby, change the stories or remake the literary meaning.

Recognizing that the literatures of Native Americans have a unique voice and that voice has not always been adequately or accurately explored in the criticism that has been written about the literature, I have begun in the last few years to be attentive to other ways of talking about the literature of the First Peoples. Particularly, I have been alert for critical methods and voices that seem to arise out of the literature itself (this as opposed to critical approaches applied from an already established critical language or attempts to make the literature fit already established genres and categories of meaning). So far, I have uncovered only fitful attempts to fashion this interpretive method or give voice to this new critical language. This essay explores the most promising of these endeavors, searches for their points of convergence, and offers some comments on the inherent critical dynamics of Native American literature.

Theorizing American Indian Literature

In her discussion "Toward Minority Theories," Nancy Hartsock writes of "those of us who have been marginalized by the transcendental voice of universalizing theory" (204). Anyone familiar with the history of Native literatures in the Americas, knows well the particulars -- translation, re-interpretation, appropriation, romanticizing, museumization, consumerization, and marginalization -- generalized in Hartsock's statement. Elements of the native oral tradition, for example, have been dismissed as primitive, rediscovered and translated into "literary" forms, used as models for contemporary literary and cultural movements, altered and incorporated into mainstream works of literature, and almost theorized into their predicted "vanishment."

Indeed, both traditional and contemporary Native works have often been framed in and read from a western literary perspective. Hertha Wong in *Sending My Heart Back Across the Years* and Arnold Krupat in *For Those Who Come After*, both talk about and call into question the western theorizing of American Indian autobiography and offer alternative understandings of the form as used by native peoples [1]. William Bevis in "*Native American Novels: Homing In*," and Louis Owens in *Other Destinies* perform similar service for the Native American novel [2]. All four critics recognize in both method and intention a difference from canonical works of the Western literary tradition. Owens' study, for example, recognizes in native stories "other destinies" and "other plots" (1992a, 1). Krupat says of Native texts: "What they teach frequently runs counter to the teaching of Western tradition, and...the ways in which they delight is different from the ways in which the Western tradition has given pleasure" (1989, 54). Quite naturally then, any "transcendental voice of universalizing theory" could not accurately interpret or represent the "other" voice and method of American Indian literature. The insistence on reading Native literature by way of Western literary theory clearly violates its integrity and performs a new act of colonization and conquest.

Hartsock says we should neither "ignore" the knowledge/power relations inherent in literary theory and canon formation nor merely "resist" them; we must "transform" them (204). Owens, in his discussion of the Native American writers' struggle with language and articulation, the conflicts between written and oral, English and native languages, also calls for a kind of transformation of the existing system. Speaking specifically of N. Scott Momaday, but seeing his case as like that of "his fellow Indian writers," Owens writes: "The task before him was not simply to learn the lost language of his tribe but rather to appropriate, to tear free of its restricting authority, another language -- English -- and to make it accessible to an Indian discourse" (1992a, 13). His comments here on creative works have implications for the language and articulation of literary criticism as well. What Owens in his own critical work and many other Native American and non-native scholars have attempted is to "tear free of its restricting authority" the existing critical language and "make that language accessible to an Indian discourse." Scholars like Owens, Gerald Vizenor, James Ruppert, Gretchen Ronnow, Arnold Krupat, Elaine Jahner and myself have employed, for example, postmodern theory, the critical language of the likes of Mikhail Bakhtin, Jacques Lacan and Jacques Derrida in the reading of Native American texts [1]. We have made use of the intersections of Native works with post-colonial and semiotic theory, and with any number of other established critical discourses.

While I believe these theories, like Bakhtin's distinction between monologue and dialogue and between linear and pictorial writing styles, have been helpful, they still have the same modus operandi when it comes to Native American literature. The literature is approached with an already established theory, and the implication is that the worth of the literature is essentially validated by its demonstrated adherence to a respected literary mode, dynamic or style. Although the best scholars in native studies have not applied the theories in this colonizing fashion but have employed them, the implied movement is still that of colonization: authority emanating from the mainstream critical center to the marginalized native texts. Issues of Orientalism and enforced literacy apply again when another language and culture, this time a critical language and the Euro-American literary tradition, take prominence and are used to explain, replace or block an indigenous critical language and literary tradition [2].

This distinction between applying already established theory to native writing versus working from within native literature or tradition to discover appropriate tools or to form an appropriate language of critical discourse, implicates my own work to date just as it implicates the work of most other scholars of native literature. I am not suggesting our critical attempts have all been for naught. However, I am hopeful that future efforts will proceed with greater awareness of the precarious situation that Native American literary criticism is heir to.

In fact, the situation is still more complicated than these comments have so far indicated because the literary works themselves are always at least bi-cultural: Though they may come from an oral-based culture, they are written. Though their writer may speak a tribal language, they are usually almost wholly in the language of English. And though they proceed at least partly from an Indian culture, they are most often presented in the established literary and aesthetic forms of the dominant culture (or in those forms acceptable to the publishing industry). The writers themselves have generally experienced both tribal and mainstream American culture and many are in physical fact mixed-bloods. Beyond this, the works themselves generally proceed from an awareness of the "frontier" or border existence where cultures meet. The criticism, too, even if written by Native Americans, is also, (and for many of the same reasons) at least bi-cultural. Perhaps to adequately open up the multicultural texts of Native American literature, it must be.

Having briefly sketched the complexities of this critical intersection, I still do not rescind my call for an "organic" native critical language. If we need a dual vision to adequately appreciate the richness of Indian literature, the native half to that vision has still been conspicuously absent. Krupat has also articulated a call for new literary criticism, most recently in *Ethnocriticism: Ethnography, History and Literature* and his introduction to *New Voices in Native American Literary Criticism*. He claims, for example:

> "In recent years some academic researchers have wanted very much to take seriously, even, indeed, to base their research upon not only Native experience but Native constructions of the category of knowledge. Still, as I have said, the question remains: How to do so? It is an urgent question" (1993 xix).

Contextual Experiments

Perhaps the most frequently employed mode for articulating what Krupat calls "Native constructions of the category of knowledge" has been oppositional. Lines have been drawn, for example, between cyclical and linear, biological and anthropological, communal and individual. In his 1985 introduction to *New and Old Voices of Wah' kon-tah: Contemporary Native American Poetry*, Vine Deloria, Jr. distinguishes Native poetic expression with just such oppositional rhetoric: "Indian poetry may not say the things that poetry says because it does not emerge from the centuries of formal western thought....It is hardly chronological and its sequences relate to the integrity of the circle, not the directional determination of the line. It encompasses, it does not point" (ix). Although this and many of the oppositional distinctions may have been necessary early on to underscore the difference, the distinct voice of Indian literature, and although they do contribute to an understanding of the native literary character, they actually proceed from and reinforce an understanding of the dominant position of the Euro-American literary aesthetic, constructing their own identity as they do by its relationship to that master template.

Again taking up the ideas of circularity, Gordon Henry more recently coined the terms "sacred concentricity" to describe both the form and the intention of much Native writing [3]. However, he framed his theory without invoking or writing itself against either the secular or the enshrined linear aesthetic. He simply set out to explain the movement and form he observed in novels like *Ceremony*, *Love Medicine* and *House Made of Dawn* whose story he felt created a sacred center (which might be place, person, event, etc.) from which emanated ripples of power and connection (and might involve healing, return, forgiveness, etc.). The aesthetic form and movement described in Henry's language has, of course, been noted in various ways and in various degrees by other scholars: the seasonal cycles of *Ceremony* have been noted, the cyclical structure of *House Made of Dawn* explored. Owens writes of the "centripetal" orientation of *Ceremony* and of the "web" it creates. Paula Gunn Allen writes of "the sacred hoop" or "medicine wheel" as the informing figure behind much Native writing (56). The emerging critical language expressing this central aesthetic characteristic of Native literature need not or should not have to base its existence or integrity on an oppositional relationship.

Several of the intriguing experiments in Native critical discourse recognizes both the differences between Native and non-Native perspectives and the complexity of the literary voice that arises from the convergence of these different perspectives. They take as their mode of operation dialogue or mediation between these two critical and cultural centers. Gerald Vizenor's "trickster discourse," Keith Basso's "code-switching" and bicultural "linguistic play," Arnold Krupat's "ethnocritiques" or "ethnocriticism," and Louis Owen's "mixed-blood metaphors" all proceed from an awareness of the border quality of native speech, writing and criticism. Although each scholar theorizes and enacts their theory in varying ways, they all seek to enrich the understanding of native literature by drawing their interpretation from the same multicultural experience which informed the creation of the text. They attempt to explore the wavering and delicate balance in the frontier text between tradition and innovation, to untangle the braided cultural contexts, to acknowledge what James Ruppert calls the "mediational discourse" which "strives to bring the oral into the written, the Native American vision into contemporary writing, spirit into modern identity, community into society, and myth into modern imagination"(210). In Vizenor and in Basso's theories, much of this mediation is accomplished playfully, with humor and self-conscious satire. Beneath or within the humor, cultural contexts and conflicts are bounced off of one another. Understanding here is always in motion.

The Predicament of Theory

However, as Jana Sequoya points out, even the theoretical position of mediation carries with it the possibility for a new form of dominance. The full representation of difference involves multiple sites of literary and cultural knowledge. However in the creation of this multicultural dialogue, this new national story, Native stories may again be changed or taken out of context. "In the oral tradition," Owens has claimed, "context and text are one thing" (1992a, 13); but it is the separation of the two that Sequoya foresees in "their expropriation for the literary market by the cultural mediator" (467). She writes of the different ways of "having" stories and claims that removing sacred oral stories from their actual culture context to place them within a literary context destroys their social role (460, 468). If this is true, to what degree might all critical endeavors be said to destroy the most immediate social or aesthetic value of those works it seeks to interpret? Alexander Nehamas speaks of the "cruelty of the commentator" and claims that the "elevation" of cultural story to the level of "literature" destroys its moral function [4]. Vizenor warns against the "dead voices" of "wordies" who situate the story in the "eye and not the ear" (7). Krupat, too, discusses the quandaries of criticism particularly as it applies to oral tradition and notes that "Indian people... have no need to produce a body of knowledge about it [oral performative literature] that is separate and apart from it" (1992, 187).

Although the task of the contemporary native theorist seems fraught with difficulty, in the last comment by Krupat we find what may be a direction to take and we find the circularity of this discussion for his comment inadvertently brings us back to the idea of criticism as existing within and arising from the literature itself. Traditional native literature has always entailed both performance and commentary with, in Dennis Tedlock's language, the "conveyer" functioning as the "interpreter" as well. We get, says Tedlock, "the criticism at the same time and from the same person" (47-48). In a similar fashion, contemporary texts contain the critical contexts needed for their own interpretation and, because of the intertextuality of Native American literature, the critical commentary and contexts necessary for the interpretation of works by other Native writers.

If we return to Owen's *The Sharpest Sight*, for example, we find the story centers partly on identity and Cole McCurtain's search for an Indian identity. Cole is told by Hoey McCurtain, "You are what you think you are" which throws Owen's text immediately into dialogue with N.Scott Momaday's "Man Made of Words," especially his oft-quoted statement, "We are what we imagine. Our very existence consists in our imagination of ourselves. Our best destiny is to imagine, at least, completely, who and what, and that we are. The greatest tragedy that can befall us is to go unimagined" (55). Owen's Cole disputes Huey (and Momaday) scoffing, "As if...you could really choose what you are going to be instead of just being what it was you had to be" (15). These statements fall early in Owen's novel. The remaining story and the various characters' searches for identity will be read in the broader context Owen's has implied. And Momaday is but one of many authors whose ideas or literary works are invoked by Owens in *The Sharpest Sight*. His text comes equipped with many of its own tools of literary interpretation.

Indeed, the dialogues enacted in and between Native texts offer scholars not only rich opportunities for interpretation, but much of the language and organizing principles necessary for the construction of a critical center. Vizenor, for example, offers us the idea of "shadow writing" and "mythic metaphors." Erdrich offers the possibility of kinship as a formal structuring principal, and the visual images of "buried roots" and "a globe of frail seeds." Momaday gives us the metaphor of the ritual "runners after evil," Owens the metaphor of an "underground river," and Janet Campbell Hale and D'Arcy McNickle offer metaphors of confinement. Our sources also provide intertextual metaphors and critical terms as the texts in their richness quote and comment on one another, and as the authors frame their own works in the context of the writings of other Native authors. Maurice Kenny, for example, titles a collection of tribal poetry "*Wounds Beneath the Flesh*," taking the phrase from Geary Hobson's "*Barbara's Land Revisited* - August 1978," and Paula Gunn Allen takes the title for one section of *The Sacred Hoop* from Vizenor's critical commentary on "word warriors." Add to this literary self-consciousness and intertextuality, the multiple connections with oral tradition and the theorizing within the literary works themselves. Add, for example, Silko's intermingling of the traditional and contemporary story, Diane Glancy's and Linda Hogan's comments on the political powers of language and literacy, and Vizenor's theories on trickster.

The critical language of Mikhail Bakhtin and Walter J. Ong may profitably be applied to Native American literature, but as Owen's Uncle Luther reminds us, we must first "know the stories of our people" and then "make our own story too." And, he warns, we must "be aware of the way they change the stories we already know" for only with that awareness can we protect the integrity of the Native American story. One way to safeguard that integrity is by asserting a critical voice that comes from within that tribal story itself.

End Notes

[1] See, for example, *Narrative Chance: Postmodern Discourse on Native American Indian Literatures* (Ed. Gerald Vizenor, Albuquerque: U of New Mexico P, 1989).

[2] I discuss literacy and Orientalism in "Learning 'The Language the Presidents Speak': Images and Issues of Literacy in American Indian Literature." *World Literature Today.* 66.2 (Spring 1992): 230-35.

[3] From conversations with Henry about his notion of "sacred concentricity" and from his verbalization of it at a lecture at the University of Wisconsin-Milwaukee in 1992.

[4] Discussed by Nehamas in a lecture "What Should We Expect from Reading? (These Are Only Aesthetic Values)" given at University of Wisconsin-Milwaukee, 1993.

Works Cited

Allen, Paula Gunn. *The Sacred Hoop: Recovering the Feminine in American Indian Traditions.* Boston: Beacon Press, 1986.

Basso, Keith H. *Portraits of "The Whiteman": Linguistic Play and Cultural Symbols Among the Western Apache.* Cambridge: Cambridge UP, 1979.

Bevis, William. "Native American Novels: Homing In." *Recovering the Word: Essays on Native American Literature.* Ed. Brian Swann and Arnold Krupat. Berkeley: U of California P, 1987: 580-620.

Deloria, Vine, Jr. "Forward." *New and Old Voices of Wah'kon-tah: Contemporary Native American Poetry.* Ed. Robert K. Dodgeand Joseph B. McCullough. New York: International Publishers, 1985: ix-x.

Hartsock, Nancy. "Rethinking Modernism: Minority vs. Majority Theories." *Cultural Critique* 7 (1987): 187-206.

Krupat, Arnold. *Ethnocriticism: Ethnography, History, Literature.* Berkeley: U of California P, 1992.

——*The Voice in the Margin: Native American Literature and the Canon.* Berkeley: U of California P, 1989.

——"Introduction." *New Voices in Native American Literary Criticism.* Ed. Arnold Krupat. Washington: Smithsonian Institution Press, 1993.

——*For Those Who Came After: A Study of Native American Autobiography.* Berkeley: U of California P, 1985.

Momaday, N.Scott. "The Man Made of Words." *Indian Voices: The First Convocation of American Indian Scholars.* San Francisco: The Indian Historian Press, 1970: 49-62.

Owens, Louis. *Other Destinies: Understanding the American Indian Novel.* Norman: U of Oklahoma P, 1992a.

——*The Sharpest Sight.* Norman: U of Oklahoma P, 1992b.

Sequoya, Jana. "How (!) Is an Indian?: A Contest of Stories." *New Voices in Native American Literary Criticism.* Ed. Arnold Krupat. Washington: Smithsonian Institution Press, 1993: 453-73.

Tedlock, Dennis. "The Spoken Word and the Work of Interpretation in American Indian Religion." *Traditional American Indian Literatures.* Ed. Karl Kroeber. Lincoln: U of Nebraska P, 1981: 45-64.

Vizenor, Gerald. *Dead Voices: Natural Agonies in the New World.* Norman: U of Oklahoma P, 1992.

Wong, Hertha. "Sending My Heart Back Across the Years": *Tradition and Innovation in Native American Autobiography.* New York: Oxford UP, 1992.

History, Nature, Family, Dream:

THE MUSICAL COLORS OF THEIR POEMS

by

Duane Niatum

Duane Niatum

Duane graduated with a B.A. in English, and received his Master's degree from Johns Hopkins University. He has also been published extensively, appearing in many publications and magazines such as; *The Nation, Prairie Schooner, Northwest Review, The American Poetry Review*, and many other literary journals and anthologies. His previous published collections of poetry are; *After the Death of an Elder Klallam, Ascending Red Cedar Moon, Digging Out The Roots* and *Songs for the Harvester of Dreams*, which won the National Book Award from The Before Columbus Foundation in 1982. He presently lives in Ann Arbor, Michigan where he is working on a Ph.D thesis on Contemporary Northwest Art. He is also the editor of *Harper's Anthology of 20th century Native American poetry.*

Introduction

This essay on American Indian poetry will emphasize the fact that the time has come for the Euroamerican literary canon to open its doors to these poets and accept their art as a legitimate part of the literature being produced by Americans today. For me, this is the major justification for writing such an essay. And if the Euroamerican reader is willing to take the plunge, he or she may learn two important things: to challenge cultural isolation and narcissism by a willingness to experience a culture in many ways different from his or her own. If the poetry is approached with a desire to understand and achieve some pleasure in the process, perhaps something new will be realized about one's own self and society.

Until recently, most non-Native Americans had a problem accepting American Indian poetry and stories because they had somehow lost faith in the truthfulness of their own words, especially in view of the massmedia overloading the individual with words so thoroughly commercialized and polluted. This no doubt inspired the English poet, Ted Hughes, to write the following lines: "Oversold like detergents," they wave "their long tails in public/With their prostitute's exclamations."

But today it is possible to introduce this poetry to a wider audience since the arrogance and attitudes of cultural imperialism have begun to weaken and erode while by no means completely disappearing. Thus, it is apparent that the various manifestations of cultural superiority which many Europeans and Euroamericans in the nineteenth and early twentieth centuries held to be the dictates of almost a god, are quietly fading away in waves of deconstruction.

We are now in the position to learn from their poems, that to an American Indian, the truth of words is no more or no less than the truth revealed in Nature. This belief relates to the fact that as a tribal poet, the word is a sacred object, a vital force of man and woman and the natural world. Since it is an oral tradition right up to the present moment, the words are the carriers of the culture from past generations to the present, and on into the future. The values of the tribe are fused into the songs and stories. This is the case because the tribal poet believes that the word, if used respectfully is invested with power and magic.

Furthermore, this sense of a word's power was so commonplace among the tribes in the past that most believed the poem or story had a life of its own independent of its narrator. This in no way threatened the ego of these poets since they knew from the beginning that they are able to create a poem or story because they are merely the vocal reeds for the expression of their people, and that a higher power than themselves gave them the gift to give back to the people something they had lost long ago on the road we are forever following into the next century.

For most poets, working from the oral traditions, believe that they are only keepers of the sacred dream wheel of the art and its music. If anything, the tribal poet thinks the song or poem gives him or her the chance to be more whole, more real, and not the other way around.

Therefore, what we find in their poems is how the word makes things dance and moves the mundane world into the spiritual. The poem is found to be a world in itself. The primal imagination uses language in such a way that the people are woven into the fabric of his or her art with the same naturalness that the surroundings and the physical world are woven into the poetic fabric. As a result, all creatures and things that exist on the earth are fit subjects for the poem.

When we look closely at the work of the best current American Indian artists, no matter what the form, we recognize that they celebrate the everyday things of the social world, its colors, shapes, sounds, textures, dreams and reason. They seem to want to convey the essence of their particular experiences by acutely observing the everyday events and things of the world down to the smallest detail. These poets strive for an unperceived reality found beneath the surfaces of the places and objects where we live and work and play. Thus, when we approach the art from this perspective, we notice immediately that the poetry attempts to cast light on the present moment in a way that allows the tribal past to shine through. Therefore, its point of view will be understood to be cyclical. And whatever element in the poem we isolate for proof or discussion, chances are some image, idea, emotion, or perception of the history of the particular poet's tribe will be found.

Moreover, this world view is organic and tells its story like the seasons, the turnings of the earth, the sun and moon, man and woman, cloud and wind. For example, as the sun gives way to the moon, the winter gives way to spring, the seed gives way to the blackberry, the smelt gives way to the smokehouse. But, this does not mean that the tribal poet and his or her audience is not aware of the fact that art is artifice as well. For generations upon generations these people have joked about the artifice of art, politics, religion, philosophy, and human society. There humor rings with satiric drums and whistles at the overly serious artist, shaman, chief, warrior or trader. What distinguishes them as contemporary poets from their shaman ancestors will only be that their aesthetic and point of view has absorbed a new dimension with the influence of "world culture" on the roots of their tribal cultures. This element of modernity plays an added role in what they create as artists. It contributes to their imaginations one more method to develop the very important element of balance and proportion, a fluid element in which the image-symbol is helped to grow and change. In one sense, this slight disruption from their cultural roots, as they enter the exile landscape of the twentieth century, is actually a mirror-image of exiled man and woman found today around the world.

This breakdown between the mind and body in the Euroamerican, the rejection that this relationship contains the key to maintaining some semblance of continuity and unity among the self, sexes, the generations, community and world, appears to be the existential demise of the urban individual who has chosen to live largely inside his or her head. Unfortunately, fantasy not grounded in some way to the physical universe can quickly surprise the one engaged in it by creating its own abstract prison. Even Isak Dinesen, true master of the visionary tale kept as a maxim for her life and art; "That you cannot neglect reality while surrendering to your dreams." In contrast to this view of the Euroamerican denying the external world, the tribal poet embraces the world beyond the self, the earth, sea, sky, bird, animal, fish and plant, stone and snowflake.

Tribal Values: Continuity

Now I will illustrate with specific poems how history is utilized in various ways by these poets. Common sense has shown their ancestors over the centuries that it is a sure method of maintaining continuity among generations. A perfect sense and example of this need for continuity among generations is found in Wendy Rose's lines from her poem, "What My Father Said." Wendy is Hopi/Miwok.

> Begin, he said, by giving back;
> as you eat, they eat
> so never be full.
> Don't let it get easy.
> Remember them
> think of those ones
> that were here before,
> remember
> how they were hungry,
> their eyes like empty bowls,
> those ribs sticking out,
> those tiny hands [1].

Also take the middle stanza from Jim Barnes', "Trying To Read The Glyphs." This sense of connection is older than his Choctaw ancestors. Jim and the stone face merge into one being, what art and the transforming spirit sometimes are able to do.

> A thousand years dead, the waterfall pour
> dry fire into my eyes, the acid of
> my seat grooves the painted face fingers
> claw into. The eyes reject my touch as I
> pull the glyph to me like a departing lover.
> I am body for the etched face I cannot
> read. Flesh and stone, my mind is full of bones
> the cames hide in webs thick as arctic snow [2].

Wholeness

Another value with similar origins is often found in conjunction with the one just discussed. It has to do with how we see ourselves in relationship to the nature of things, both animate and inanimate. Like other values we will soon discuss, it is found in the art and society of countries around the world. It is the simple yet profound idea that "all is one." This is true even though many writers and artists of the twentieth century have adopted the attitude that "the idea of unity" or "oneness among living creatures and things" is a sham, and "disunity" and "fragmentation" are the real concepts that define ourselves and the natural world. They would replace "all is one" with "all is fragments." Donald Barthelme [3], for example, has a character say in one of his stories that he believes that the only thing that seems real to him is the fragment. And Helen Vendler [4], a critic, praises Louise Glück [5] for her "cryptic narratives," a la minimalism. But only in our age has the fragmented and vague been considered seriously as an element of art, no matter what the form. Before the 1920s and the appearance of Surrealism and Dadaism, they were thought of as "cheap shots." Although this may be the aesthetic view for the Euroamerican artist and individual, the American Indian and tribal artist from around the globe would be committing cultural suicide if they accepted this view for themselves. Such a self-destructive attitude undermines the very foundations of their tribal heritages. This attitude that reinforces the chic cynicism of consumer culture, of course, is not a new fashion. It has been in the air at least as long as the Nihilist Movement of the nineteenth century. In fact, several theories of modern science, in their own devious ways, have contributed to this view as it caters more and more to politics and the marketplace. But with most American Indians you are as much a part of what you see as what you see is a part of you.

This world view is apparent in the next poem section by Jim Barnes. For years I have been amazed at the sudden sound of the tap, tap, tap of the flicker, but never became one with this bird quite like Jim Barnes in this stanza from "Tree Songs From A Texas Oilfield."

> In pecking order
> the flicker is king
> of ground and trunk:
> dressed in black tie
> and hammered vest,

he speaks with the authority
of a pile driver [6].

The Idea of Place

The hive of place is another way in which these tribal poets bed down in reality and dream there might be a tomorrow. They cannot ignore the ambivalent path of illusion whether asleep or awake, but illusion is balanced in their poems with the feeling of knowing briefly what their present place in the larger context of things and world actually is at the moment. The tone and vision of their poems often defines the larger context of things and world and how they see themselves in relationship to the world in which they live.

We discover from these poets that form is inextricably connected to melody and movement. Any adequate rendering of their work would have to convey in Native figures, the many sensory paths of imminent world-overturning and spiritual reestablishment in the Oneness of nature and the brotherhood of man, animal, and universe.

The idea of place, its significance to the tribal poet, can easily be recognized in N. Scott Momaday's "To A Child Running With Outstretched Arms in Canyon de Chelly." Momaday is a Kiowa from Oklahoma, but he has lived in the past for many years on the Navajo Reservation in Arizona, where the Canyon de Chelly is found.

> You are small and intense
> In your excitement, whole,
> Embodied in delight.
> The backdrop is immense;
>
> The sand drifts break and roll
> Through cleavages of light
> And shadow. You embrace
> The spirit of this place [7].

Like the tapestry of morning light, what holds these separate voices in a single circle is the wonder in singing back to life ancestral connections. What is meant by ancestral connections is a belief the

American Indian has in never looking upon the land or river or lakes or mountains surrounding his village without seeing the homes and paths of his grandfathers and grandmothers. Therefore, 'by singing, the soul of the singer is put in harmony with the essential essence of things' [8].

"My flowers shall not perish
nor my chants cease:
they spread, they scatter."

Here I want to mention another historical fact. There has always been a place for poetry in the life of American Indian people. From the birth of the first tribe there was a path of transformation of life's experiences into song. Tribal myths and legends and jokes tell of the people singing of almost every event in their lives. There are songs of birth, death, fertility and renewal, joy and sadness, work and play, dream, planting and harvesting crops, hunting and fishing, loving and hating, fearing and trusting. "The old ones," (tribal ancestors), felt there was no experience that could not be made into song for the breath and dance of the people. Of course, there are differences to be recognized between the ancient songs and the new. The ancient songs were not isolated from the broader social and spiritual canvas of the community, for example. Songs in the old days were not called art. Art objects such as poems, paintings, sculptures, pots and rugs were considered expressions of the community as a whole, not as personal, egocentric works. To do the work of an artist was simply an integral part of the normal routines of the tribe. Art, work, play, religion, and society, to name just a few of the things we do as a group, were linked to each other as the tribe's single thread of experience.

So there, cultures were devoid of a Shakespeare, a Keats, an Emily Dickinson. This was, due in part, because most songs were created anonymously. In such communities self-indulgence and egotism was considered a destructive force and in bad form. Individual will and the creative act were subjected to the needs and desires of the tribe. As an artist you were expected to keep a very low profile. As N. Scott Momaday has aptly put it:

71

In order to understand the true impetus of contemporary
Native American poetry, it is necessary to
understand the nature of the oral tradition. Until
quite recently, the songs, charms, and prayers
of the Native American--those embodied exclusively
within the oral tradition;that is, their existence
was wholly independent
of writing [9].

Therefore, if we listen and read carefully the poems of these contemporary authors, we will recognize certain fundamental beliefs and attitudes about the nature and spirit of language and literature, and man and woman's continued belief in the sacred power of words. Natalie Curtis said in *The Indian's Book,* "Song is the breath of the spirit that consecrates the act of life."

Perhaps the most prevalent unifying tribal value you will discover in their poetry is the soul chanting for kinship. Every American Indian artist that has inspired me has woven this important thread into the material of the work. "Dream of Rebirth," by Roberta Hill Whiteman, an Oneida from Wisconsin, certainly demonstrates the kinship value in the form nearest to the oral tradition, namely, the brief lyric. The Oneida were originally from the New York area and were members of the legendary Iroquois Confederacy. Her words show the healing power of song--how it can become a wing or a mediation to an ailing body and a weary spirit. This is the final stanza:

> I dreamed an absolute silence birds had fled.
> The sun, a meager hope, again was sacred.
> We need to be purified by fury.
> Once more eagles will restore our prayers.
> We'll forget the strangeness of your pity.
> Some will anoint the graves with pollen.
> Some of us may wake unashamed.
> Some will rise that clear morning like the swallows [10].

There is an ancient Aztec song that declares the true artist is one who creates from the heart and works with delight. This poem of

Whiteman's echoes in her unique way that rigorous standard. It speaks with sagacity when it says: "Worn-out hands carry the pale remains of forgotten murders," yet manages in the end to unify the lost selves, regain the lost ground, turn the pain into a vision of healing. We are likely to enter her verbal canvas because she meets unflinchingly the slipping and sliding of life, the despair of the soul of her people and herself with a sense of engagement and wonder.

In the following passage, we witness the strong sense she has of her relationship to the community of her people and even the stars. These are the last two stanzas from "Star Quilt":

> Star quilt, sewn from dawn light by fingers
> of flint, take away those touches
> meant for nosier skins,
>
> anoint us with grass and twilight air,
> so we may embrace, two bitter roots
> pushing back into the dust [11].

But we see no forced sense of tribal values in these lines. There strength lies in how much values are fused into the weave of the poem as if the quilt was the narrator, as it probably is. She tells us in the notes at the back of the book that the star quilt was made by the Plains Indian women for their children and grandchildren. They are so important to the Plains people that a young man may take one of these blankets on his vision quest into the sacred mountains of his ancestors. Thus we see how it weaves one generation into the fabric of life of the next generation and all succeeding generations, since much of its value stems from the passing on of its spirit from one generation to the next.

Let us now look at how Simon Ortiz, an Acoma Pueblo from the Southwest, ties into a sacred bundle, all the values we have discussed in this essay. His poem, "A Story of How a Wall Stands," brings to us an experience where his father shows, while working with mud and stone on something he is building, how a stone wall 400 years old is a grandfather to both him and his son, and how, if one looks closely at its nature, the smallest details of its design and form, it will show how to hold all of one's parts together in a harmonious relationship to the land around one and the land within one. Here is the first stanza of the poem:

> My father, who works with stone,
> says, "That's just the part you see,
> the stones which seem to be
> just packed in on the outside,"
> and with his hands puts the stone and mud
> in place. "Underneath
> what looks like loose stone,
> there is stone woven together."
> He ties one hand over the other,
> fitting like the bones of his hands
> and fingers. "That's what is
> holding it together" [12].

In the following passage of another poem Ortiz gives us a sense of how natural is the Pueblo's feeling about being brother or sister to all things before us, whether land, water, or animal. Ortiz is with his father in their corn field. The title is *"My Father's Song"* and the third and fourth stanzas are these:

> My father had stopped at one point
> to show me an overturned furrow;
> the plowshare had unearthed
> the burrow nest of a mouse
> in the soft moist sand.
>
> Very gently, he scooped tiny pink animals
> into the palm of his hand
> and told me to touch them.
> We took them to the edge
> of the field and put them in the shade
> of a sand moist clod [13].

We see from these stanzas how a poet does not speak just for himself, his family, and his tribe, but for everything around him including a creature so tiny as a field mouse and her babies.

Before discussing other ideas about their work, I would like to return to a few passages by Whiteman. In an interview with Joe Bruchac she tell us that to write a poem is very much like a woman weaving a quilt. She says her writing has a lot to do with engaging oneself in the mysteries of life and trying to better understand and appreciate that relationship. She implies that being and knowing she is an Oneida is very important to her as an artist. Incidentally, this echoes much of what other American Indian artists have said. The attraction could be thought of as a home and what that connection offers. She confirms what many other writers and artists have said in terms of her strong feeling of accepting her dispossession and how important it is to try and put it all back together. With many other writers, the first experience of learning and feeling yourself as an exile in your own land is experienced in childhood.

Another dimension to her art is witnessed in *"Woman Seed Player"* when the poet shows us the wondrous exchange possible between two arts. In this poem, she is narrating the story from a painting by the late Lakota artist, Oscar Howe. It is a descriptive poem since the focus is on a woman seed-player in a whirlwind dance as she tosses seeds to the earth. The seed-player expresses a feeling for life being reborn and the words reveal the dance of the poem, for example:

> When running shadow turns rattler,
> her concern is how the mountain rises
> beyond its line of sorrow. Then,
> shooting her seeds, she bids
> the swallow fly over rolling hills [14].

The poet offers us symbolically the two polarities that keep us wondering about ourselves and the world, that is, in the way the rattlesnake of the earth and the swallow of the sky, the two poles of flesh and spirit are brought together in a new unity. In a few lines later she speaks directly to the artist:

75

> You said no one had ever gone full circle,
> from passion through pattern and back again
> toward pebbles moist with moonlight [15].

Awareness of our finiteness makes us want to fly or crawl forever. We long to believe there exists a unity between life and death, earth and sky, yet we know full well nobody has returned from the dead to tell us if it is true or possible. But, in other lines, Whiteman shows us a healing source whose significance is related directly to the art she sees in nature:

> How easily the rain cross-stitches
> a flower on the screen, quickly
> pulls the threads, varying the line [16].

We should have it so good she might be implying, and perhaps, in our own small way we do, as these lines hint:

> The leaf light dust and her stable hand
> allow my will its corner of quiet. [17]

Louise Erdrich, a poet and novelist, is a member of the Turtle Mountain Band of Chippewa from North Dakota. She has mentioned in an interview that it is important for those who read her work to remember that she is from a very mixed-blood background and culture, one that certainly includes Chippewa, German and French. This is also the case for other American Indian authors, such as, Leslie Marmon Silko, N. Scott Momaday, Wendy Rose, Paula Gunn Allen, Maurice Kenny. This fact, Erdrich assures us, has had an immense influence on her as a person and a writer. It often dictates how she writes and what she writes. She says she never tries to consciously control what she writes, but lets it flow as if by its own volition. She equates a poet or fiction writer to being something like a medium at a seance. You let the voice of the characters speak through you. She tells us what many other tribal writers have said in their own ways. That is, if you are a mixed-blood, you are never allowed to forget you are an outsider, an alien living in the mainstream of America. The forces of the mainstream never tire of telling the mixed-blood how she or he does not fit into their social framework. As she says, the strongest voice guiding your art may very well be the voice of your tribal ancestry.

"Indian Boarding School: The Runaways" is a perfect introduction to her poetry because it symbolizes a caged reality that all junior and senior high Indian students must come to terms with in their young lives. Generally, Bureau of Indian Affairs schools across the nation are hundreds, if not thousands of miles away, from the tribal lands of their students. As a result the students are uprooted from their tribal and family support systems at a very impressionable age.

Furthermore, the poem reflects an entirely different running away than what white youths experience. White children flee the homes of their parents while the Indian students flee the impersonal and sterile environment of the BIA school for their parents' homes and friendly territory. (These schools include the residential as well as church schools that remove children from their homes and cultures). It is an old white technique to force the students into acculturation. As Erdrich says in the poem, in desperation, some Indian students recognize that they must act on their own if they are to free themselves from the boarding school's trap:

> Boxcars stumbling north in dreams
> don't wait for us. we catch them on the run [18].

Soon we discover the hopelessness of their efforts to reach freedom, the fact that the escape is always going to be of short duration:

> ...We watch through cracks in boards
> as the land start rolling, rolling till it hurts
> to be here, cold in regulation clothes.
> We know the sheriff's waiting at midrun
> to take us back. His car is dumb and warm [19].

In the sheriff's car on its way back to the school, these students learn more about life the hard, routine way of alienation.

> The highway doesn't rock, it only hums
> like a wing of long insults. The worn-down welts
> of ancient punishments lead back and forth [20].

But with the cold eye of irony, another teacher of the road our lives take us down, these youth learn survival regardless of how many times they are caught on the run and taken back to the school. They learn quickly that pain earned on the road is a better teacher than any found in the school. These youth learn by transforming that pain in flight as they tell us in the poem, while scrubbing the sidewalks:

> Our brushes cut the stone in watered arcs
> and in the soak frail outlines shiver clear
> a moment, things us kids pressed on the dark
> face before it hardened, pale, remembering
> delicate old injuries, the spines of names and leaves [21].

"Jacklight" illustrates how easily an American Indian in tune with his or her ancient tribal traditions can take on the voice of an animal, a blue jay, or a stream, and convince us of the naturalness of the transforming act:

> We have come to the edge of the woods,
> out of brown grass where we slept, unseen,
> out of knotted twigs, out of leaves creaked shut,
> out of hiding [22].

We are at first surprised to find that these are not men hunting in the forest, but the animals that are being hunted. Lines further along confirm it:

> We smell the raw steel of their gun barrels,
> mink oil on leather, their tongues of sour barley. [23]

But, it seems apparent that these animals who have come to the edge of the forest are there for a purpose since we learn that they have been coming to this edge too long now and it is time for a change:

> It is their turn now,
> their turn to follow us. Listen
> they put down their equipment.
> ...
> And now they take the first steps, not knowing
> how deep the woods are and lightless [24].

Chances are these animals are showing us and the hunters that they are our lost family, what we all have been searching for, their path back to where we came from, what we have lost on the road to the urban abstractions, the cities so many of us now call home.

"After all, what is writing but controlled dreaming?"
- Borges (1899-19??)

When you are forced to survive socially, economically and spiritually, completely at the mercy of a dominant and predatory culture that still does all it can to break down further your sources of power, you would be a fool not to continue the tradition of dreaming a path of transformation beyond the paradox of your physical prison. So it will come as no surprise that each cultural region in Native North America has a dream pattern it uses as a springboard to freedom. Each finds that springboard by turning to the untapped sources of their tribal images and symbols, ancient and modern. This is powerful medicine because the image-symbol with a soul and body, the one breathing from within and without its form, draws us to it no matter whether we come from California, Washington, France, South Africa, Peru, the Netherlands, Ohio, or China. What artists have learned for the last 150 years, and modern science confirms, is that there is but one fluid circle of connections through which the several planes of being and doing, feeling and thinking, seeing and dreaming, living and dying, are interrelated spokes on the single wheel of experience. This is the golden light between our worlds. It shows us how we may see the other, man and woman, child, fish, mountain and stone as more than a stranger, a type. This idea of unified vision is a characteristic of the work of nearly every artist from American Indian country I have encountered. Like the vision seekers of First People, these contemporary poets add their songs to the elders' dream-wheel, and chant for survival and renewal.

Since the tribes have always tried to live in harmony with the physical laws of Nature, their sense of time has been seen in terms of the way it is experienced in the natural world. This kinship is important to the people and nurtures their spirits. In contrast, it seems a view that their Euroamerican contemporaries have rejected, or deny exists. Is this one reason why Santayana, the modern American philosopher, said many years ago, "Those who cannot remember the past are the first to repeat it?"

But it is equally important to stress the various ways they use the spirit: spiritual reality may be their major mode of expression, no matter what the art. And didn't Vasily Kandinsky, in 1912, one of the major innovators of modern Western art, make the following comment on the spiritual in art:

> To speak of mystery in terms of mystery.
> Is that not content? Is that not the
> conscious or unconscious purpose
> of the compulsive urge to create [25]?

Still the main purpose, however, has been to show you how these poets uncover the limitless ways the spirit expresses itself in a people, and how the Mohawk, Pueblo, Blackfeet, Oneida, Chocktaw, Hopi and Miwok, and many other tribes from the first morning fire have miraculously united the physical and spiritual worlds in the same space and moment in time. This centeredness and integration of opposing opposites, the light and dark planes of reality, continues to be the broadest canvas of their art, and what may prove the soundest link in the sacred ring of their imagination.

Finally, we could find over and over again how these poets

challenge their Euroamerican critics who claim American Indian cultures and spirits are a small and broken thread in North America's past and present, beyond recognizing, and doomed to extinction. For if we choose, we can with certainty hear the unique cadence of these poets and with what I call an active, open look, see the words of their blood dance in these poems fuller and deeper than any river of summer.

End Notes

[1]. Rose, *The Half-Breed Chronicles* (Los Angeles: West End Press, 1985).

[2]. Barnes, *La Plata Canta* (West Lafayette: Purdue University Press, 1989).

[3]. Donald Barthelme, American novelist and short fiction writer, considered by some critics to be one of the most innovative writers in America since the 1960s.

[4]. Helen Vendler, American Post-New Critic, The supposedly feminine counterpart to Harold Bloom.

[5]. Louise Glück, American poet.

[6]. Barnes, *La Plata Cantata.*

[7]. Niatum, ed., *Carriers of the Dream Wheel* (New York: Harper & Row, 1975).

[8]. Mary Austin, from her introduction to *American Indian Poetry,* edited by George W. Cronyn, XIV (New York: Ballantine Books, 1972).

[9]. Momaday, *Carriers,*

[10]. Whiteman, *Star Quilt* (Minneapolis: Holy Cow Press, 1984).

[11]. Ibid, p.1.

[12] Niatum, ed., *Harper's Anthology of Twentieth Century Native American Poetry* (San Francisco: Harper & Row, 1988).

[13]. Ibid, p. 147

[14]. Whiteman, *Star Quilt.* p. 74

[15]. *Ibid*, p. 74.

[16]. *Ibid*, p. 74.

[17]. *Ibid*, p. 74.

[18]. *Harper's Anthology,* p. 334.

[19]. *Ibid.* p. 334

[20]. *Ibid.* p. 334.

[21]. *Ibid.* p. 335.

[22]. *Ibid.* p. 335.

[23]. *Ibid.* p. 336.

[24]. *Ibid.* p. 336

[25]. Highwater, *The Sweet Grass Lives On* (New York: Lippincott & Crowell, Pub., 1980, p. 15.

TWO VIEWS INTO CONTEMPORARY NATIVE POETRY

by

A. A. Hedge Coke

A.A. Hedge Coke

A.A. Hedge Coke is Huron/ Tsa la gi/
French Canadian and Portugese. She is a
graduate of the Institute of American
Indian Arts. She has also been published
in journals and anthologies including;
Voices of Thunder, *It's Not Quiet
Anymore*, *Caliban*, *Bombay Gin*, *Exit
Zero*, *Naropa Summer Magazine*,
Neon PowWow, *Poetic Voices*,
Sparrow Grass, *Anthology O: Subliminal Time*,
The Little Magazine Gatherings IV,
Reinventing the Enemy's Language,
and an upcoming chapbook by
Tender Buttons Press.

Among the Dog Eaters is a collection of poetry written by Adrian Louis and published by West End Press (1992). Louis is a Paiute journalist from Nevada who teaches English at Oglala Lakota College (O.L.C.) on the Pine Ridge Reservation of South Dakota. Louis has an editing background in tribal newspaper where he was nominated twice for Print Journalist of the Year (National Indian Media Consortium).

Among the Dog Eaters follows the highly acclaimed *Fire Water World* (also published by West End Press), which was chosen co-winner of the Poetry Center Book Award as San Francisco State University as best book of poems published that year (1987). Louis has written several volumes of poetry and has been awarded fellowships from the Bush Foundation. In addition, Louis co-founded the Native American Press Association.

I find the work in *Among the Dog Eaters* to be a unique look at reservation life. The look at reservation life depicted by Louis is, however, not unique within the Native community at large. Louis has succeeded in bringing to light raw perspectives in dealing with blatant racism, oppression, economic devastation, alcoholism, and many other contemporary likelihoods of being Indian in a not-so-Indian world. I applaud Louis in his success in gifting the world community with these inside views. I liken the work to a similar key-hole point of view as utilized by Paddy Chayefsky in his writings. This wonderful place of perception gives pure, unadulterated, insight to the reader without judgements typically made by an alien to the source community.

Louis is primarily writing about life on the Pine Ridge Reservation, of which he is not a Native, though he manages to develop such accuracy it is as if he has always been a part of it. This is due to his being an Indian himself, to his working at O.L.C. since 1984, and to his personal involvement in the community there in South Dakota. The outlook on the world from Pine Ridge is genuine Indian viewpoint. As there is a great lack of easily obtainable published work from deep within Indian Country, I believe Louis has made an excellent gift to the outside world and to the community in setting groundwork for the people there to begin sharing more about the experiences they live.

The work is honest, as real as that spark of life we cling to in survival, as open as a mule deer crossing the Badlands, and as precise as the language in the Fort Larmie Treaty. The voice of Louis is pure "rezzer". The afflictions and tribulations which Louis witnesses are witnessed by all those who choose to retain Indian rights and lands. This volume will both agitate and excite the reader with its realistic approach to presenting life at hand.

> On a Hill
> north of Pine Ridge
> in a furious spring sunlight
> under crashing clouds, in face-slapping wind
> more than a hundred Sioux are crying.

(from: AT THE BURIAL OF A BALLPLAYER
WHO DIED FROM DIABETES)

Through pictorial portrayal of anguish in poetic voice, we witness Indian resiliency and character. The truth of what it means to be an Indian today is partially revealed within this text. The message is clear. This is contemporary life with all its ugliness and beauty, with all its injustices and equity, with a brash unbiased look at peers and separate nations within Indian Country. The breath of desire is puffing throughout this work. The pieces satisfy the curiosity readers may have upon opening its pages. It fulfills a void in written works long overdue. The inclusions of colloquial "Indianisms" such as "ennut", as well as straight out Lakota, help the reader to feel a part of the rhythm and beat of the land and its people. Place is an important part of Indian cultures; the land is the sole connection to the mother of all. This is why the broken treaty issues are so extremely important. The land is sacred to the people just as the "Holy Lands" are sacred in the Middle East. In *Among the Dog Eaters* this reverence for land is evident in many "Pine Ridge" pieces and also in the memory of "NEVADA RED BLUES" -- a reference to Louis' own homelands. The love and loss in his travels from Nevada, through Colorado, to Brown University (where he completed MA studies in Creative Writing), and to Pine Ridge show what this country is to an Indian male helping his people in teaching and on his way to being fulfilled in life.

The Lakota Times gave this volume great reviews. Elizabeth Cook-Lynn reserved commentary when the *Rapid City Journal* asked her to give a review. She told me she wasn't sure that what Louis exposed in his books needed to be explored by the outside world. She felt, rather, that it was meant to be held by "Indians only," as a protective measure. We are often so grossly misportrayed by the outside world, I have to take this into consideration and see that we do need to get this honest portrayal out into the world. I say this in hopes that we may convey our own portrayals and messages without being mistranslated. I do, however, have some difficulty with the inclusion of "THE SWEAT LODGE" as I believe this sacred and best omitted.

All in all, the unique success in bringing this voice to the general populace is an honoured accomplishment in Indian Country. There are many counter-peers in Indian Land writing and achieving success in literature, but few as brash and bold as Adrian C. Louis. I suggest this book as a must read for all interested in life, love, sociology, Indian Studies, and community.

When white men come into Indian land
and try to lead by forlorn example.
I want to laugh and cry at the same time.
If only they understood:
the savages don't want to be tamed!
We wanted to help *the people...*

- Among the Dog Eaters

A Breeze Swept Through is a collection of poetry by Luci Tapahonso published by West End Press (1987, 1989, 1991). Tapahonso is a Dineh (Navajo) woman from Shiprock, New Mexico. At the time of publication she was assistant professor of American Indian Studies, Women Studies, and English at the University of New Mexico in Albuquerque. This volume is her third book of poetry, following "ONE MORE SHIPROCK NIGHT"and "SEASONAL

WOMAN," The works have been partially supported by grants from the National Endowment for the Arts.

A Breeze Swept Through is an impression of life for a southwestern Indian woman and her daughters. It is again unique in that it brings the reader a marvellous take on Indian participation in life from a feminine perspective. From witnessing a "tall cowboy at the store" with her girlfriend in RAISIN EYES, to a mother telling her children:

> remember now, my clear-eyed daughters
> remember now, where this pollen
> where this cornmeal is from
> remember now, you are no
> different

and on sending her four year old to school for the first time in FOR MISTY STARTING SCHOOL, we get a sense of grounding in contemporary Indian female life. The balancing effect of Tapahonso's story-telling skills make obvious the beauty in life and living -- the beauty of being Navajo. The mesmerizing quality or tone present in her language lifts the reader above the page into the cloud of vision evoked by rhythms and currants as sweet as a river, as pleasant as a breeze sweeping through the arid southwest home of the author. The personal quality of the work is inviting and exciting to be a part of in audience.

This volume includes references to symbols used by the author's people (both ancestral and contemporary). It also includes verse similar to traditional songs. This effect of culture on the word is harmonious and integral to the working of the literature for Tapahonso's purposes. Even the cover portrays symbolism and ties of past to present for native women in the works of Jaune Quick-To-See Smith, a highly acclaimed Flathead painter. I prefer to compare Tapahonso's work to Emmi WhiteHorse's (Navajo) paintings, however, because Emmi is known for her aesthetics whereas Jaune is better noted for her political activism. I make the direct comparison to Tapahonso's work in aesthetics through the Beauty Way. The Beauty Way is the way that Navajo live properly. A spiritual path. I find that Tapahonso utilizes this approach in her poems. In SHEEPHERDER'S BLUES (for Betty Holyan--who did herd sheep between film and art school), we absolutely feel the woman to woman, heart to heart, Indian to Indian, Navajo to Navajo, measure of small exchange in conversation between friends who haven't seen one another for a while. FEAST DAYS AND SHEEP THRILLS could only have been penned by a Dineh lady, no one else would own this sense of "Indianism" in a test. This sharing if being "Indian" to the world is a joy to this reader.

This is not to say that Tapahonso is not political. I do find politics at work within this volume, in that being Indian in this time is political.. One cannot simply ignore the disastrous effects of oppression on a people. The honesty and truth in life lies, however subtly, between the lines and is in the work. Although it is customary to italicize words from languages other than English, I find not choosing to italicize Navajo words makes Dineh language equal to English. It is a way of indication this is a living language, not a romanticized version of dominant English. I am very grateful Tapahonso and West End did not opt for the more "standard" way of doing things.

Female that she is, Tapahonso brings a softer touch to Indian reality. Though the reality of being Indian in this era is no more soft to a woman than to a man, Tapahonso manages to bring personal beauty into word, into experience, into life in portraying its meaning to the outside world. Her writings are not necessarily written for that purpose, as it is most definite her Indian audience is well established. Cook-Lynn says of Tapahonso, "She is wonderful. Have you read her?" I believe this is a voice necessary to literature and to Indian Country. The male/female roles of Indian society are still of great importance in preserving and enhancing the culture.

I am taking time to compare these two authors to demonstrate that "all Indians are not alike". Rarely is time given in literary review to compare distinctly separate native writers. This contributes to more stereotyping and generalizations in the outside world view.

I find Adrian C. Louis to be a didactic poet. Graphic illustration of the world he knows gives the reader a sense of knowing what he/she should think after reading the works included in this volume. Maybe this is an important statement to make given the wrongful illusion generally believed by the mainstream American public. It is necessary for a people to portray themselves adequately before outside peoples can understand what it is, this reservation life. I believe it is of utmost importance in working toward peace and compassion. It is in the open now more than ever before.

I have a hard time relating to all of the perspectives Louis subscribes to. I have lived on Pine Ridge and I am from another tribe, just as Louis, so possibly it is because I am female. I have a hard time with Hemingway, too. Both of these writers seem to be a man's man in pen. Louis' writing may well transcend cultures but, I think that he does not transcend gender. The book is an obvious male statement of the life Louis lives, as well it should be. He writes what he sees, and I appreciate the insight into this male perspective myself. I have great respect for his willingness to be so open and take such risks in his work. I know the voice of Louis is an accurate representation of many male voices in this and in other Native communities.

Tapahonso, in comparison, has a definite, aesthetic female voice. The works deal with this femaleness throughout day-to-day life and experience. Motherhood, dating, school, work, grandmothers, and daughters are all included and spoken from the author's point of view. Storytelling is the age old approach to growth and understanding. Tapahonso tells the story of one Navajo woman. I believe Tapahonso transcends the culture gap in her works out of the sheer beauty of the language she utilizes.

Tapahonso's imagery and word play are startling and effective. Her use of track lines and white space are successful in providing breath spaces and one relishes the deliverance of this language. Reading Tapahonso, one is inspired to read Tapahonso aloud--the sense of timing brings music to the ears and the taste of the words on the tongue is delectable.

Both of these authors speak of the past and the present without skipping a moment in time. To do this eloquently is simply Indian to begin with. The past is the present, everything relative, and everything meaningful. To correct images of the past in contemporary literature, we share their unique cultural viewpoints throughout the world. I encourage all interested in extending their own world view to read these two volumes.

DOG ROAD WOMAN

They called you
grandma
Maggie   like
Maggie Valley
I called   on you
for your knowledge
of pieced cotton
I worked clay
to pottery
and thread   to weave
but   had no frame
nor understanding
of pattern
in quilting.
Climbing high
in sacred wood,
which feeds the
di ni la wi gi u no do ti,
I captured hickory
twigs   you wanted
for a toothbrush

to dip snuff.
Ninety-two year old
leathered fingers
caressed stitch
and broadcloth
into blanket.
You with your apron
and bonnet
and laughter
at *gold dollars*
and processed meats.
You who taught
me to butcher
without waste
and who spun
stories   on your
card whenever I
would listen,
we fashioned stars.

DISPELLING
and
TELLING:

SPEAKING NATIVE REALITIES IN MARIA CAMPBELL'S HALFBREED AND BEATRICE CULLETON'S IN SEARCH OF APRIL RAINTREE

by

Kateri Damm

Kateri Damm

Kateri is a band member of the
Chippewas of Nawash, Cape Croker
Band on Georgian Bay, Ontario and of
mixed Ojibway/Polish Canadian/
Pottawotami/English descent. She was
born in Toronto where she lived for several years before her family moved to the
Cape Croker area in 1976. She received
her Honour's B.A. in English Literature
at York University in 1987 and is currently completing her Master's degree in
English Literature in Ottawa, Ontario
before moving to the Cape Croker reserve with her two dogs, Otis and A.J.
my heart is a stray bullet was her first
collection of poetry.

Jeannette Armstrong, in her discussion, "The Disempowerment of First North American Native Peoples and Empowerment Through Their Writing" says that the 'social problems' of Native peoples are caused by the domination, disempowerment and aggression wrought by foreign peoples who sought to damage and destroy them. She asserts that "[t]he dispelling of lies and the telling of what really happened until *everyone*, including our own people understands that this condition did not happen through choice or some cultural defect on our part, is important" (Armstrong, p. 209). She suggests that "as Native writers" our task is twofold: "To examine the past and culturally affirm toward a new vision for all our people in the future, arising out of the powerful and positive support structures that are inherent in the principles of co-operation" (Armstrong, p. 210). Healing, she says, "can take place through cultural affirmation" (Armstrong, p. 209).

Maria Campbell's *Halfbreed* and Beatrice Culleton's *In Search of April Raintree* take up the challenge to Native writers expressed by Armstrong. Both Campbell and Culleton present an alterNative perspective of the history of Canada and in so doing, affirm and preserve Native views, Native realities and Native forms of telling, while actively challenging and re-defining dominant concepts of history, truth and fact. Both upset stereotypes of Native peoples, and particularly of Native women of mixed-blood, by providing a context which speaks to some of the popularized, widely held images of Native peoples that have been created and maintained by the history and literature of the dominant "White" culture in Canada. They question, blur and displace fixed delineations of genre, culture and race and assert their own space. They show how the "social problems" plaguing Native peoples in Canada are caused by aggressive, oppressive and violent social, political and governmental systems which reflect embedded notions of imperialism, colonization and assimilation and not through defects in the people or characters they are portraying.

By speaking in their own voices, Campbell and Culleton give voice to the silence(d). They speak not <u>for</u> Native people in Canada but "of what it was like...what it is still like" (Campbell, p. 9) to be a Native in Canada, to be of mixed First Nations and European blood, to be a Metis woman, to suffer at the hands and history of the dominant culture. From a personal, First Person, autobiographical perspective, both tell something about "what it is like to be a half-breed woman in Canada, about the joys and sorrows, the oppressing poverty, the frustrations and dreams" (Campbell, p. 2). They enter the healing circle by speaking the unspoken, by speaking the disempowerment of Native peoples, by empowering themselves through the telling of memories that they have been socialized in the dominant system to want to forget "but [that] won't be forgotten" (Culleton, p. 9).

Culleton and Campbell are both concerned with the history of the Metis people and the way in which this history has been falsely represented by the dominant colonizing culture and how these false representations have been presented as fact in the government and education systems controlled by the dominant culture. Both texts address the ways in which 'White lies' about Native peoples, their histories and cultures, are used in the education system as a form of indoctrination into the White society. Further, both texts link this form of cultural violence and domination with the assimilation, oppression and poor self image of Native peoples which has led to the various forms of self-destruction and internal violence evident in Native communities. Stereotyping, for Campbell and Culleton, is a reflection of the inherent racism of Canadian society and is one of the factors which is directly responsible for the 'social problems' of the Native people about whom they are writing. Alcoholism, drug abuse, family violence, suicide, prostitution are the products of hopelessness, despair, poverty and loss of identity arising from the "the loss of cohesive cultural relevance...and a distorted view of the non-Native culture" (Armstrong, p. 208).

Culleton in particular uses her text to examine and denounce the portrayal of Metis people in the education system. Through the essays and comments of April's younger sister, Cheryl Raintree, who identifies more closely with her cultural heritage than April but whose highly romanticized view of Metis people is as unrealistic as April's negative perception of them as "gutter creatures," Culleton reveals the lies and tells how the telling of lies affects the lives and well-being of Native peoples.

At one point Cheryl confronts the education system which tries to 'teach' her "how the Indians scalped, tortured and massacred brave white explorers and missionaries" (Culleton, p. 57). She loudly asserts that this version of 'history' is "all a bunch of lies!" (p. 57). Although the teacher tries to silence her by ignoring her point of view, Cheryl refuses to be unheard; she refuses to allow the lies to remain unchallenged:

> "I'm going to pretend I didn't hear that," the teacher had said calmly.
>
> "Then I'll say it again. I'm not going to learn this garbage about the Indian people," Cheryl had said louder, feeling she couldn't back down.
>
> ..."They're not lies; this is history. These things happened whether you like it or not."
>
> "If this is history, how come so many Indian tribes were wiped out? How come they haven't got their land anymore? How come their food supplies were wiped out? Lies! Lies! Lies! Your history books don't say how the white people destroyed the Indian way of life. That's all you white people can do is teach a bunch of lies to cover your own tracks!" (Culleton, p. 57).

Cheryl bravely takes on the entire education system in this scene but as the novel then shows, the dispelling of lies can be a costly undertaking. For her attempt to revise the history being taught about Indian people, Cheryl is threatened and then beaten with a strap by the school authorities. When she continues to refuse to "co-operate" her White foster 'mother' is called in to control her. Using the threat of separation from her sister, Mrs. DeRosier is finally able to dominate Cheryl into acquiescence. Later Cheryl is further punished when Mrs. DeRosier cuts her hair down to the stubble in a sort of symbolic 'scalping.' Although she is forced into a temporary silence, Cheryl continues to attack the portrayal of the Metis people throughout her education in the White school system and regularly writes and sends letters and essays to April which present this alterNative history.

Both Culleton's and Campbell's texts tackle the lies entrenched in the education system and both are written as the memoirs or lifestories of a young Metis or "halfbreed" woman who recounts her personal and family history from within the context of her social and cultural positioning. However, though there are many similarities in the form and content of both stories, there are also some important, relevant differences which must be acknowledged and understood if a reader hopes to read the text responsibly from where it is positioned within its social and cultural context.

Although it contains a disclaimer that, "Names of persons and places have been changed in some cases" (Campbell, p. 7) Maria Campbell's text is autobiographical, based on her experiences as a "half-breed" woman in Canada. Campbell's story begins with an introduction in which she quickly situates the reader, writer and text and establishes the retrospective point of view from which she/I is telling her story, documenting her history, and writing her past. It also clearly outlines Campbell's reason for undertaking the project: to tell "what it is like to be a halfbreed woman in our country" (Campbell, p. 2). Inherent in this statement is the suggestion that Other accounts of "what it is like" are false, distorted and/or incomplete and that Campbell, by speaking about her own life, is presenting a more honest or 'true' depiction. By telling from an insider's point of view, she confronts the lies of history with the realities of her life story.

The story/text moves from the introduction into a relatively brief history of the Metis "halfbreeds" and their land. This history re-presents a Native view of the historical, social and political conditions of the Metis people and challenges the accepted "White" view of the both the Red River Rebellion and the Riel Rebellion. Campbell presents an alterNative view of the people involved and consequently challenges the history book portrayal of Louis Riel, the "Halfbreeds," the white settlers, the treaty Indians and the Conservative Government of John A. Macdonald.

> ...[E]ight thousand troops, five hundred NWMP [North West Mounted Police] and white volunteers from throughout the Territories, plus a Gatling gun arrived to stop Riel, Dumont and one hundred and fifty

Halfbreeds.

The history books say that the Halfbreeds were defeated at Batoche in 1884.

Louis Riel was hanged in November of 1885.
Charge: high treason.

Gabriel Dumont and a handful of men escaped to Montana.

Poundmaker and Big Bear surrendered, were charged with treason, and sentenced to jail for three years.

The other Halfbreeds escaped to the empty pockets of North Saskatchewan.

The total cost to the federal government to stop the Rebellion was $5,000,000 (Campbell, p. 6).

Clearly, Campbell's telling rejects the "history book" portrayal of Louis Riel as "madman." However, instead of opposing this popular "historical" portrayal of Riel directly (by re-stating it and perhaps risking validating or reinforcing it) she simply offers another version of what happened, and in outlining the costs in both human and monetary terms, suggests that it was John A. Macdonald, his government and the NWMP who were "mad" and irrational in their response to the petitions and grievances of the Metis people. Her telling of the history suggests that it was racism on the part of the White government and not insanity or 'savageness' on the part of the Metis people which led to the Rebellion and resulted in the government-sanctioned deaths of those whose primary goal was not to annihilate the White settlers and their government, but to obtain justice by retaining some of their land. Campbell's account of the history of her people tells of the events and people from a Native point of view and can leave no doubt that "totalitarianism and genocide" (Armstrong, p. 208) were motivating factors in government decision-making.

This is an important statement on Campbell's part and one which obviously falls within the realm of action later advocated by Armstrong in her essay. However, as Culleton's text has also shown, this sort of rejection of the versions of 'history' propagated by the dominant culture continues to be necessary and will continue to be so until the lies are completely erased. Since they are not, Armstrong's challenge remains necessary and will continue to be an essential role for Native writers, storytellers and artists for as long as the lies exist and are taught to our children. Fortunately though, this role has already been assumed by several writers including Campbell, Culleton and Lee Maracle whose experience with the school system is remarkably similar to those described by Campbell and Culleton. In her self-published book *I Am Woman*, Maracle says that schools are "ideological processing plants" (Maracle, p.113) that inculcate racism in the students who are taught the colonizer's narrative of integration and hatred of difference. Like the fictional character, Cheryl, Maracle, as a school child, also confronted a teacher about the portrayal of Metis people and later recalled the experience in her life writing:

> The teacher called my turn. I glanced at the clean white page with black characters all over it. 'Louis Riel was a madman, that was hanged...'. I could not buy that anymore than I could the 'cannibalism' fairy tale of fifth grade. I could not forsake my ancestors for all your students to see (Maracle, p.111).

By confronting the hegemonic, racist underpinnings of the colonial, oppressive powers in the dominant society, the lifewriting of Native women can be, and in the cases of Campbell, Culleton and Maracle are, as Doris Sommer suggests in her essay, "'Not Just a Personal Story': Women's *Testimonies* and the Plural Self," "a medium of resistance and counterdiscourse, the legitimate space for producing that excess which throws doubt on the coherence and power of an exclusive historiography" (quoted in Smith and Watson, p. xiii). Lifewriting is in this way, political, disruptive and empowering. In her essay "Construction of the Imaginary Indian," mixed-blood writer Marcia Crosby contends that lifewriting is a way to confront and resist the homogenization of First Nations people and the imposition of "the West's postmodern centre/margin cartography" (Crosby, p. 267). Crosby goes on to state, "I...consider it an act of affirmation to speak in the first-person singular, refusing an imposed and imaginary difference in order to assert my own voice" (Crosby, pp.267-268). Campbell asserts her own voice by telling her version of the history of her Metis people then moving forward to tell of the history of her own community and family. At this point, Campbell also briefly recounts her personal family history and genealogy beginning with her "Great Grandpa Campbell" and finally stretching forward to her children's generation. In this telling, history is not linear, chronological and progressive, it is a spiral in which there is no clear beginning or end. It is a web in which people, actions and events are interconnected and not easily disengaged or delineated. Cause and effect are not simply revealed through a listing of successive dates of events but are enmeshed in a tangle of events, emotions, histories, beliefs, values....

Campbell begins her community and family history by tracing the movement of several halfbreed families to the Prince Albert region of Saskatchewan where they were gradually dislocated and forced by unjust government policies to live as squatters on their own land before finally being left as homeless, disenfranchised outcasts dwelling on the thin margin of "crown land" set aside on either side of planned and completed roads. Living as squatters on road allowance land, these Metis descendants of the First Nations and early settlers had no treaty rights as Indians and no land rights as settlers and so were left without legal or political power and recognition. Campbell, in an interview with German scholar Hartmut Lutz, says that the Metis were "Forgotten People," marginalized geographically, politically, socially and economically:

> You know, Indian people went to school, my people didn't because we weren't allowed to go to school until 1951. We couldn't go to Indian schools, and we couldn't go to white people's schools, because we didn't pay taxes, we weren't landowners (Campbell in Lutz, p. 51).

In *Halfbreed*, Campbell suggests how this neglect contributed to a long-term cycle of poverty and despair which even now continues to effect Metis communities. Campbell says that when the Metis half-breeds, who had been "a proud and happy people," (Campbell, p. 9) became "Road Allowance People" it began a miserable life of poverty which held no hope for the future. That generation of my people was completely beaten. Their fathers had failed during the Rebellion to make a dream come true; they failed as farmers; now there was nothing left. Their way of life was part of Canada's past and they saw no place in the world around them, for they believed they had nothing to offer. They felt shame, and with shame the loss of pride and the strength to live each day (Campbell p. 8).

Campbell clearly links the hopelessness and despair which arose from their history of oppression and injustice to the cycle of self-destructive 'social problems' which are apparent in contemporary Native communities:

> You sometimes see that generation today: the crippled, bent old grandfathers and grandmothers on town and city skid rows; you find them in the bush waiting to die; or baby-sitting grandchildren while the parents are drunk. And there are some who even after a hundred years continue to struggle for equality and justice for their people. The road for them is never-ending and full of frustration and heart-break (Campbell, p. 8).

Obviously, in Campbell's eyes, the Metis people and their descendants are not to blame for the situation in which they find themselves. Disempowered by what Armstrong terms "the siege conditions of this nightmare time" (Armstrong, p. 208), their responses are both understandable and, in many ways, unavoidable: whether they assimilate or continue to resist they face annihilation by a dominant culture with a racist, colonizing mentality.

Talking at the Women in View festival in Vancouver in 1991 Campbell said:

> Sometimes it seems I've spent my whole life dealing

with racism. As an Aboriginal woman in Canada it's part of our daily life. We get up in the morning, we check the weather and we dress for it. As Aboriginal people, we've had to do that to survive (Campbell in Kelley, p. 7).

Her experience of the reality and pervasiveness of racism in Canada is supported by Lee Maracle who has also asserted that "[r]acism is for us, not an ideology in the abstract, but a very real and practical part of our lives" (Maracle, *I Am Woman*, p. 2).

The ways in which racism effects Native women in Canada are enacted in both Campbell's and Culleton's texts and challenge the predominant beliefs that Canadian society is not racist or that racism in Canada is "polite," "subtle," non-violent; in other words, that is, it has few 'real' impacts on its victims and is, therefore, tolerable. For Campbell, as a Metis woman:

Canada's history, the history of Canadians, is that they are killing us with their liberal gentleness. Helping us, being kind to us. "We don't have horrible racism in this country," is one of the things they say. They tell us, "We never had slavery here, we never had this," but some of the horrible things that have happened are worse, or every bit as bad. Because the kinds of things that have happened to Aboriginal people in Canada are things that were so "nice" that nobody's ever bothered to record them because they were done in such a "nice" way, or if they were recorded they were changed.

It's okay to report the atrocities of other countries, and what they do to their peoples, but heaven forbid that Canadians would ever do something like that!

We were busy in the 1940s hearing about the horrible things Germany was doing. Nobody would ever believe that in Saskatchewan at the same time people were loaded into cattle cars, not having bathrooms or facilities, and were carted off, hauled some place, and dumped off in the middle of the snow - and some of those people dying. We never hear about things like that because Canada doesn't do things like that. We need to write those stories ourselves (Campbell in Lutz, pp. 58-59).

Throughout her work as a storyteller, Campbell articulates and demonstrates the way in which racism and poverty are linked: how poverty becomes a form of violence, control and oppression used against those who are considered inferior. In *Halfbreed* she shows how racism has affected her people, her community, her family and her self as an individual. Moving from the political and social realms to the individuals within them, Campbell demonstrates how racism affects society as a whole as well as each individual within the society so that 'social problems' of the Native people are seen as both the result of the widespread impact of systemic racism on a whole race or culture as well as the product of the destruction of individuals within the society. So, while Campbell's story is, as autobiography, both unique and intensely personal, it also suggests that other Native women (and men) in similar situations have their own equally valid stories of how their lives have been damaged by the effects of racism. Her story, by dispelling lies and telling "what it was like...what it is still like," advances the understanding that what happened to her and her people did not "happen through choice or some cultural defect." For Campbell, the situation of her people and her own experience living what Culleton calls "the native girl syndrome" is not a simple case of cause and effect but an intricate web of social, political, geographic, economic and personal circumstances.

She repeatedly maintains in her storytelling that poverty is one of the most effective tools that has been and continues to be used by Canadian society as a means of subjugating, dominating, exploiting and even destroying the human targets of its racism. In *Halfbreed* she recounts how her people were denied land and treaty rights and later speaks about how her family was so poor that her father had to become a poacher in the National Park in order to provide meat for his family.

She then tells a story about how as a young girl she was tricked into 'selling out' her father to game wardens for an "Oh Henry!" chocolate bar. While her father was imprisoned the family had no money and no meat and they became even more dependent on poached game for their subsistence. Her conclusion, while controlled and at times indirect, clearly articulates the bitter irony of the situation and her anger, her sense of betrayal and her awareness, even as a child, of how racism was affecting her life:

> The Law will do many things to see that justice is done. Your poverty, your family, the circumstances, none of it matters. The important thing is that a man broke a law. He has a choice, and shouldn't break the law again. Instead, he can go on relief and become a living shell, to be scorned and ridiculed even more. One of my teachers once read from St. Matthew, Chapter 5, Verses 3 to 12: "Blessed are the poor in spirit for they shall inherit the Kingdom of Heaven." Our class discussed this, using Native people as examples. I became very angry and said, "Big deal. So us poor Halfbreeds and Indians are to inherit the Kingdom of Heaven, but not till we're dead. Keep it!" My teacher was furious...and I had to kneel in the corner holding up the Bible for the rest of the afternoon....I used to believe there was no worse sin in this country than to be poor (Campbell, p.61).

Here Campbell also tackles the idea that Native people have the same choices available to others in society and so are responsible for their 'problems.' It an idea that reappears in her writing at the time she 'decides' to become a prostitute. Although she says "I could say at this point that I was innocent and had no idea what I was getting into. I have even tried to make myself believe this but that would be lying" (Campbell, p.133), Campbell suggests that she was so beaten and abused and abandoned by her White husband and by a society that viewed her as a worthless non-entity, that she was trapped and unable to see her way out. She says, "I feel an overwhelming compassion and understanding for another human being caught in a situation where the way out is so obvious to others but not to him" (Campbell, p.133). She then uses her childhood as an example of how following dreams blindly "can lead to the disintegration of one's soul" (Campbell, p.133). Although she accepts some responsibility for her "choice" and avoids making excuses for her life, Campbell shows how she was so disempowered as a Halfbreed woman that she had few real options available to her and felt so powerless and hopeless that even the few she might have had were not apparent to her.

Jeannette Armstrong, in her essay "Racism: Racial Exclusivity and Cultural Supremacy," explains how racism functions and, in Canada, how "culturally supremacist racism" continues to subjugate and destroy Native peoples where the death rate "no less than in other colonized countries where physical force is used, continues to rise without gunfire" (Kelley, p. 80). According to her, "[o]nce coercion has been exerted to the point of subjugation, control is enforced through the functions of society which transmit culture. Continued attempts to force acceptance of principles which are culturally reprehensible results in psychological oppression and an internalized spiritual disintegration" (Kelley, pp. 79-80).

This spiritual disintegration, in Campbell's case, led to drug addiction, prostitution and near death. Emotionally, spiritually and physically abused because of her identity as a Halfbreed "squaw," Campbell lost her sense of cultural pride and personal self worth. During this time she says "[s]omething inside of me died. Life had played such a joke. I had married to escape what I'd thought was an ugly world only to fine [sic] a worse one" (Campbell, p.134). After this she refers to herself as being a "a walking zombie," "numb and depressed" (Campbell, p.136), "like a block of ice" (Campbell, p.138) and at one point says "I was using pills and drinking a lot, but instead of finding any escape, I became more and more depressed, and began to hate myself" (Campbell, p.137).

As the narrator of her own history, Campbell gains the perspective and distance to eventually realize that her self hatred and spiritual disintegration were not her fault. After telling about an incident in which "two little Indian boys" are taunted by a group of drunk white men and about the misdirected anger, hopelessness and despair she felt in response, she recalls her Cheechum telling her "that when the government gives you something, they take all that you have in return - your pride, your dignity, all the things that make you a living soul. When they are sure they have everything, they give you a blanket to cover your shame" (Campbell, p.159). To come out from under the blanket is to face an ugly reality and a painful process of healing.

Campbell eventually comes out from under her blanket and begins the process of healing by confronting her painful past. For Campbell writing is a form of storytelling and as a storyteller she has said that she considers her role to be that of "a community healer and teacher" (Lutz, p.42). In writing *Halfbreed*, Campbell teaches by presenting other views of reality and by using different ways to communicate her message. She uses storytelling as a way to teach her audience but she also, more importantly, uses this telling to heal herself and her community. She began telling her (life)story by writing about the negative aspects of her life and says, "I needed someone to talk to and there was nobody around" (Kelley, p.7). In the "Introduction" to *Halfbreed* Campbell says that she returned home to "find again the happiness and beauty" (Campbell, p.2) she had known as a child. It was there amidst the "broken old buildings" that she finally realized that "the land had changed, my people were gone, and if I was to know peace I would have to search within myself" (Campbell, p.2). This internal, spiritual journey is also a quest for healing and occurs for Campbell through the process of writing. She says the act of writing *Halfbreed*:

> ...helped me to go through a healing process, to understand where I was coming from. It helped me to stop blaming the victim, and start blaming the criminal. It helped me to realize that it wasn't my fault, that racism was real, that you could reach out and touch it, and that a lot of what happened in my life was a result of racism (Kelley, p. 7).

Since writing *Halfbreed* Campbell believes her work "has not only served to heal myself and my family, but also to make change in my community and the communities I live in" (Kelley, p.7).

Telling her story became a revitalizing, culturally affirming experience for Campbell. It empowered her by providing her with an opportunity to analyze her life, her community, and the society around her, in a way that helped her to reconnect with her culture and regain her identity as a Metis woman. However, it became more than a personal, literary act of autobiography. It became an important public act of telling and was therefore, both a social and political act. By speaking out, Campbell, through her story/telling gives voice to a silence born of oppression, hardship and domination. It speaks the unspoken, the unspeakable. It lifts the veneer of complacency in Canadian society and shines a bright light on the ugly racism supporting our nation state. A telling story, *Halfbreed* is an act of self-determination, of defiance, and of liberation so that by the end of the telling Campbell, as storyteller, teacher and healer, can confidently assert: "I no longer need my blanket to survive" (Campbell, p.184).

Culleton's semi-autobiographical novel *In Search of April Raintree* follows a form that is very similar to Campbell's. Like Campbell, she begins with brief section which establishes the narrator's retrospective position and her reasons for telling her story. She writes, "I always felt most of my memories were better avoided but now I think it's best to go back in my life before I go forward" (Culleton, p.9). For April Raintree, the narrator of the story, the telling of her life story is a process of personal healing, an opportunity to confront the past and resolve the painful issues that haunt her. For author Beatrice Culleton, the writing of the book was also a process of healing and resolution. Culleton says that, like April Raintree, she was moved to write the book as a result of the suicide of a family member. Culleton began writing the novel after

> the second suicide of a member of my family. I have two sisters and a brother. Both of my sisters committed suicide at different times....So it was after the second suicide that I really thought, "Why are my family members alcoholics?" And "Why do we have so many problems?" (Culleton in Lutz, pp.97-98).

It was upon thinking about these questions and the events in her own life that Culleton decided:

"If I write it [the book], maybe I can figure out some
of the answers,"or something. At least rethink the way
I've been living. Kind of blind, with my head in the
sand, or something. And eventually it came out as a
book. As I wrote, it wasn't going to be about a search
for identity. But while I was writing that's what I
realized about myself: that I had to accept my identity....
(Culleton in Lutz, p.98).

Clearly, Culleton strongly and closely identifies with the narrator
in her book who she says is profoundly affected by her sister's suicide
and ultimately "decides she has no choice but to accept who she is"
(Culleton in Lutz, p. 100). In many ways, the events in April Raintree's
life intersect with events in Culleton's own life: the alcoholism of her
parents, her separation from her family and placement in foster care,
her experiences with racism resulting from her identification as a
"visible" minority, the suicide of a sister, and the decision to write her
story as a way of confronting suppressed memories, of searching for
her self and of finally accepting her identity as a woman of Native
descent. *In Search of April Raintree*, can, therefore, legitimately be
read as fictionalized lifewriting since it shares many of the same
strategies, themes, structures, and forms as the lifewriting of 'real'
people.

Culleton wrote the first draft of the book in April 1981 as part
of her personal healing process. Although thinly disguised as fiction,
the book is clearly an attempt by Culleton to come to terms with a
personal, family and cultural history filled with grief, love, sorrow,
confusion, anger, despair, separation, humour, suicide, survival. The
main character and narrator/writer of *In Search of April Raintree* is
April Raintree, a 24 year old Metis woman who recalls the experiences
and events of her life and tells her lifestories or memoirs/memories so
that she can go forward, so that the memories, the past she once
avoided, can be freed and can set her free. She begins with a personal
statement about the importance of memories and about her desire to
finally confront her own so that she can move forward.

April begins her life story with a description of her family and a retelling of her childhood memories of her family's life together. Her description of her parents emphasizes that they are of mixed-blood and (significantly) includes a description of their 'colouring.' Her father, she says, is "of mixed-blood, a little of this, a little of that and a whole lot of Indian" (Culleton, p.9). Her younger sister, Cheryl, "inherited his looks: black hair, dark brown eyes which turned black when angry, and brown skin." There was no doubt they were both of Indian ancestry (Culleton, pp.9-10). Her mother, however, is "part Irish and part Ojibway" and, presumably, because she and April have "pale skin" (Culleton, p.11), their ancestry is less readily apparent.

The voice and perspective in this childhood section of the novel shift several times (sometimes inconsistently and perhaps even unconvincingly at some points). At times the point of view is clearly retrospective: from April's more mature 24 year old point of view. At other times there is a childlike naivete to the descriptions and observations which suggest that the scenes are retold from April's point of view as a five or six year old child. In both cases, the style is simple and direct and it is easy to believe that the memoirs are the work of the 24 year old Metis narrator characterized by Culleton. Perhaps, though the voice is too convincing: at times the straight-forward narration seems simplistic rather than simple. So, although Culleton manages to create an appropriate voice for April, she does so at great risk. The voice of April Raintree risks becoming monotonous and unimaginative, not in terms of what the story recounts, but in terms of how it is told.

Culleton herself acknowledges that April is not a particularly likable or sympathetic character, especially once she becomes an adult. April is, however, a very believable character who experiences many of the real problems faced by others in her situation(s) and who very often does not react in a particularly admirable way. Like any real person, April has no wise, omnipotent voice of authority guiding her choices and so, she makes mistakes. However, despite all of the oppression and suffering April is a survivor. As a young woman, she survives being violently attacked and raped by three men by using the same strategies she has employed throughout her life to survive the cultural oppression, domination and systemic violence of the colonizing society: by becoming silent, by acquiescing, by enduring the pain, by becoming emotionally numb. In a sense, the rape scene is a graphic enactment of the violence perpetrated against April throughout her life and of her means of surviving it. She is not a hero, a resistance fighter, or a warrior except by virtue of her ultimate survival against her attackers and her determination to protect others from the same suffering. She is a survivor not because she is extraordinary or superhuman but because she finds the strength and will to survive and make things better.

Both Raintree and Culleton, like Campbell, enter into the writing of their texts, the writing of them/selves, with the purpose of creating a better future for themselves and the people around them. April Raintree is motivated by the responsibility she has for her nephew, Henry Lee, to strive for a better tomorrow, "For my sister and her son. For my parents. For my people" (Culleton, p. 228). Culleton is similarly motivated by her need to understand the problems she and her family and her foster sisters experienced. Like April, Culleton also was disconnected from her family traditions and cultural heritage by the "child welfare" system in Canada which deprived Native children of the rich social and spiritual foundation which so strongly informs art and creativity. The work of Maria Campbell, for example, addresses some of the same issues, histories and experiences but is able to draw on a wealth of cultural traditions in both the form and content of its presentation and representation.

Campbell, who had very strong, intimate ties to her Metis community and family throughout her childhood and adolescence, uses the fertile ground of Metis, Cree and French symbolism and traditions to create a highly aesthetic, imaginative auto-biographical (hi)story which borrows from the storytelling traditions passed to her through her cultural education within her Metis community. In contrast, the stark, plain style of the (creative) writing in *April Raintree* is far less dependent on imagery, metaphor and symbolism to communicate its message. However, this deceptively simple style becomes an extremely effective and genuine form for reflecting both the narrator's and author's cultural deprivations. The lack of Native symbolism and tradition is consistent with the experience of one who has been deprived of familial and cultural affiliations. In this way, the novel represents a compelling and extremely disturbing enactment of the destructiveness of the cultural oppression, colonialism and racism endured by generations of Native children. In a very real way, through *April Raintree,* Culleton makes tangible the 'invisible,' often unacknowledged, spiritual and emotional damage inflicted on apprehended children and their communities. Thus, the systemic violence of the child 'welfare' system is revealed in the impoverishment of Raintree and Culleton as evidenced in their writing. For them, as for all writers, their writing is a form of cultural expression, which, though personal and specific to the individual, reflects the reality of cultural and social positioning. Unfortunately, in Culleton/Raintree's case the cultural inheritance has been stolen.

April's disconnection from her culture, her isolation, her deprivation scream out in every line of her story. Her difficulty in telling her story then becomes further evidence of the losses and damage she has suffered through the social 'welfare' policies which separated her from her family and her community. Although, unlike Campbell, she has not learned how to tell her story, even to herself, she has, even more importantly, recognized the value of telling and the need to be pro-active and responsible so that a better future can be created.

> As I stared at Henry Lee, I remembered that during the night I had used the words "MY PEOPLE, OUR PEOPLE" and meant them. The denial had been lifted from my spirit. It was tragic that it had taken Cheryl's death to bring me to accept my identity. But no, Cheryl had once said, "All life dies to give new life." Cheryl had died. But for Henry Lee and me, there would be a tomorrow. And it would be better. I would strive for it. For my sister and her son. For my parents. For my people (Culleton, p.228).

As Metis women Raintree and Culleton had been silenced by the dominating society; they had been brainwashed to "look down on Natives and not want anything to do with them" (Lutz, p.101) but ultimately their true voices as Metis women who have been apprehended, abused and deprived refuse to be silenced. They speak the truth, they tell what happened though they have not yet been healed, though their communities have not yet been healed. They are the "stakeholders" referred to by Armstrong, they are the ones who need the system to change and who therefore begin to see themselves as "undefeatably pro-active in a positive sense" (Armstrong, p. 210).

Writing, for Armstrong, for Campbell, for Culleton, for Maracle, for Raintree, for Crosby...is empowering. It is a means of recognizing and acknowledging the strength, the beauty, the value and the contributions of Native peoples. It is a means of affirming the cultures, of clarifying lies, of speaking truth, of resisting oppression, of asserting identity, of self-empowerment, of survival, of moving beyond survival. As readers, it is our responsibility to join this circle humbly, to listen actively, to accept responsibility, to become more informed, to recognize our complacency, to face our pasts, to remember, to confront the vestiges of imperialist thought which still cling to the edges of our minds, and to create new opportunities for telling and dispelling through our audience. In words, the healing continues.

So, the story goes....

Bibliography

Armstrong, Jeannette, "Racism: Racial Exclusivity and Cultural Supremacy," in *Give Back: First Nations Perspectives on Cultural Practice.* Caffyn Kelley, editor. North Vancouver: Gallerie Publications, 1992.
——"The Disempowerment of First North American Native Peoples and Empowerment Through Their Writing" in *An Anthology of Canadian Native Literature in English.* Daniel David Moses and Terry Goldie, editors. Oxford: University of Oxford Press, 1992.

Campbell, Maria. *Halfbreed.* Halifax: Goodread Biographies, 1983.

Crosby, Marcia. "Construction of the Imaginary Indian" in *Vancouver Anthology: The Institutional Politics of Art.* Stan Douglas, editor. Vancouver: Talonbooks, 1991.

Culleton, Beatrice. *In Search of April Raintree.* Winnipeg: Pemmican Publications Inc., 1983.

Lutz, Hartmut. *Contemporary Challenges: Conversations with Canadian Native Authors.* Saskatoon: Fifth House Publishers, 1991.

Maracle, Lee. *I Am Woman.* Vancouver: Write-on Press Publishers, 1988.

Sommer, Doris. "'Not Just a Personal Story': Women's *Testimonies* and the Plural Self," in Smith and Watson, editors. *De-Colonizing the Subject: The Politics of Gender in Women's Autobiography.* Minneapolis: University of Minnesota Press, 1992.

Thomas King's
Medicine River
A REVIEW

by

Gerry William

Gerry William

Gerry is a member of the Spallumcheen Indian Band in Enderby, B.C.. He currently teaches English and Creative Writing classes at the En'owkin Centre in Penticton, B.C. He received his Bachelor of Arts Degree in English Literature in 1975 and has published <u>Roseanne</u>, a poem, in ***Gatherings IV***, also published by Theytus Books. Gerry is currently at work on the second novel of a trilogy called "Enid Blue Starbreaks," a space fiction set in the far future.

Medicine River is a wonderful series of stories set in the fictional town called Medicine River. Despite its slim weight, the novel sets up many interesting dynamics that can be studied in different ways by those who read it. The story is for the most part a humorous and ironic look at a fictional native community on the Canadian plains.

I will examine "Medicine River" (from now on called 'MR' for brevity's sake) as a self-contained unit, with few references to outside sources. The areas covered will include the following: setting, narrative point of view, characterization, themes and techniques.

The first question is in terms of what choices Thomas King makes in MR. Where does the story take place and when does it happen? And in what ways are the location and the time important to this story? The answers to these questions help to define the setting of the story.

Let's start with the first question, the one about location. Medicine River is located east of the Rocky Mountains in Canada. As the story begins there is a sense that this community could be any small prairie community. Nor is there anything later in the novel that changes this sense, nothing that gives Medicine River a character different from other towns in Alberta, Saskatchewan or Manitoba. In this, King follows the method used so successfully by Margaret Laurence in her Manawaka tales. Here is how MR first opens:

> Medicine River sat on the broad back of the prairies. It was an unpretentious community of buildings banked low against the weather that slid off the eastern face of the Rockies. Summer was hot in Medicine River and filled with grasshoppers and mosquitoes. Winter was long and cold. Autumn was the best season. It wasn't good, just better than the other three. Then there was the wind. I generally tried to keep my mouth shut about the wind in Medicine River.[1]

Notice that in the description of the town, the narrator shows a dry and ironic sense of humour. More on this later. For now, it is worthwhile to note that the location is important in one way. It illustrates the universal nature of the community.

The sense that people are where they come from is firmly established by the second paragraph, where the other main character is introduced, not in terms of other people or even in terms of himself, but in terms of the setting which Will has described in the opening paragraph: "Harlen Bigbear was like the prairie wind. You never knew when he was coming or when he was going to leave" (p. 1).

Indeed, Harlen is like the wind, since he sweeps in and out of Will's life at random, stirring things in Will that he doesn't recognize or acknowledge and yet that are inextricably a part of whom Will is.

What kind of community is Medicine River? Well, for one, there is an odd and unspoken polarization within the community. Although Will's photography business is in the town of Medicine River, there is hardly any noteworthy interaction between the natives and the non-natives. King mentions hardly any non-native people in Medicine River. Will's stories revolve around his relations with Harlen and the native side of his family. The exception to this, Will's relationship to his white father, is discussed later in this essay under "Characterization."

The non-native community is not directly involved with the major emotional or social issues the natives face in the story. In fact, Will seems displaced partially because he tries to make sense of the native part of his heritage; he reconciles with it but the native community itself seems to exist separate from the non-native community.

Other examples of this native centrality abound. When Will joins a basketball team, it is a native team. When he is asked to do a group photograph, a pivotal moment in the story, it is a photograph of Joyce Blue Horn's extended native family. When he goes for drinks, it is with the native friends he has. The most serious personal involvement he gets into besides his friendship with Harlen is his relationship with a native woman, Louise Heavyman.

This process points to the situation in many native communities. Native communities like the one in this novel exist parallel to the non-native community, with little social interaction between the two parts of the community. If this is coexistence, then it is a discrete coexistence, with a bare acknowledgement of one to the other. From now on, when I refer to Medicine River, I am speaking only of the native part of the community.

Thus, Medicine River is not the bleak non-native world in which Jim Loney futilely struggles for understanding of his identity and past. Nor is it the separate worlds in which April and Cheryl Raintree live apart from one another. Understanding comes to Will through his acceptance into the native community, where the novel's energies are directed.

In Medicine River. everyone seems to know what everyone else does. If there are secrets, then they are well hidden. There is scarcely anything which Harlen doesn't know about his native friends and neighbours. Nor does he leave Will in the dark. Again, this sets up some humorous conflicts, as when Harlen wants to tell Will something and Will doesn't want to hear it:

> "Seeing a man live alone is sad, Will. You get all drawn out and grey and wrinkled. Look at Sam Belly."
> "Sam's over ninety."
> "And he's not married."
> "Sam was married for over fifty years, Harlen."
> "Course he was. Wouldn't have lived this long without a good woman. But do you think he'll live another ten years?"

(p.27)

There are other settings, such as the one in Calgary, where Will spent some of his childhood before the family moved to Medicine River. There is also Will's work in a photography store in Toronto, from where Harlen draws him like a spider draws a fly. Yet Will isn't at home in any setting until the novel draws to an end. He is drifting on a spiritual level just as his brother James drifts and as Harlen's brother drifts.

The time in which the many stories occur is just as important to the story's setting as is location. There are four levels of time in the story. The first two deal with the different time senses between Harlen and Will. Will has a European sense of time, always worried about its passage, while others in the novel, especially Harlen, have a different time frame from which they operate. This difference sets up many humorous conflicts between the two friends. In the opening pages, Will protests but follows Harlen to a restaurant, leaving his place of business reluctantly but leaving it nonetheless.

Take another incident that shows how Harlen never seems to sleep:

> "Will, you awake?"
> "Harlen?"
> "Will, wake up. It's important.
> "Harlen, it's the middle of the night...I'm in bed."
> "Will, Louise is pregnant. I'll be by in ten minutes."
> "Harlen..."

"Okay, twenty."

(p. 30)

There are two other levels of time that play an important role in the story. These levels are connected with the structures of many chapters, which form separate parts, one part dealing with an earlier time in Will's life or in the life of those around him, and another part in which time unfolds even as the narrator lives it. Again, King establishes this process on the opening page by preceding Will's commentaries with a letter written by Will's father:

Dear Rose,

I'll bet you never thought you'd hear from me again. I've thought about calling or writing, but you know how it is. How are you and the boys? Bet they're getting big. Bet you're probably mad at me, and I don't blame you. I'm going to be in Calgary for a rodeo. Thought I might drop in and see you . . .

(p. 1)

This letter is from Will's childhood. It is the first of several letters scattered throughout the first chapter. The cumulative effect is to have the story of Will's father unfold during the same time as Will's first adventures in Medicine River as an adult unfold.

Besides the four levels of time in the novel, the setting is ambiguous about the exact time of the story as a whole. We know only that it is contemporary to airplanes and cars. Again, this ambiguity is as deliberate as the general nature of the town itself; this story is a story universal to the time and place of modern day prairie life and to native communities in general.

Having examined some general patterns of setting and looked at the relationship of time to setting, how do Will and Harlen relate to their environment?

Will as photographer tries to stay in his shop but Harlen regularly manages to drag him away from it. This although Will does not feel a part of any community until near the end of the story. Look, for example, at the way he remembers Toronto when he talks to his brother

120

James:

> "I may go to San Francisco," [James] said.
> "Always wanted to go there. What do you plan to do?"
> "Stay in Toronto, I guess."
> "Pretty exciting?"
> "I guess."

(p. 94)

And later, in Toronto, after Will has lost his job, there is the same feeling of detachment:

> I looked around Toronto for a few months, took the occasional free-lance job, but nothing seemed to settle. I was sorry I had thrown out the folder.

(p. 96)

At this stage, at least emotionally, Will is like his brother James in that neither feels attachment to the communities they happen to live in.

Harlen is the complete opposite to Will in this way. Harlen not only knows everyone, he has a deep understanding of place and its importance. He feels an emotional commitment to the place where he lives. This respect for place is shown in the following passage, where he talks of a place he's never been to:

> ..."Man's a world famous photographer, you know. Worked in Toronto." And he took his time with each syllable in Toronto, as if the word was magic.

(p. 99)

Harlen belongs to Medicine River and is as much a part of its setting as he is a part of its people. There is that wonderful scene where, after months of indecision, Will returns from Toronto to find Harlen waiting at the airport. It's as though Harlen has never left the airport in the months following the funeral of Will's mother.

And, of course, Harlen's relationship with the place he lives is often the cause of humorous events. Harlen may be a part of the setting, but he is not always in control of it. There is the time when he and Will are looking for a gift and head out to the reserve:

> We left the road, climbed a low embankment, and headed out on to the prairies.
> "This is just like the explorers, Will," said Harlen.

121

"Head south. Those trees over there look familiar."
We headed south. We got lost. We headed north.
We got lost. We headed west. We got lost.

(p. 138)

The rest of the chapter follows the perilous journey Harlen undertakes, forging a river to avoid a washout that, as it turns out, was repaired some time before.

The pivotal scene in the novel comes when Will undertakes to do a group photograph of a native family. This picture is not taken within the sterile confines of the studio, where Will wants to take the picture, but near the river where Joyce Blue Horn brings her entire family, including relatives. This setting is appropriate, for this is also the beginning of Will's acceptance into the community. From now on he is no longer on the outside looking in as the neutral observer. Instead, he becomes more serious about his feelings towards Louise, helping her to find a house and making love to her for the first time.

The novel ends at Christmas with the whole world opening up to Will. He finds out that Louise has turned down a marriage proposal by South Wing's father and that they're both heading back to Medicine River. His brother James phones to let him know everything is all right in San Francisco. And Will takes a symbolic walk in the snow as the winter sun emerges from an overcast day. There is a mood of happiness and peace in the final lines of MR. This process is completed by Will's walk outdoors, just as the process of acceptance earlier in the novel was completed by the pictures Will took on the banks of the river.

When we look at the narrative point of view we find that in MR, the story from the beginning is Will's story. In those opening lines to the novel quoted above, we see and hear a detached and almost impartial observer called Will who, in the first person narrative point of view, manages to show his detachment. This is no easy feat to achieve. The first person narrative point of view is usually taken up by those who wish to approach a story from a personal point of view. One thinks of April Raintree, who's approach is emotionally charged, in sharp contrast to Will's more detached observations. Compare, for example, the intensely intimate opening of *In Search of April Raintree* with that of the lines quoted at the beginning of this review:

MEMORIES. SOME memories are elusive, fleeting, like a butterfly that touches down and is free until it is caught. Others are haunting. You'd rather forget them but they won't be forgotten. And some are always there. No matter where you are, they are there, too. I always felt most of my memories were better avoided but now I think it's best to go back in my life before I go forward. Last month, April 18th, I celebrated my twenty-fourth birthday. That's still young but I feel so old.[2]

Memories and feelings. The use of the butterfly as a metaphor. The realization and understanding at the beginning of the novel ("I feel so old...") opposite to Will's attempt at the start of his story to "shut up" and move through the story as the detached observer.

There are, of course, reasons for the choice of the first person narrative point's of view in *April Raintree* and MR, although these choices are different from one another.

April Raintree is the personal story of two sisters. There is only one way to tell it, and that is with a personal first person narrator. MR's structure, particularly its use of different time periods within a single chapter to unfold two separate events, demands a narrator who can withdraw from the scene and become, for all intents, the storyteller who holds an audience spellbound and captive.

So why not a third person point of view in MR? If Will is the detached observer who oversees the story, why not tell the story in the third person?

The use of first person has three advantages in this story. First, there are times when Will the observer is all but invisible and the story takes over. The story of the community is as important as the narrator of it.

But Will's detachment is a facade that is gradually worn down through the story as Harlen, Louise and the rest of the community increasingly involve him in the events that are important to them. If Harlen is the busy-body, he is also the one who spins enough webs to bind Will until he cannot escape the webs of the community even if he wishes to. The irony is that Will, who belongs nowhere at the start of the novel, doesn't want to escape at the end. He proves a willing captive to the community and its needs, which draw him out of his self-imposed isolation. The ending of the novel describes a very personal sense of warmth and affirmation set against Christmas itself. Such a feeling of warmth and joy would have been difficult to get in the third person.

The second reason for a first person perspective is that there is another party that is drawn into this web, a party that usually is as detached and isolated an observer as Will himself. Through Will's eyes and senses that party is drawn into the story in a way that cannot be done from a third person narrative point of view. That party is, of course, the reader. The story wants the reader to become as involved as Will in the events of Medicine River. The irony and self-deprecation works more easily at this level than it does in the third person.

And finally, King draws the map of Medicine River with broad strokes. Not for him the increasingly remote refinement of techniques so prevalent in James Joyce's later works. By starting the narrative point of view as seen through Will's detached perspective, King places the community on a sound base with the reader before he begins to spiral Will towards commitment.

Will in effect becomes the storyteller who on occasion seems aware of the reader. His memories of the past and the stories he recollects from his childhood are all part of this storytelling technique. The novel is in one sense the long series of memories of a narrator, showing the development of his character. In this sense King uses the same techniques as does Beatrice Culleton. At times both April Raintree and Will are intensely introspective in their attempts to make sense of what is happening around them. Witness this passage from MR:

> So I took some pictures of Lionel, and they turned out good. I put one up next to the picture of Harlen and the basketball team. The next week, I took four of the best pictures out to Lionel's house. I had never been out to that part of the reserve. Harlen gave me directions, and I got lost. By the time I found the house, everyone had eaten, but Lionel took me in the kitchen and warmed up some of the moose-meat stew that his daughter had made.
>
> (p. 175)

Clearly Will is reminiscing but in his remoteness he seems to be talking to the reader as much as to himself. He knows this information, but he thinks of it anyway, as though aware that other people are watching the story through his eyes and wouldn't know the information he knows without his speaking of it in his internal voice. Yet the voice is also casual and informal, a friendly monologue that the reader overhears which gives information without obstructing the storyline.

The voice of Will becomes intensely personal only towards the story's end or in moments of emotional interaction between he and other characters in the story. It's interesting how we can see the story through Will's eyes and yet not feel that we are Will himself, but someone observing Will. That's where Will's detachment becomes a valuable tool:

> The nurse at the desk smiled at me and came over to where I was standing. "This must be your first," she

> said. "Which one is yours?"
> Harlen and the boys were at basketball practice,
> and Mr. and Mrs. Heavyman had probably gone back
> to the reserve. Louise was in her room. South Wing
> lay in her bassinet wrapped in a pink blanket.
> I looked down the corridor. It was clear.
> "That one," I said.
>
> (p. 42)

Will as narrator could have said that he felt confused or proud or secretive, all of which he does feel, but he keeps his emotions at a distance and lets his physical actions speak for themselves. First, he mentions other people not being there. Then he looks down the hall. We see at once the continual process of self-deprecation and the need for Will not to embarrass himself in front of others. That glance down the hall speaks volumes about Will without overstating it through a long emotionally descriptive passage.

This brings up what Will is like as a person as compared to other characters in the story. By now you might think that Will is an emotionally-crippled human being. He isn't. He is an observer who spends more time listening than he does talking, a practice guaranteed to make more friends. Which explains why Harlen is drawn to Will and why Will in return may feel more close to Harlen than his observer status would let on. Will's emotions must be implied from what he does, not what he says.

Let's look at an example of this friendship. In Chapter Seven some gossiping friends of Harlen talk about Harlen's going on a drinking binge. Will cannot believe it but states his disbelief in a roundabout way that he has learned from being around Harlen:

> Bud smoothed one of his braids and set his beer
> down. "Floyd says Harlen's drinking again. Saw him
> down at the American the other afternoon. Looked
> pretty bad, Floyd said. Heard him in the bathroom
> throwing up."
> "Harlen doesn't drink."
> "Something must have happened. Figured you
> might know, you being good friends and all."
>
> (p. 96)

The humorous thing about Medicine River is that while gossip abounds as it does in all communities, there is rarely any malicious intent involved, just a state of confusion in which no one is sure of the truth. So when Will goes looking for Harlen, now afraid that the rumours may be true, he runs into the person who seems to have seen Harlen during his binge and whose friends above have said started the story of Harlen's drinking binge:

> The smoke in the American was thick and blue. I could hardly breathe. "No, thanks. You guys see Harlen?"
>
> Floyd looked at Elwood, and Elwood looked at the table.
>
> "Haven't seen him tonight," said Floyd.
>
> "Someone says they thought he was drinking again."
>
> "Yeah, I heard that, too," said Floyd. "Heard he was at some bar the other day. Looked real bad, I heard. Throwing up in the toilet."
>
> "Anybody know where he is?"
>
> "Could be anywhere, Will. Man starts to drink, he loses track of where he is," and Floyd turned to the women. "Am I right?"
>
> (p. 98)

This roundabout way of speaking is one that is shared by most of the characters in the story. The result is that characters avoid confrontations except in the most extreme of circumstances. Will doesn't accuse Floyd of being the source of the rumours nor does Floyd acknowledge where the rumours began. But Will's continued pursuit of the whereabouts of Harlen speaks of a deep and abiding friendship that remains unspoken between the two. Will is worried and doesn't give up his search until he finds Harlen at home:

> "Harlen," I said, "you okay?"
>
> Another moan.
>
> "You want the bucket?"
>
> "God, Will, I feel awful. What are you doing here?"
>
> "Thought you might need some company. I've got some coffee on."
>
> ...Bertha Morley walked in. "Will," she said. "What are you doing here?"
>
> "Thought I'd come by and see if I could help."
>
> "That's nice," said Bertha. "People should help like that. How's he doing?"
>
> "Still pretty drunk . . ."
>
> "Drunk?"
>
> "Don't know what started it. Bud Prettywoman

said Harlen just started drinking. Didn't know why.
You got any idea?"
  "Bud see him drinking?"
  "Floyd told him."
  ..."Harlen's not drunk, Will. He's just got the flu.
You had it yet?"
  "Flu?"
  "Everybody's getting it. Harlen got it Friday. It
was my birthday. We went to the American for lunch.
He was pretty sick then, but you know Harlen. Spent
most of lunch in the bathroom."

(pp. 100-101)

The above passage reveals a refreshing gullibility to Will. In
another chapter Floyd tells Will about Harlen hurting his ankle and
not being able to dance at powwows. Only later, after some confusion
on Harlen's part, does Will find out that Harlen hurt his foot in a
basketball game.

There are many distressful stories in MR, although most of them
do not directly involve Will. Will as narrator manages in his way to
inform the reader of these stories. For example, in Chapter Four he
recalls the story of an abused woman friend of his mother's without
directly condemning such abuse. In the confrontations between Harlen
and Joe, David Plume and Ray Little Buffalo, Eddie Weaselhead and
Big John Yellow Rabbit, Will is there but he is the observer who skirts
in and out of direct involvement with the antagonists.

Yet by the end of the novel we have built up a picture of Will as
a Will who is self-deprecating, kind, gentle towards women, and always
thoughtful. We get this picture through a method of indirect
accumulation of impressions, inferring from what Will does because
he rarely says what he feels about events and people. King uses this
method because Will is only one of many, only one of a community of
people whom he watches, involved and uninvolved. We care for Will,
but we also care for Harlen, for Louise, for South Wing, and for the
rest of the extended family that is the native part of Medicine River
itself.

If Will is detached, then surely part of it is caused by his father's
lack of commitment to his family, a dysfunction that, like all
dysfunctions, repeats some of its patterns upon those closest to the
dysfunctional behaviour.

And so, as the first chapter shows, we see the letters from Will's
father as a background to Will's own reluctance to participate in the
activities around him. Appropriately enough, the two different times
are linked by Harlen himself, who brings Will the letters that are quoted

from in the chapter. If this is a story of personal angst and ultimate commitment, then it is a limited reconciliation, for although Will becomes a part of the community he never comes to terms with his father.

The impersonality and detachment in Will is not always good, becoming a mask that he hides behind without realizing it. Note how he describes the man who is his father: "There was one picture of my mother...Kneeling behind her was a man in uniform..."(pp. 4-5). Will cannot recall his father; he has no memories of his father which mean anything at the emotional level. The one time he does try to find something of his past through his father, Will's mother unwittingly becomes part of the problem when she finds Will rummaging through the chest that contains his father's letters to her. She hits Will and he bolts out of the house, leaving the issue of his father forever unresolved between he and his mother.

Finally, Will may think the worse of other people such as Raymond Little Buffalo, who reneges on a business deal, but he never condemns anyone outright. As the observer, this refusal to show how he feels is another sign of Will's detachment and seeming objectivity.

It is this sense of ironic self-deprecation and the friendship Will feels for Harlen that distinguish him from the bitter self-alienated man like Jim Loney. And the past helps, for while Will hardly remembers his father, he remembers many other things from his past with a clear vision that is absent from Jim Loney.

Let's examine some of the other characters, none of whom are complex. They are people who simply live out their lives the best way they know how. Each of them has their own personality, no easy feat to do in a novel of this length. Each brings a distinct and particular world view and set of problems. Even people with similar standing in their community are developed in different ways. Take two people who unknowingly are more like one another than they would care to admit.

Big John Yellow Rabbit is the Director of the Friendship Centre. He dresses in suits and is stubborn in his ways. He tries to change the community to his way of doing things. Some of the traditional people are worried about him. Harlen talks to Will about him:

> ...There were a few complaints. Some of the traditional people didn't care for the three-piece suits that Big John liked to wear.
>
> "Them suits make us think of Whitney Oldcrow over at DIA," Bertha Morley told Big John at one of the powwows. "And why'd you cut your hair?"

(p. 53)

One of John Yellow Rabbit's staff members is Eddie Weaselhead, who figures he should be Director because he's worked there longer than John has. Eddie goes to the other extreme of dress:

> ...He always wore a ribbon shirt to work and a beaded buckle. He had four or five rings and an inlaid watch-band that he wore all the time and a four-strand choker made out of real bone with brass ball bearings, glass beads and a big disc cut from one of those shells.

(p. 55)

It is both ironic and fitting that it is Bertha again who points out how funny Eddie looks in his clothes, "like a walking powwow poster" as she puts it. What sets the two off is the fact that they dislike one another. They point at the way the other dresses and behaves. They don't see that their own clothes reflect an attitude that sets them apart from the other Indians. The real irony is that each is more like the other than they are to the community they try to serve.

When we look at the structure of MR, we see that all of the chapters have their own themes, ranging from love to hate to abuse to deception. In their entirety and multiplicity, they give a complete picture of a community and its residents. But there is one general theme at which I hinted at earlier. That theme is one of Will's reconciliation, not with the past, but with the community itself. At the start of the novel Will is detached, the observer who sees everyone but himself in an analytic way.

In almost every major encounter, Will rarely speaks of how he feels, letting his actions and words be his interpreters. He is a man of few words. When he speaks, his responses are short cryptic remarks and questions aimed at prodding the other person to open up. As said before, this facade is broken down by Harlen and others within the framework of the different stories.

The climax of the reconciliation theme occurs in Chapter Fifteen. Harlen asks Will to take pictures of Joyce Blue Horn's family. During the scenes that follow, three separate processes develop the idea of reconciliation and its influence on Will.

The first two processes deal with the concept of the extended native family. The extended family involves the sense within native communities of the relationships of people with each other. People within a native community often feel that they are a part of a larger unit than just their so-called 'nuclear' family. Their sense of responsibilities therefore include more than just their immediate family. It involves the issue of inclusiveness that is the opposite to the concept

129

of the nuclear family.

As Will mingles with the many people along the banks of the river Lionel introduces Will to Floyd's grandmother:

> "Her boy," said Lionel, "was a real good storyteller. Always had a funny story to tell...Granny says you remind her of him. She says maybe she should adopt you."

(p. 211)

Here we have an elder who is willing to include Will as part of her family, although they may not be related to one another through blood lines.

Joyce Blue Horn initiates the second process that draws Will into the community. It is on her suggestion that Will ceases to be the man behind the cameras and becomes instead a part of the family picture that is eventually taken on the banks of the river. One doesn't have to think about this very hard to see the metaphors implicit in the actions of this chapter.

By the end of the chapter, in fact, the concept of family, and of Will's being a part of a larger family, are firmly cemented through his association of his nuclear family's picture (which forms the second story in this chapter) with the family photos of Joyce Blue Horn's extended family:

> I worked late that night, got the portraits packaged up and ready to mail. When I got home, I tacked the picture of Mom and James and me up on the kitchen wall. Right next to it, I stuck a picture of all of us down at the river.
>
> I was smiling in that picture, and you couldn't see the sweat. Floyd's granny was sitting in her lawn chair next to me looking right at the camera with the same flat expression that my mother had, as though she could see something farther on and out of sight.

(p. 216)

Notice that Will gets as close as he ever does to saying how he felt ("I was smiling...."). He also mentions Floyd's granny in the same sentence as he does his own mother, thereby reinforcing the concept of the extended family as well as the sense that Will is no longer alone, that he can depend on more the nuclear family that he rarely has looked to for support in the past few years. And, of course, by this time Will

130

has no father or mother, just his brother James.

MR uses this sub-theme of extended family units to tie Will into the larger theme of reconciliation with the community. In other words, the major direction of the novel is to move Will away from the detached and remote character who is on the sidelines looking into the community. Will is tied into being a part of everything around him, including the family ties implicit in his relationship with Louise Heavyman and her daughter, South Wing, to whom he has become a surrogate father figure.

The third process of reconciliation involves Will's immediate family, the 'nuclear' family that is traced through another photograph, this of his mother, his brother and himself. There is a stark contrast between the family portrait of Joyce Blue Horn's family compared to the unsmiling figures in this picture:

> The photographer kept telling us to smile, and James and me did our best. I don't guess Mom ever smiled. At least the portrait we got had her staring at the camera, her face set, her eyes flat.

> (p. 213)

The sense of discomfort is carried through afterwards when James and Will struggle in their uncomfortable clothes, itching to get out of them because they are so formal and starched. This discomfort is a metaphor related to Will's own memories and feelings towards his family. It reflects a sense of guilt, unhappiness and loneliness that is directly opposed to Joyce Blue Horn's family:

> Then, too, the group refused to stay in place. After every picture, the kids wandered off among their parents and relatives and friends, and the adults floated back and forth, no one holding their positions. I had to keep moving the camera as the group swayed from one side to the other. Only the grandparents remained in place as the ocean of relations flowed around them.

> (p. 215)

The reconciliation here is not between Will and the community, but between Will and his last surviving family member, James. Will drags out the faded photograph of his 'nuclear' family to make a copy to send to his brother as a reminder of their past. The reconciliation is developed in a later chapter when Will finally gets up enough nerve to talk to his brother about how badly he feels about the stone-throwing incident in their childhood. For now, though, it is enough that Will is making a connection with his brother in this way and not simply leaving things as they are.

There are two major techniques that dominate MR. The use of irony sharpens the humour of the novel while the split storyline mentioned in other parts of this essay contrasts the way in which people handle similar issues in the story.

MR is replete with irony, a technique seldom used or needed in *April Raintree*. Irony is one of those terms that bring on endless debates and differences among writers and scholars. Everyone's definitions differ.

Irony as I use it within MR is a reference to the fact that so many situations and comments in the story are understated and opposite dependant upon the characters themselves. This irony is more effective when it is placed against opposing forces, as it is so often, for example, when the emotional powers of Harlen conflict with the reluctant detachment of Will. Again, note how the opening contrasts and emphasizes this difference:

> Harlen Bigbear was like the prairie wind. You never knew when he was coming or when he was going to leave. Most times I was happy to see him. Today I wasn't. I had other things to do. There were photographs in the wash and three strips of negatives that had to be printed. But that didn't stop the wind from blowing, and it didn't stop Harlen.

(p. 2)

Harlen is an elemental force, the metaphor of the wind a sharp contrast to April's memories as a butterfly that is blown here and there by forces greater than herself. Harlen is seldom pushed into doing things by others; he is the proactive Prometheus or the predecessor to the elemental Coyote archetype that dominates King's next novel. Compare him to Will, who at the beginning is essentially helpless to resist this great force when it pushes him.

Will often tries to resist Harlen's wiles, but his attempts prove not only futile, but humorous because they are never successful. And Will accepts Harlen's overpowering friendship in an understated way that makes the reader sympathize with him even as the reader knows and hopes for Harlen's positive efforts.

This understatement is more effective just because the story is seen through the victim's eyes, and the victim never protests much nor is he bitter or hurt by his defeats. Harlen is Harlen, and who is Will to oppose such a force? Time and again we see Will bend before this wind; time and again we see Harlen's wile and savvy overcome Will's protests. But Will does so with grace and a self-deprecation that makes him a more sympathetic character in the reader's eyes:

> "Wind's starting to blow pretty good, Will. We better start climbing down."
> "No," I said. "I'm going to jump."
> The wind blew a little harder. Harlen was holding onto the girder with both hands. The backs of his knuckles were pale.
> "You going to jump?" I said.
> "Don't think so."
> "Why not?"
> "Same reason you won't jump."
> "I'm going to jump."
> "Don't think so, Will."
> A gust of wind almost blew me off the girder. I sat down next to Harlen. "I'd jump," I said, "if the wind wasn't blowing."
> "Blowing pretty hard, that wind," said Harlen. "You got your good shirt on, too. No sense ruining it. Maybe we should climb down now."

(p. 163)

And, of course, the striking thing about the above passage is that Harlen is careful not to damage his friend's dignity in a potentially embarrassing moment.

Next, let's look at one chapter to see how its structure (aside from the different time frames) is used to show different stories related to the same theme, thereby reinforcing each other and the theme itself.

In Chapter Six the two stories are as follows. In the first, Will meets Raymond Little Buffalo, who gets him to take pictures for a proposed calendar to raise money for the Friendship Centre. In the other story, Will tells people what his father has done in his life. Both stories are about deception, one innocent and harmless, the other a more insidious one that Will in his inimitable way implies more than states.

Will tells stories about his father out of no maliciousness. Instead, it fills a part of his past with colour although he knows the stories are fabricated. The stories hurt no one and they provide him pleasure in the telling, the closest to a storyteller that Will gets. It is another indication of Harlen's influence on Will. It is also an attempt, however misguided, to make some sense of the past that Will does not have:

> Most of all, I liked to point out, he loved his family,
> and I was always getting postcards and letters with
> pictures of him standing against some famous place
> or helping women and children take sacks of rice off
> the back of trucks.

(p. 84)

There is wish fulfilment here, simply because Will's father is the opposite to how Will speaks about him to others. His father has shown no commitment to the family.

Raymond acts out of a more conscious motive called greed. He profits from the schemes he gets others to participate in and has neither the intention nor, in the end, the means to repay those who fell for his plans. What Will feels about Raymond is unstated yet the inferences can be made from what Will does when he meets Raymond:

> Ray had on his suit. He looked clean and neat sitting
> in the chair. "Sorry to hear you had to take out a loan,"
> he said. "Harlen and me figure that as soon as the
> money starts to come in next year, you"ll get paid first
> with interest. Damn, but I wish I knew what happened
> to that bill."
> I guess I wasn't smiling when I sat down.
> "Expenses will sure eat into the profits quick."
> Ray wasn't smiling either. "They sure will."
> Ray ordered another pitcher, and I sat there staring
> at him until he disappeared in the smoke and the noise
> of the evening.

(p. 87)

Again, we must infer what Will is feeling by projecting ourselves into his situation, for Will's anger is never stated outright. Ray has used Will and others and feels no compunction in defrauding them, taking advantage of their good natures never to push matters too far or to hold him accountable for his deception. But this deception is only part of what makes Ray what he is. Ray also beats up David Plume, the 'AIMS' activist, in another chapter, stealing David's jacket in the process. It is another irony that Ray in a way kills himself in the subsequent encounter with David, falling on a bottle he carries with him when David starts shooting at him.

The two types of deception in this chapter are different in nature from one another. Will's lies are built around him trying to make

134

connections with his past in the best way he can. He hurts no one in the process. The lies apparently stop when his mother sends him a picture of his father, a picture that he cannot relate to and which serve to sever him forever from having to make further efforts to understand his father and what he represented.

Ray's deceptions are ugly and hurt people. They are a part of a broader pattern of dysfunctional behaviour that eventually comes full circle to exact its revenge.

In summary, I have used a fairly formal approach to look at several elements within MR. But I have not exhausted the topics chosen. There is a wealth of material to be looked at in the comparison of stories and themes within the dual-story chapters, for example. One could also look at Harlen and study his character in a number of ways. One could look at the family values expressed in a number of ways in the novel. Then there are the other characters in the story (such as Louise Heavyman) whom I only touched on in my discussions.

The fact that letters influence the story in different ways or that the spinning top and the rattle are used in a symbolic way could be studied.

There is also a lot to be said for examining any story in terms of its psychological, spiritual, or mythological contents. Similarly, the reader, if he or she knew the writer, could examine the story in terms of how it was or was not an expression of the writer's own life and philosophy. Then there is the historical and cultural perspective that would ask the questions related to how a story fits into the history of the area and how it was the expression of a particular culture, some of the latter having been dealt with in this essay.

But the real point of any story, regardless of its complexities, is how well it stands as a story. Is the reader going to enjoy the story on its own merits and prior to any subsequent analysis or commentary? On this level I would have to say that *Medicine River* is one of the best novels I have read. The narrative is straightforward, the stories are simple and easy to read, and the characters are interesting and intriguing in their separate ways. I have yet to meet a student who did not enjoy the story. One of the fascinating things about this novel is that a deep and abiding sense of humour and compassion run through the stories and provides some of the framework within which the story unfolds. Read the book. I know you"ll agree with me that this is an excellent first novel by Thomas King.

References

Culleton, Beatrice. *In Search of April Raintree*. Winnipeg, Manitoba: Pemmican Publications, Inc., 1983.

Frye, Northrop. *Anatomy of Criticism: Four Essays*. Princeton, New Jersey: Princeton University Press, 1957.

King, Thomas. *Green Grass, Running Water*. Toronto: HarperCollins Publishers Ltd., 1993.

——*Medicine River*. Toronto, Canada: Penguin Books Canada Ltd., 1989.

MacLennan, Hugh. *Two Solitudes*. New York: Duell, Sloan and Pearce, 1945.

Maracle, Lee. *Ravensong*. Vancouver, B.C.: Press Gang Publishers, 1993.

Welch, James. *The Death of Jim Loney*. Markham, Ontario: Penguin Books Canada Ltd., 1987.

HALFBREED:

A REVISITING OF MARIA CAMPBELL'S TEXT FROM AN INDIGENOUS PERSPECTIVE

by

Janice Acoose

Janice Acoose

Janice graduated with a Double Honours Degree in both Native Studies and English. She has also received a Master's Degree in English from theUniversity of Saskatchewan. As a writer she has had several poems, some short stories, and has been published in an array of journals and anthologies. She also writes for the *Saskatoon Star Phoenix* as well as *Saskatchewan Indian* and *New Breed*, with an upcoming guest editoial column for <u>Windspeaker</u> out of Alberta. A mother of two, she enjoys being with her special partner, and spending time with her children. She is currently on leave from her lecturing position with the Saskatchewan Indian Federated College (S.I.F.C.) as an English Professor. Janice is co-producing and scriptwriting for a 13 part T.V. series focused on Indian artists

Indigenous people who reside within the country now known as Canada have roots in this land that can most appropriately be described as immemorial. Over the years, our peoples maintained a curatorial relationship to the land and the land reciprocated by providing for our needs. Because of this relationship to the land, and for many contemporary Indigenous peoples, the memory of it, we were able to survive despite many very deliberate genocidal attempts to do away with our cultures. [1]

Nonetheless, Indigenous peoples' very numerous and distinct cultures have been transmitted from one generation to another through languages, songs, dances, traditional economic practices, and governing structures. These specific Indigenous ways continue to provide a spiritual, social, political, and economic context that distinguishes Indigenous peoples from non-Indigenous peoples and thus contribute to the formulation of the self. Throughout the long history of relations between Indigenous and non-Indigenous peoples in North America, many writers and scholars have attempted to articulate this complex relationship.

In Canada, numerous non-Indigenous writers and scholars continue this tradition through educational institutions and the media. However, few (if any) non-Indigenous writers and scholars have had extensive first-hand knowledge of our ways and thus were and are unable to correctly represent our distinct social, political, and economic ways of life. Some of these writers misrepresented specific Indigenous peoples by imposing their own Eurocentric world view, while others fragmented our ways by writing about only one aspect of a specific Indigenous culture.

Over the years, the political ramifications of this kind of representation contributed to the formulation of social, political, and economic ideals upon which non-Indigenous peoples modelled very racist and sexist attitudes and behaviours. Currently, as many contemporary Indigenous and non-Indigenous peoples agree, this situation is extremely problematic.

Maria Campbell's 1973 autobiographically-based *Halfbreed* intervened in the Canadian literary tradition that had, until then, constructed Indigenous women in ways that were contrary to our real lived experiences. Campbell's text challenges existing stereotypes and images of Indigenous women by providing a vivid spiritual, social, political, and economic context of her own Halfbreed (and to a limited extent Cree Indian) way of life. [2] As one of the first Indigenous women speaking out, or writing her way out of what Adrienne Rich's "When We Dead Awaken" describes as the assumptions that women are drenched in (18), Campbell begins to understand how her identity has been constructed for her. Through the act of writing, the author begins to search her past for evidence of her authentic self.

Inevitably, she helps other Indigenous women to begin the same kind of reclamation and re-connection of their selves.

In this way, Ms. Campbell's somewhat fictional autobiography is extremely important because it functions as an important model for achieving wholeness and connectedness for Indigenous women in North America, who were like so many other Indigenous peoples, as Howard Adams maintains in *Prison of Grass*, very "isolated and individualized people" (178). Lastly, her text is an important legacy for Indigenous women because it represents Indigenous women in the persons of Cheechum, Grannie Campbell, Qua Chich, Grannie Dubuque, and her mother to a somewhat lesser extent, as survivors of the oppressive colonial regime, and abusive relationships, as well as systemic racism and sexism.

Maria Campbell's text intervened in a literary tradition that had constructed Indigenous women's lives from within a White-Euro-Canadian-Christian patriarchy. Her text, albeit written in the English colonizer's language and thus seemingly privileging the patriarchal hierarchy, consistently resists conforming to the Christian patriarchy. The author's first act of resistance manifests itself in the construction of her text. As so many previously colonized writers (who are variously cited throughout this thesis and who have struggled to de-colonize themselves) maintain, the act of writing is a political act that can encourage de-colonization. In this context, Campbell is one of the first few Indigenous women who appropriated the colonizer's language to name her oppressors, identify the oppressor's unjust systems, laws, and processes, and subsequently work towards de-colonization. Ms. Campbell prefaces her text by defiantly addressing members of the colonial world. She asserts, "I write this for all of you, to tell you what it is like to be a *Halfbreed* woman in our country"(2). Campbell's reference to herself as a *Halfbreed* disturbs many liberal White-Euro-Canadians who think of the term as derogatory and are thus puzzled by her continued use of it. Howard Adams (a staunch Metis activist originally from the Duck Lake area and one of the first Indigenous people to achieve a doctorate in the Euro-Canadian educational system) writes:

> To the whites of Canada, "Metis" means a light coloured Indian. In Canadian history, "halfbreed" refers specifically to the group of people who are part Indian and part white. These halfbreed people did not have a choice as to whether they would be Indians or white or in-between; society defined them as members of the native society and it still does today. Halfbreed was the original name used by white traders in the early fur-trading years, but today this word has become

unacceptable to mainstream society. To whites, halfbreed became a vulgar expression, so they adopted the name Metis—the French expression for mixed blood—which seems to be a more polite term. Most hinterland natives, however, still use halfbreed or simply "breed", while urban natives use Metis (ix).

Maria Campbell, and many other contemporary people, still use the term Halfbreed; some refer to themselves as Halfbreeds with a strong nationalistic pride, while others use the term as a kind of blatant reminder of Canadian society's racism towards them. [3]

Campbell's language, which repeatedly shifts from English to Mitchif to Cree, is an important site of resistance. Examples of this resistance are most evident in Campbell's names for her female relatives. Her greatest influence and confidante, whose name and term of reference according to the English-Canadian patriarchy is greatgrandmother Campbell, is fondly referred to in Mitchif as Cheechum. Another maternal relative, who according to the patriarchy is the author's great-aunt, is simply referred to as Qua Chich.

Campbell's text also resists conformity to the Euro-Canadian patriarchy by looking back at her life with a re-awakened self. In doing so, she challenges the White-christian-patriarchal constructs of Indigenous women, which are both racist and sexist, by firmly contextualizing her book as proceeding from a Halfbreed-Indigenous ideology. This context is embodied in the author's very strong sense of community and family, or as Thomas King describes it in the preface to *All My Relations*, the web of "kinship that radiate[s] from a Native sense of family"(xiii). By firmly rooting the text in her Halfbreed-Indigenous ideology, Campbell challenges the squaw drudge, Indian princess, and suffering victim images because she remembers the women in her family as resourceful and dynamic women who were vital to their community.

The author maintains that her Cheechum is her greatest source of inspiration, strength, and love. She remembers Cheechum as a small woman who tenaciously clung to her own way of life despite numerous and powerful threats from the various agents of colonization. She writes,

> Cheechum hated to see the settlers come, and as they settled on what she believed was our land, she ignored them and refused to acknowledge them even when passing on the road. She would not become a Christian, saying firmly that she had married a Christian and if there was such a thing as hell then she had lived there; nothing after death could be worse! (15)

That Christian is the author's greatgrandfather Campbell, who the old people called "Chee-pie-hoos" or "Evil-spirit-jumping-up-and-down"(14). The author implies that Chee-pie-hoos, who came from Edinburgh, Scotland and ran a Hudson's Bay store, regarded Cheechum as a loose woman in accord with the stereotype of Indigenous women as whores. Indeed, old man Campbell's White-Euro-Christian patriarchal influence encouraged him to think that his "wife was having affairs with all the Halfbreeds in the area"(14).

Although Cheechum married the Scottish immigrant, Campbell insists that the old lady defiantly resisted any kind of domination. During the 1885 Resistance at Batoche and while greatgrandfather Campbell worked with the North West Mounted Police, Campbell maintains that Cheechum collected information, ammunition, and supplies to give to the so-called rebels. When the old man found out, he punished his wife by stripping her naked and beating her in public. Some time after, Great Grandpa Campbell died mysteriously and Cheechum went to live with her mother's people in the area now known as Prince Albert National Park. Cheechum's mother's people were, according to Campbell, "Indian," even though "they were never part of a reserve, as they weren't present when the treaty-makers came"(15). The author proudly remembers that Cheechum scorned offers of so-called help in the form of welfare and old age pension. Instead, the old woman remained completely self-sufficient and therefore hunted, trapped, and planted a garden. Campbell writes,

> Cheechum built a cabin beside Maria Lake and raised her son. Years later when the area was designated for the Park, the government asked her to leave. She refused, and when all peaceful methods failed the RCMP were sent. She locked her door, loaded her rifle, and when they arrived she fired shots over their heads, threatening to hit them if they came any closer. They left her alone and she was never disturbed again (15).

The subsequent marriage of her son, Maria's Grandpa Campbell, to a "Vandal" woman whose family had been involved in the 1885 Resistance marks a continuation of Cheechum's pattern of resistance. Campbell describes grandmother Campbell as a fiercely strong woman who after her husband's death "went to a white community...to cut brush for seventy-five cents an acre"(16). Grandma Campbell kept her children warm while they worked by wisely choosing to wrap their feet in an Indigenous way with rabbit skins and moccasins, as well as using material (old papers) from the White culture. Her adaptive powers are vitally important and grandmother Campbell conforms to the powerful, dynamic, and resourceful women pattern that the author subsequently adheres to. Grannie Campbell, the author remembers, was also very physically strong. She writes, "Because they (Grannie Campbell and her children) had only one team of horses and Dad used these to work for other people, Grannie on many occasions pulled the plough herself"(16). Grannie Campbell, like Cheechum, was totally self-sufficient; in fact, when Maria's father suggested that he could take care of her "she became quite angry and said he had a family to worry about and what she did was none of his business"(17). Till she was quite old, "she brushed and cleared the settlers' land, picked their stones, delivered their babies, and looked after them when they were sick"(17).

The representation of Grannie Campbell's older sister, Qua Chich, also resists the stereotypic images of Indigenous women because she survives the government's treaty-making interventions, relocation to an Indian reserve, a marriage which left her widowed, and destitution and poverty which afflicted her sisters and brothers. Campbell remembers Qua Chich as a strange old lady who cussed at her dog in Cree. Also, according to the author, Qua Chich was considered quite wealthy because "she owned many cows and horses as well as a big two-storey house"(22). Qua Chich maintained her home and property long after her husband's death. While Campbell remembers that "she was stingy with money, and if someone was desperate enough to ask for help she would draw up formal papers and demand a signature," Qua Chich's business skills exemplify another aspect of the strong and resourceful women who pattern the author's family(23).

The variety of female personalities Campbell presents in the book resists the very limited and confining stereotypical images that imprison Indigenous women. Campbell's mother, whom she describes as "quiet and gentle, never outgoing and noisy like the other women" also challenges the very limiting stereotypical princess/squaw images(17). While the author acknowledges that her mother, like so many others "was always busy cooking," the author recognizes that she was quite unlike the other Metis women because "she loved books and music and spent many hours reading to us"(17).

The author's maternal grandmother also resists the stereotypical confines that non-Indigenous peoples construct for Indigenous women. Campbell describes her as "a treaty Indian woman, different from Grannie Campbell because she was raised in a convent"(18). Campbell's Grannie Dubuque marrie Pierre Dubuque, a French immigrant who "arranged his marriadge...through the nuns at the convent"(15).

In her early years, Campbell cannot comprehend the devastating damage Christianity has inflicted on her culture. However, as a young de-colonizing writer looking back upon her life with fresh eyes, she begins to understand how Christianity has constructed and defined her in accord with the patriarchy. Indeed, she realizes that Christianity is a powerful agent of colonization; and therefore, it constantly attempts to impose controls. As indicated previously, the author's mother and grandmother Dubuque were both raised in convents and thus Christianity severely eroded any connection they may have had to their original way of life. Grannie Dubuque's life was arranged by the convent nuns who married her off to Pierre Dubuque. Campbell remembers that her people never talked "against the church or the priest regardless of how bad they were"(32). Remembering her mother's undaunting and unquestioning faith in God, even when the fat priest selfishly eats what little food they have, Campbell recalls that her mother "accepted it all as she did so many things because it was sacred and of God"(32). The priest, by comparison, showed no respect for what was sacred to the them. Campbell bitterly remembers that he took things "from the Indian's Sundance Pole,...[things] that belonged to the Great Spirit"(30). Unlike the mother, Cheechum clearly understood the power politics manifested in the priest's actions and thus thoroughly resisted domination. Campbell insists that Cheechum hated the church, the Catholic God, and the priest. The author writes, "Cheechum would often say scornfully of this God that he took more money from us than the Hudson's Bay store"(32).

As an Indigenous woman, Cheechum's knowledge, values, and belief system, unlike Christian dogmatism, was derived from a closeness to the land. As a result of her closeness to the land, Cheechum had tremendous insight into human relations, as well as a rich understanding of plants and animals. Having lived through many kinds of changes, she was extremely opinionated about the politics of war, the church, the role of men and women, and the government. After Campbell's mother dies, she finds comfort in Cheechum's words. She writes:

> I have never found peace in a church or in prayer. Perhaps Cheechum had a lot to do with that. Her philosophy was much more practical, soothing and exciting, and in her way I found comfort. She told me not to worry about the Devil, or where God lived, or what would happen after death She said that regardless of how hard I might pray or how many hours I spent on my knees, I had no choice in what would happen to me or when I die. She said it was a pure waste of time that could be used more constructively. She taught me to see beauty in all things around me; that inside each thing a spirit lived, that it was vital too, regardless of whether it was only a leaf or a blade of grass, and by

recognizing its life and beauty I was accepting God. She said that each time I did something it was a prayer, regardless of whether it was good or bad; that heaven and hell were man-made and here on earth; that there was no death, only that the body becomes old from life on earth and that the soul must be reborn, because it is young; that when my body became old my spirit would leave and I'd come back and live again. She said God lives in you and looks like you, and not to worry about him floating around in a beard and white cloak; that the Devil lives in you and all things, and that he looks like you and not like a cow. She often shook her head at the pictures I gave her of God, angels and devils and the things they did. She laughed when she saw the picture of the Devil turning people over with a fork in the depth of Hell's fire, and remarked that it was no wonder those people looked so unhappy, if that's what they believed in. Her explanation made much more sense than anything Christianity had ever taught me (72-73).

Cheechum's simple ways were often contradicted by Campbell's maternal relatives whom the author describes as both strict Catholics and superstitious "Indians." Also, contrary to Cheechum's subtle teachings about striving for spiritual and cultural riches, Grannie Dubuque often implicitly encouraged the author and her siblings to ambitiously seek out material wealth. Campbell writes that while Grannie Dubuque visited she encouraged them to pretend they were rich. Although their food was only meat, potatoes, bannock, lard, and tea, Grannie Dubuque urged them to pretend they were eating fancy salads and dishes like chicken-a-la-king on a fancy table cloth (80). If only briefly, Campbell's maternal grandmother allowed them to forget their poverty but the harsh reality of their lives often intruded upon their games. Moreover, Grannie Dubuque's idealization of White culture only reminded Maria's family of unattainable goals.

To a certain extent, Campbell's language reflects the author's subtle conformity to the White-Euro-Canadian-Christian patriarchy when she begins to fragment Indigenous peoples. Referring to the differences between "Treaty Indian" and "Halfbreed" women, she makes broad generalizations that are more stereotypical than factual; the author explains that "Treaty Indian women don't express their opinions, Halfbreed women do"(27). Those differences, according to Campbell, represent part of a pattern between "Indian" and "Metis" people. She elaborates the differences in the following passage:

There was never much love lost between Indians and Halfbreeds. They were completely different from us-- quiet when we were noisy, dignified even at dances and get-togethers. Indians were very passive--they would get angry at things done to them but would never fight back, whereas Halfbreeds were quick-- tempered--quick to fight, but quick to forgive and forget.

The Indians' religion was very precious to them and to the Halfbreeds but we never took it as seriously. We all went to the Indians' sundance and special gatherings, but somehow we never fitted in. We were always the poor relatives, the awp-pee-tow-koosons [half people]. They laughed and scorned us. They had land and security, we had nothing. As Daddy put it, "No pot to piss in or a window to throw it out." They would tolerate us unless they were drinking and then they would try to fight, but received many sound beatings from us. However, their old people, our "Mushooms" (grandfathers) and "Kokums" (grand- mothers) were good. They were prejudiced, but because we were kin they came to visit and our people treated them with respect (26-27).

In later years, more wisely looking back upon life, in a conversation with Hartmut Lutz in Contemporary Challenges, Ms. Campbell insists that "when it comes to Aboriginal people in Canada, we have the church to "thank" in all areas, whether we are Metis, non-status or whatever, for the dilemma that we are in now!" (47). Indeed, she insists that the Catholic church has always been "the `man coming in front of' the colonizer" (47). A more articulate and mature Campblell explains to Lutz that up until 20 years ago "the priest had total power in the community....It is still there, but not the kind of influence they had before"(46). She also points out that because the church has been losing control, it is now incorporating Indigenous ceremonies and rituals. Campbell astutely maintains:

But that's the history of Christianity. When you can't completely oppress a people, if you are losing them, then you incorporate their spiritual beliefs. And that's even uglier than the other way, because then people think "Oh,well, now it's okay, because the priest is now doing our ceremonies." So the priest ends up becoming the shaman in the community (47).

If her comments sound bitter, one must try to examine those comments from within Campbell's own cultural context. As a young girl, Campbell's dreams, hopes, and ambitions are shattered by Christian patriarchal intrusions, her mother's death, extreme poverty, racism, and sexism.

Maria Campbell was 33 years old when she wrote her story. It grew out of her anger and frustrations. In the interview with Hartmut Lutz she talks about the writing process which led to *Halfbreed*:

> When I started to write *Halfbreed* I didn't know I was going to write a book. I was very angry, very frustrated.
>
> I wrote the book after I had the dream! I had no money, and I was on the verge of being kicked out of my house, had no food, and I decided to go back out in the street and work. I went out one night and sat in a bar. And I just couldn't, because I knew that if I went back to that, I'd be back on drugs again.
>
> I always carry paper in my bag, and I started writing a letter because I had to have somebody to talk to, and there was nobody to talk to. And that was how I wrote *Halfbreed* (53).

Her writing thus becomes an act of resistance. Through the construction of her text, Campbell looks back upon her life with a renewed vision and a stronger connection to those powerful, resourceful, and dynamic women who came before her. What she writes has rarely been said by Indigenous women in North America. The racism and sexism that she suffers is something that too many Indigenous women have suffered. Her voice allows this suffering to be heard. Campbell has first-hand knowledge of this suffering and has survived the genocidal attempts to do away with her people's ways, and survived too the colonial oppression, abusive men, and systemic racism and sexism. She refuses to let her ancestors' sufferings be white-washed by liberal do-gooders. Speaking with Lutz she states:

> Canada's history, the history of Canadians, is that they are killing us with their liberal gentleness. Helping us, being kind to us. "We don't have horrible racism in this country," is one of the things they say. They tell us, "We never had slavery here, we never had this," but some of the horrible things that have happened are worse, or every bit as bad. Because the kinds of things that have happened to Aboriginal people in Canada are things that were so "nice" that nobody's ever bothered to record them because they were done in

such a "nice" way, or if they were recorded they were changed. It's okay to report the atrocities of other countries, and what they do to their peoples, but heaven forbid that Canadians would ever do something like that!

We were busy in the 1940s hearing about the horrible things Germany was doing. Nobody ever would believe that in Saskatchewan at the same time people were loaded into cattle cars, not having bathrooms or facilities, and were carted off, hauled some place, and dumped off in the middle of the snow — and some of those people dying. We never hear about things like that because Canada doesn't do things like that. We need to write those stories ourselves (58-59).

Her voice refuses to let Canada erase what has been done to her people. But, she also addresses the way Indigenous people have internalized colonialism. Remembering Cheechum's words, she writes in *Halfbreed*:

Many years ago, she [Cheechum] said, when she was only a little girl, the Halfbreeds came west. They left good homes behind in their search for a place where they could live as they wished. Later a leader arose from these people who said that if they worked hard and fought for what they believed in they would win against all odds. Despite the hardships, they gave all they had for this one desperate chance of being free, but because some of them said, "I want good clothes and horses and you no-good Halfbreeds are ruining it for me," they lost their dream. She continued: "They fought each other just as you are fighting your mother and father today. The white man saw that was a more powerful weapon than anything else with which to beat the Halfbreeds, and he used it and still does today. Already they are using it on you. They try to make you hate your people (47).

In this passage, Campbell points to colonialism internalized and manifested in family violence, and Metis privileging the White ideal-- symptoms of the colonial disease. When she remembers how her father was beaten and died inside after unsuccessfully attempting to politicize their community, she writes with anger and a real sense of loss:

> Daddy started to drink that summer and I began to grow up. Our whole lives, and those of our people, started to go downhill. We had always been poor, but we'd had love and laughter and warmth to share with each other. We didn't have even that anymore, and we were poorer than ever. Daddy still trapped, but only because it was an escape for him. He would be gone for long periods at a time, then when he was home he drank and often brought white men home with him. Sometimes he'd hit Mom, and she would take the baby and run away until he was sober. He seldom smiled and he hardly ever talked to us unless it was to yell. When he sobered up he'd try to make up, but it never lasted long. Once he even slapped Cheechum (67).

The author's family had lived through extreme poverty but they were able to stay together and help each other. Maria maintains that when the people lost their collective dreams and their hopes they lost their self-respect. Her father lost self-respect after his own people turned on him. As Frantz Fanon in *The Wretched of the Earth* and Dr. Howard Adams in *Prison of Grass* argue, colonized people turning on their own people is symptomatic of the colonial disease.

Campbell also remembers being victimized by colonialism when as a child she internalized the White ideals. Wishing for what the Germans and Swedes possessed, she thought they

> must be the richest and most beautiful on earth. They could buy pretty cloth for dresses, ate apples and oranges, and they had toothbrushes and brushed their teeth every day (27).

This dream--which represents idealization of White culture--carries her all the way to Vancouver where she once again remembers childhood dreams of "toothbrushes and pretty dresses, oranges and apples, and a happy family sitting around the kitchen table talking about...tomorrow"(114). Many hopes and dreams shatter as she remembers the men and women who were bought off or silenced by the government. The most prominent symbol of the government's co-opting is embodied in the Indian in the suit. During her re-awakening, recounted towards the end of her narrative, she meets many Indigenous people who have sold their dreams. Witnessing the way the oppressor uses Indigenous neo-colonial puppet rulers to further the goals of the colonial oppressor, Campbell is devastated.

However, she does not allow herself to be beaten. Like the very strong, vital, and resourceful women within her family, she survives. Campbell survives colonial rule in its absolutely worst oppressive states, abusive men, systemic racism and sexism, and drugs and alcohol addiction. She does not die a victim of Canadian society's racism and sexism, like Margaret Laurence's beaten-down Piquette Tonnerre, or a hopeless whore with no strength or determination to liberate herself, like William Patrick Kinsella's Linda Star. As a survivor, she leaves an important legacy for other Indigenous women.

More importantly, because of Campbell's courageous gestures to speak out, to name her oppressors, and to re-claim her self, she lifts the cloak of silence from other Indigenous women who find themselves prisoners in similar situations. For example, many contemporary Indigenous women who are writers look to Maria Campbell's text as the one which encouraged them to also speak out, name their oppressors, and re-claim their selves. As a result, many of these writers found comfort in solidarity with other Indigenous women. Thus, just as Campbell's Cheechum wisely foretold, she did find her self and many more sisters and brothers.

End Notes

[1]. In Canada these genocidal policies were initiated by a very paternalistic colonial government for the so-called good of Indigenous peoples. For example, the Indian Residential School system was utilized in Canada to supposedly "civilize" and "christianize" Indigenous peoples. Also, throughout Canadian history various Acts of Parliament were passed to do away with Indigenous peoples. In relation to the Metis, land was taken from us unjustly (some even say illegally) through the scrip system.

[2]. Prior to the imposition of the Indian Act, Indigenous peoples had a simple way of indentifying individuals. If a person lived among Indigenous peoples and respected our ways, values, and beliefs, they were generally accepted as one of the people. Currently, the Canadian constitution recognizes the Metis, which is synonymous with Halfbreed, as one of the Aboriginal (Indigenous) peoples of Canada.

[3]. For example, Howard Adams much more so as a gesture of defiance refers to himself as a Halfbreed or a Breed. My mother and her relatives also refer to themselves as Halfbreeds.

Native Women/ Native Survival

A REVIEW OF JANET CAMPBELL HALE'S

"THE JAILING OF CECELIA CAPTURE"

by

Victoria Lena Manyarrows

Victoria Lena Manyarrows

Native/Mestiza (Eastern Cherokee) and 37 years old, I was raised alongside reservations and within mixed communities in North Dakota and Nebraska. As a young person I spent a year in various foster homes. Since 1981, I have worked extensively with community arts and alcohol/substance abuse programs in the San Francisco Bay Area, and have a Master's degree in Social Work (MSW)

My essays and poetry have been published in various Native and multicultural publications in the United States and Canada, including the anthologies *Without Discovery: A Native Response to Columbus; Piece Of My Heart, Gatherings III: The En'owkin Journal of North American First Peoples;* and *Voices of Indentity, Rage and Deliverance;* and the journals *The Four Directions; The Raven Chronicles; Calyx; Gallerie: Women Artists' Monographs (Issue 10); Eclectic Literary Forum; Northwest Literary Forum; Orphic Lute; Common Lives; Matrix; Sacred River; Sidewalks; Sinister Wisdom;* and *Social Work Perspectives.*

is to use written and visual images to convey and promote a positive Native-based world-view.

She remembered the old man in the bar in the Mission district telling her, "We are the biggest tribe of all, us displaced ones, us urban Indians, us sidewalk redskins." He was right.

(p. 199)

In her 1985 novel *The Jailing of Cecelia Capture* Janet Campbell Hale tells the story of a 30-year old Native (American Indian) woman law student, the weekend she spends in jail on drunk driving charges, and her memory of the events and experiences of her life which led to her jailing. Throughout the novel the protagonist, Cecelia Capture, is presented as a woman unhappy with her life and struggling to survive and maintain her identity and integrity as a Native woman in white society, despite the obstacles and isolation she feels. Eventually, it is her closeness to death, and her realization that she has a life to live and be remembered for, that instills in her a sense of hope and meaning—and confidence that she will be able to overcome any difficulties and obstacles that she may yet encounter.

Writing from her own experience as a Native woman who grew up in post-WWII urban California and on rural western Indian reservations, the author introduces themes endemic to Native survival in contemporary society—alcoholism and substance abuse, physical and emotional abuse and violence, psychological and social displacement and isolation, and societal and internalized racism and sexism.

Alcoholism, substance abuse, and other methods of physical and emotional abuse and self-abuse are often-present aspects of Indian life. The racism of the dominant white society often turns inward. The result of this "internalized" racism is low self-esteem, confusion, and all-too-often self-inflicted physical and emotional abuse and violence. Alcohol and suicide are seen as doorways of escape from a life lacking in hope, and filled with pain and unhappiness.

In the novel, Cecelia uses (abuses) alcohol in the same way her Indian father did—to escape from an unhappy life and to cover her pain. Hale suggests that alcohol is an inevitable part of Indian life and that it was not surprising that Cecelia would follow in her father's footsteps and become an alcoholic. Ironically it had been her father's father who had established the tribal law prohibiting alcohol consumption on the agency grounds, and it had been her father who had broken the law one day, by leaving a tribal council meeting to sneak a drink.

As she was growing up, it had been her father's apathy and alcoholism that had made her become more angry and tired of him. As the youngest of four girls (her next oldest sister was 12 years older), Cecelia had always tried to please her father. It was her father who wanted her to become a lawyer, and Cecelia assumed that she was his last attempt to have a son, who perhaps could become "the athlete he had always thought he had the potential to become...[or] the lawyer he had wanted to be but had failed to become" (pp. 57-58). Her father had sent her to predominantly white schools because he felt that to "compete successfully in a white man's world, you had to learn to play the white man's game" (p. 58). He prevented her from learning her native language so that she would be forced to think only in English and see the world as other English--speaking people see it. Understandably, Cecelia came to feel that "like many Indian people of his generation, her father seemed...in some curious way ashamed of being Indian, although he would have denied it vehemently" (p.59).

As the years passed and her father's drinking became more abusive, Cecelia felt that he lost interest in her schooling and didn't care for her anymore. His alcoholism angered her and she lost respect for him. However, this alcohol-induced apathy and neglect which she witnessed and was forced to endure as a child was not strong enough to later prevent her from turning to alcohol when she became an adult. Rather than subscribe to the set of beliefs that some alcoholism counsellors espouse today, that American Indians have a *genetic* predisposition to alcoholism, I believe that Cecelia's eventual reliance on alcohol for relief from life's pressures was rooted in greater "environmental," psycho-social causes--her isolation in white society and her isolation from other Native people and Native support base, and the racism and sexism she experienced in both white and Indian communities.

Psycho-social displacement and isolation are acute realities for most Native people living in this racist and a historical society, which is generally ignorant and disrespectful of Native people and Native needs and wants. More than any other racial or ethnic group in U.S. history, Native people have been misunderstood and stereotyped into oblivion. The only way that we can be "understood" or perceived by the dominant white society and its believers is through stereotypical images and ideas, usually based on mythical images from the past and images of suffering past and present, which generally serve to not acknowledge our current and living existence, nor take us seriously as contemporary participants in society.

It is this isolation of Native people that can be most destructive. There is the reality of isolation within the larger and dominant white society, and isolation from one's own community and people, which can occur when a Native person enters and participates in white-

established and white-dominated social/educational/cultural institutions, and/or becomes involved in interpersonal, especially sexual,
relationships with white people. Not only did Cecelia feel a great deal
of isolation as a Native woman from the time she left her family and
the reservation (she was 16 when she left her family and moved to
San Francisco), but her isolation was complete and deeply personal,
in that she had little contact and no meaningful relationships with
Native people, or Native culture.

Once, during her "welfare mother" days, when she was in her
late teen's and living alone with her infant son in a San Francisco
hotel, Cecelia, "yearning for the companionship of other Indians," went
to the American Indian Center, but was discouraged by its run-down
appearance and the presence of only "a couple of disreputable-looking
men playing pool." She then went to a neighbourhood Indian bar,
ordered a beer, and then couldn't even finish it because she was so
discouraged and disappointed by the alcoholism and hopelessness of
"these...displaced people...She preferred being alone to being one of
them. She had seen such awful desperation in their Indian faces. Big-
city Indians. She was truly cast adrift, without people of her own..."
(pp. 111-112).

Cecelia's interpersonal and sexual relationships were primarily
with white men. Shortly after first arriving in San Francisco in 1966,
Cecelia met Bud, her first boyfriend and the father of her first child,
and she experienced a taste of the isolation and ignorance of Native
people that white society promotes. Young Bud, soon to be shipped
to Vietnam and be killed, asked her:

> "Are you Indian, Cecelia? You look like maybe you
> are." She had to laugh. He couldn't tell for sure. He
> had to ask. How funny it was. He was a white guy,
> and he thought her being Indian was neat and exotic
> (p. 134).

Five years later, after her father had died and she felt more lonely
and isolated than ever, Cecelia met and married Nathan, a young white
college professor from a socially prominent and privileged family - a
man whose "family tree went all the way back to the *Mayflower*" (p.
164). After she married Nathan, Cecelia herself began drinking. Her
isolation from other Native people was thorough. At one point, Cecelia
recalls how she "had once had such disdain for white people that she
couldn't stand blond furniture or light-colored dogs and cats, and
now she was married to a blond white man" (p. 51).

After graduating from UC-Berkeley, Cecelia had wanted to continue on to law school, but her husband preferred that she "stay home" and take care of their two children. He didn't think that law school was appropriate for Cecelia and he thought that she should "consider a more realistic career goal, such as becoming a social worker or a teacher of young children" (p. 164). Cecelia became increasingly bored with home life and resentful of her husband's attempts to restrict her. She began drinking more "to relax, to keep from thinking too much, to put up with Nathan" (p. 164). His privileged background began to irritate her, even though it had been one of the things that had initially attracted her to him. And she resented his condescending attitude toward her.

A climactic point in the novel, and an incident which illustrates the racism and deep isolation that Cecelia endured within the context of her relationship with her husband - an extremely arrogant and ignorant man - was the night they went to an all-white party, hosted by Nathan's friends. Cecelia felt alienated from the white people at the party, isolated herself from them, and began to drink herself into a stupor. She overheard Nathan and his friends mocking the title of Dee Brown's book, *Bury My Heart at Wounded Knee*, and she grew angry and increased her drinking, all the while thinking of the historical reality of Wounded Knee and how ignorant these 20th century white partygoers were:

> There were photographs of the massacre. It happened long after the battles, long after the treaties were signed. Cecelia had seen those old photographs. They were much worse than anything she had seen from My Lai. The Indian bodies lay frozen in the snow, and they were not the bodies of warriors. They were all kinds of peoples: old people, women, children. None of them was armed. They were gunned down by the U.S. Army at Wounded Knee (p.167).

When they arrived home that night, they argued and physically scuffled. When Nathan told Cecelia that she was a drunk just like her father, Cecelia stopped fighting and cried. The next day they made up and she agreed not to drink around him again, if he would "allow" her to go to law school.

Racism and sexism — both societal and internalized — create heavy burdens and demands on Native women. Expectations of how Native women should behave and appear to others, both within the dominant white society and within Native families and communities, have for too long been shaped by the roles and mores of the larger white-and male-dominated society. The racism and sexism of the larger society becomes internalized in the psychological and social fabric of Native communities, families and individuals -- and Native women are the ones who suffer.

Cecelia Capture was a woman, as her name suggests, "captured" not only by the physical jail cell, but by the demands and expectations of the Native and white people who she related to, and the societies and communities they represented. It is a reality that Native people are often unjustly imprisoned and murdered by racist governments, not only in the United States, but in almost all countries of the Americas. Indeed, Cecelia's father had been imprisoned for a year on a trumped-up murder charge, and now Cecelia found herself in an institution familiar to Native people.

Marriage, especially for women, is depicted throughout the novel as a type of "prison." a holding tank for women until they die, or divorce, or their husbands pass on. That the novel ends on this theme accentuates its reality for Native women:

> The drizzle turned into downpour. She would soon be soaked to the skin, but she didn't care. Her long-dead marriage was really over, and knowing this gave her a great feeling of relief. No longer constrained. Not hemmed in. She was not able to return to the beginning, of course, and remake her life more to her liking, but now she was free to go on with the life she did have (p.201).

For years, Cecelia had witnessed her mother's misery in an unhappy and harmful, alcohol-tinged marriage. Early on, Cecelia had resolved that she would never be like her mother, whose white family had virtually disowned her, and who suffered throughout her marriage from arthritis:

> her life wasn't going to overtake her that way and make her a prisoner and a cripple, miserable, mean and bitter. She would not wind up like her mother. Her life was going to be her own... She would be free (pp.74-75).

Years later, after Cecelia quit law school to accompany her husband to his new teaching job in Spokane, Washington, she began to feel like a "prisoner" in her marriage, but she accepted it as many women do, by rationalizing her pain and loneliness - "Nobody had a perfect marriage, after all, and theirs was certainly not as bad as some." (p. 176). It was only when she feared that she had inherited her mother's arthritis ("she felt a nagging ache in the joint of her right shoulder") that she called Berkeley and made plans to re-instate herself in law school. Despite being a key institution of oppressive white society, (law) school represented freedom for Cecelia--freedom from an oppressive and unhappy past, and a path to a future uncertain, but full of change and hope.

Cecelia's experience with the racism, ignorance and brutal alienation of white society was recounted throughout the novel. Racism touched her life, from her experiences as a child in school, when the white children "taunted and teased and called her names, or..ignored her and made her feel as alone as if she were the only person in the world," (p. 76) to the scene in the bar on the night of her arrest: "He thought she was a Mexican. They always thought that. Especially in California. Even Mexicans in California mistook her for one of them." (p. 33)

And, on a more subtle level, racism from within her own family affected her psyche and emotional development. Cecelia's mother, who in many ways symbolized white society and its disdain and disregard for Native people, had always focused on, and "nagged" Cecelia about her hair:

> "Long and straight and stringy. Why don't you get it cut and put in a good perm? You look just like some old witch. You look like Geronimo. You look like some damned reservation kid" (which her mother knew that she was but did not like to recognize) (pp. 54-55).

For Native people, long, straight hair has always been a symbol and evidence of one's "Indian-ness." White society restricts Native hairstyles in prisons and discourages Native hairstyles and culture on an insidious psycho-social level, and it is also true that many Native and mixed-heritage families and their communities have in the past and continue today to internalize the racism of the larger and dominant white society, and use this racism to restrict and impede Native-defined culture and expression. Such internalized racism can lead to confusion and identity problems for Native people, which in turn can lead to alcoholism and substance abuse, and other forms of physical and emotional abuse and violence - too often used against our own people and against ourselves.

The Jailing of Cecelia Capture is a very moving and personal story which is firmly grounded in the real life experiences of contemporary Native women. This reader recognized and identified with many of the experiences and difficulties of Cecelia's life. I grew up in an environment of alcoholism and abuse, anger and violence, and internalized and societal racism and sexism. For me, psychological and social displacement and isolation occurred when I left my mother's home at age 18 to attend school at a white-dominated college, where Native students were a rarity. But like Cecelia, I was eager to leave home and unhappiness behind, and school represented freedom, change and hope.

My mother was an alcoholic and an Indian, who was herself unjustly and cruelly institutionalized, dehumanized and abused by my father, and she turned this abuse and racism against us, her children. Like Cecelia, I heard all the negative words about long, straight and "stringy" hair, and I was frequently compelled to curl my hair, or have it cut. I was also subject to name-calling and derisive terms, such as "half-breed," "mixed-breed" and "Pocahontas." For a year, my younger brother, sister and I endured the alienating experience of living in white foster homes -- another "common" Indian experience, but not one that Cecelia shared. Jail, the courts, detention centers, foster homes, social workers, hospitals and untimely deaths are all very familiar to me.

I have experienced the racism of ignorance and non-recognition of Native peoples like Cecelia, who was often seen as "Mexican" in California. In California and the Southwest United States, and also in Mexico and Central America, I have often been seen as "Mexican" or "Chicana." In Mexico and Central America, however, my American Indian identity has been readily accepted and understood, as there is less denial of Native culture, lineage and history in these more mixed-blood, *mestizo* lands.

Thus far, I have not succumbed to any "genetic" pre-dispositions to become an alcoholic, and I am confident I never will. Being very aware and respectful of Native culture and values, the lessons of history and the evils of racism and sexism, and having grown up in a comparatively liberalized and activism-oriented era (the 1970's, when Indian activism was at its strongest and most visible position so far in this century; and the 1980's, when Central American struggles and the Native-positive and Native-oriented Nicaraguan Sandinista Revolution flourished) I recognize the choices and privilege that I have been allowed, which have enabled me to resist disease and despair in my own life. So, too, by the end of the novel Cecelia had renounced her "long-dead" marriage, her scarred and painful past, and regained her strength to resist disease and despair and start anew -- to "remake her life more to her liking."

Victoria Lena Manyarrows

References

Hale, J.C. *The Jailing of Cecelia Capture.* New York: Random House. 1985

Inside Looking Out:

READING "TRACKS" FROM A NATIVE PERSPECTIVE

by

Armand Garnet Ruffo

Armand Garnet Ruffo

Armand was born and raised in Northern Ontario and draws on his Ojibway heritage for his work. He holds B.A.'s from York University and the University of Ottawa and a M.A. from the University of Windsor. His prose and poetry have appeared in numerous journals and anthologies, including *An Anthology of Canadian Native Literature in English* (Oxford University Press 1992).

In her introduction to *Studies in American Indian Literature, Critical Essays and Course Designs,* Paula Gunn Allen, a Laguna Pueblo poet and critic, says that "Professors who intend to embark on the teaching of courses using American Indian materials -- traditional or modern -- must study carefully the traditions, history, and present day settings of the tribe from which the document comes or to which it refers...context and continuity are two of the most important areas to be taken into account in the teaching of American Indian literature" [1]. Clearly what this position calls for is a degree of cultural initiation. Those coming from outside a culture must seek out the necessary prerequisite information so that any attempt to address its literature will be more than merely superficial or, in the extreme, inaccurate. "The critic, therefore, not only must clarify symbols and allusions but also must define or describe whole perceptual-interpretative systems" [2].

In considering the problem of cross-cultural interpretation, Elaine Jahner, a non-Native critic, notes in her article "A Critical Approach to American Indian Literature" that "We have to rely on ethnological information to interpret the metaphorical structures and their thematic import" [3]. This position, however, in referring to a scientific approach in the context of culture, raises the fundamental question of how one culture communicates to another and ultimately to the even broader problem of human communication itself, specifically, the production and exchange of meanings. John Fiske provides rudimentary insight into the nature of the problem through an examination of semiotics when he says, "All codes depend upon an agreement amongst their users and upon a shared cultural background. Codes and culture interrelate dynamically" [4].

It is this position that provides an avenue of approach in considering a novel such as Louise Erdrich's *Tracks.* What is immediately evident in the work is an elaborate system of coding which subsumes a complex body of information central to plot, structure, character, and even theme, and yet, ironically, information which is not readily available to the culturally uninitiated. This is not to say the novel is incomprehensible to a non-Native audience but rather that it operates according to different levels of understanding and, hence, meaning. Specifically, through the voice of its two narrators, *Tracks* draws heavily on the Native American oral tradition and even "seems to aspire to the status of 'pure' storytelling" [5]. So while critics may state that "encoding invites decoding" [6] such a work necessarily raises questions: How much goes unnoticed? How much is left unknown? How much can the 'outsider' really know and feel? Again the problem of cross-cultural interpretation comes to the forefront. The point here is to proceed by examining specific aspects of the novel in light of Anishnawbe culture in order to attain some insight into these "perceptual-interpretative systems," and by doing so attain a better understanding of how the novel builds upon Native American culture.

By employing principle characters as narrators speaking to a like-minded audience, Erdrich posits implicit information within the text which not only adds to the complexity of the work but which is crucial to a thorough understanding of it. Drawing upon the given that "literature reflects the deepest meanings of a community" [7] Erdrich begins her narrative using the collective pronoun "We" heard through a first person point of view. In doing so, she immediately establishes both an immediacy and intimacy between narrator and listener, Nanapush, a narrator bound to community (or in this case what is left of it) and the traditions of that community, tells his story to his 'granddaughter' Lulu. In this manner Erdrich gives us the impression of overhearing a family conversation, of almost eavesdropping, so that the process of reading implicates the 'listener' into becoming an active participant in the experience of the story -- a quality of the oral tradition -- rather than merely a passive observer. This is no less so when we turn to the novel's second narrator, Pauline, and again "hear" a similar kind of voice, but directed not to any particular character within the text but instead directly to the reader. For while Pauline, contrary to Nanapush, may deny and finally reject her community and traditions, she is nonetheless a product of her culture and therefore intimately a part of what she is so desperately trying to leave and ultimately destroy.

From the first page, then, Nanapush is heard telling Lulu the history of her tribe and family, particularly of the devastation of the "spotted sickness" [8] and how their people were forced to flee their home lands -- which resulted in an "exile in a storm of government papers" (1). Thus Erdrich immediately establishes that the world is out of balance; man and nature are no longer in harmony. For the Anishnawbe the significance of this cannot be overstated. Imbalance means destruction and death -- which itself has many implications, for to kill without considering the spirit of that which is dying is akin to destroying one's own spirit. It is a view of creation as one complete whole; the world of objects and the spiritual world, the conscious and the unconscious, thought and feeling, are the embodiment of one great and powerful essence. Thus the ability to commune with the spirits is premised upon the inherent belief in a highly ordered and moral universe in which the earth, planets, animals, men and women all function in harmony and in accordance with the vision of Kitche Manitou (the Great Spirit or Great Unknown) [9].

As the universe is ordered and defined so is the immediate world of humans, where life is bound to a vast array of symbolic elements -- a vital part of the concept of communion and spiritual power. It is for this reason that Nanapush can say to Lulu, "Granddaugher, you are the child of the invisible" (1). He doesn't merely say that she is a child of the dead, which would imply an incommunicability between the physical and spiritual realms of being; instead, by saying that the other form of existence is merely "invisible," Nanapush, in essence, is telling Lulu that the reality in which her relatives live is as real and as present as the one she is presently living, and therefore more a communicative continuation than a disjunctive separation. Such statements become all the more significant if the 'listener' realizes that the spiritual world is an integral part of the Anishnawbe view of existence, and that the concept of family and community includes both the living and the invisible world. Another example is when Nanapush says, "They say the unrest and curse of trouble that struck our people in the years that followed was the doing of dissatisfied spirits" (4). He even goes further to say that "We feared that they [the spirits] would hear us and never rest" (5). Here the influence of the spiritual world upon the physical and vice versa is clear. Embodied within whole concept of spirituality then is the basic tenet of continuity and completeness -- the circularity of being -- and the notion of influential power through which there is interaction with the physical world. It is this upon which the novel develops.

Characters, therefore, either function within or in response to these traditional concepts of existence, which in turn shape events, dramatic action and, accordingly, the whole structure of the novel. Thus the central conflict is one of cultural integrity versus cultural disruption. Specifically, it is whether or not Nanapush and Fleur can save the Pillager land allotment on Lake Matchimanito from the faceless lumber company. Although conflict between characters is important and undeniably propels the novel forward, it is nevertheless subsumed under this main conflict. The importance of land to the Anishnawbe cannot be overstated, "The Anishnawbe predicated fatherhood on the sun. In the same way they proclaimed motherhood in the earth. Both sun and earth were mutually necessary and interdependent in the generation of life. But of the two pristine elements, Mother Earth was the most immediate and cherished and honoured" [10]. In semiotic terms, Fleur, the Mother Earth figure is pitted against invading, disruptive forces which threaten her existence by threatening the land. In this respect, such characters as Pauline, Napolean, Sophie, Bernadette, the Morrisseys and Lazarres, Nector and to some extent Margaret and even Eli (It is Margaret who protects her own property over Fleur's and Eli who ends up working for the very lumber company that is doing the destroying.) are either disruptive agents or, in the least, products of cultural disruption and alienation.

In response to the destruction of the land, Nanapush says early in the novel that "I weakened into an old man as one oak went down, another and another was lost, as a gap formed, a clearing there, and plain daylight entered" (9). Here Erdrich sets up the contrast between traditional Native beliefs and those of western Christianity. The Native person's belief that the dark forests are indeed sacred is put into sharp contrast to the cleared, sun lit fields normally associated with Christianity. The role of Nanapush then, may be likened to a guardian of traditional culture, which stems from his spiritual bond to the land, evinced in the novel by his close relationship to Fleur (33). This, however, is not to say that Nanapush is a static and doomed character lost in the past. Far from it, for although he laments the last buffalo hunt, the fact remains that he does move to Margaret Kashpaw's land, joins the tribal council, and is able to save Lulu from residential school, who in the end is an adopted Nanapush and bearer of (oral) tradition. And so with Nanapush's adaptability and ability to survive in the 'new' world is the survival of the whole culture.

What is most obvious to those familiar with Anishnawbe culture is Erdrich's variation on the name Nanabush, who according to Anishnawbe tradition was "born of a human mother, [and] sired by a spirit, Epingishmook, (the West)" [11]. Essentially, Erdrich playfully changes the name of Nanabush to Nanapush (in good old trickster fashion) and injects her story with another layer of meaning. Thus to fully understand the role that Erdrich assigns Nanapush, it is necessary to understand the significance of Nanabush. Perhaps the most significant fact is that in his (or her) role as "trickster" he is both a cultural hero and a teacher of human nature -- and existence in general -- among the Anishnawbe people. It is equally important to remember that despite this hero/ teacher role, Nanabush's behaviour is not always benevolent, but at times downright hostile, certainly mischievous. Take, for example, the traditional story in which Nanabush, disgruntled from fasting, discovers his grandmother making love to his grandfather and burns his grandfather's buttocks and then kills him. Later, he even tricks his grandmother into cooking and eating the old man. This is obviously a departure from the comical, foolish Nanabush who finds himself dancing with bullrushes instead of people, or the Nanabush who kindly gives names to the animals. Basil Johnston points out, in *Ojibway Heritage*, that "He could be true or he could be false, loving or hating. As an Anishnawbe, Nanabush was human, noble and strong, or ignoble and weak. For all his attributes, strong and weak, the Anishnawbe came to love and understand Nanabush. They saw in him, themselves" [12].

Therefore, by knowing that Nanapush is indeed a variation of Nanabush, the Trickster figure, and that as a guardian of an age-old tradition his presence carries the weight of an entire culture (through all those stories associated with him), the 'listener' obtains insight into the importance of the Nanapush in relation to other characters and levels of meaning. The implications are clear when he says, "My girl, listen well. Nanapush is a name that loses power every time it is written and stored in a government file" (32) or "My father said, 'Nanapush...its got to do with trickery and living in the bush'" (33). In telling Lulu about himself, Nanapush is in fact telling her about cultural survival, about remaining true to traditions. Later he says "power dies, power goes underground and gutters out, ungraspable. It is momentary, quick of flight, and liable to deceive" (177). Here no doubt he is referring to his own role as Trickster, and his own power within Native culture -- which only now is resurfacing after years of being 'underground.' Also, by understanding Nanabush, the 'listener' realizes that there is a long tradition behind Nanapush's bawdy stories, such as the one about "the sticking-out thing." (147). Nanapush best explains this mischievous side of himself in his own words when he tells Lulu how she came to be a Nanapush: "There were so many tales, so many possibilities, so many lies. The waters were so muddy I thought I'd give them another stir" (225). Such an explanation not only tells Lulu who she is, but moreover reveals succinctly who Nanapush is -- in that it reveals his use of trickery to save her (He transforms himself into a bureaucrat so that he can draw her home.) which in turn exemplifies his role as a guardian of tradition.

Like Nanapush, Pauline also functions in a dualistic role as both narrator and character, although, in contrast to Nanapush, she carries the weight of cultural imperialism and embodies the profound effect Catholicism in its extremity has had on Native people -- which Arthur Solomon calls "cultural and spiritual genocide" [13]. In semiotic terms, both Nanapush and Pauline define each other's role as referents, so while Nanapush is a guardian of culture and tradition, Pauline becomes the death of culture and tradition. As signifers, they are bound to both cultural and historical determinants. And so, when Nanapush says, "Our tribe unraveled like a course rope," (2) Pauline may be viewed as one of the loose strands no longer bound to the Native community. Parentless and rootless, she is a product of acculturation/ assimilation, first moving away from the north to work at "Kozka's Meats," and then becoming hired help on the Morrissey farm, determined at all costs to give up her Native identity and join the community of Christ. (We should note that Pauline represents the kind of Church doctrine that says 'Thou shall not kill' and yet tacitly, if not explicitly, sanctions war.) Yet, although Pauline does succeed in getting what she wants and eventually joins the nunnery and takes up her vows and becomes sister "Leopolda," nonetheless, she continues to rely on her Native heritage to interact with the spiritual world. And when this interaction does occur, she takes it for granted as something inevitable and normal, as anyone coming from outside the culture could not. In this sense Pauline straddles both the non-Native and the Native worlds right up until she adopts a whole new identity. This however does not lessen the fact that she originates from the same culture as Nanapush and Fleur, and that because of this, they know her intimately and call into question both her integrity and reliability. When Nanapush tells Fleur that Pauline has come from Argus with a story, Fleur's comment is simply "Uncle, the Puyat lies" (38). Nanapush himself says, "As I said, she was born a liar, and sure to die one" (53). What such statements in fact do is bring into question the reliability of Pauline as narrator. Is the 'listener' to believe her when she says that Misshepeshu, the "water man" or "monster," who lives quietly in Lake Matchimanito, is really a "devil?" Without Erdrich precisely telling us, how can the 'listener' possibly know, unless he or she comes to the story with some prior knowledge of culture?

It is when considering how the concept of vision operates within the text that knowledge of culture becomes imperative. This is particularly important as vision functions to propel character interaction and shape events and, in doing so, lend structure to the novel. Devoting a chapter to the subject, which he subtitles "Self Understanding and Fulfillment," Basil Johnston gives an idea of the importance of this concept in Anishnawbe culture: "No man begins to be until he has seen his vision. It was through vision that a man found purpose and meaning in life and to his being" [14]. Added to this is the variable of different kinds of vision; with its own particular parameters, kinds of vision depend on whether or not the meaning of the vision is complete and clear or fragmentary and unclear, and whether it occurs during vigil or in the dream state, dream being "the simplest and first form of vision" [15]. What then is a vision? The dictionary defines it as "an experience in which a personage, thing, or event appears vividly or credibly to the mind, although not actually present" [16]. To the Anishnawbe this definition is however inaccurate, if not false, in that it indicates that a vision is essentially unreal, merely hallucination, a phenomenon that occurs only in the mind. In Native American culture, it is much more. Johnston goes on to explain that "the vision as a force could alter conduct, mode of life, and even character" [17]. What is important to recognize here is that the term is a culturally coded concept emboding a force or power which can profoundly affect the individual, so much so that to reveal a private vision of self-revelation is comparable to giving away one's "soul-spirit."

Throughout her novel, Erdrich uses certain basic principles of the concept of vision and imaginatively shapes them to function within the context of her story. In other words, although she employs the concept as an Anishnawbe would understand it, as something powerful and real, the manner or context in which she uses it is uniquely her own. In writing a work of fiction, Erdrich has shaped her understanding of traditional practices to suit the purpose and demands of her story. One of the most powerful examples of vision in the novel is the death scene between Pauline and Fleur. Here Fleur has just given birth to her baby and like the baby is on the verge of dying. Pauline comments, "I saw that she was dying. She would take me as well" (158). Just prior to this elaborate vision or 'voyage' to the place of the dead, Fleur pins Pauline to the cabin floor with her knife, and although Pauline says "A swirling blackness lowered, lifted, and when I pulled away, the knife from between my thighs dropped" (158) at the conclusion of the scene, she adds "I was once more pinned tight by the knife" (162). Physically, Pauline and Fleur never leave the cabin and, yet, despite western culture's notions of what is and what is not possible, they do travel in a very real and physical sense in that what they encounter profoundly affects them. In fact, because Fleur loses the first round of cards to the "invisible/ dead," she loses her baby, and the baby dies. It is this seemingly illogical contradiction emphasizing how cultures perceive existence that reveals the fundamental truth of the scene and not necessarily what occurs in it. This is not to say that Erdrich does not make use of certain beliefs that are central to the Anishnawbe. For even though Pauline and Fleur travel to a place that is strictly the product of Erdrich's imagination, they do indeed travel "a path that broadened when it swerved...to run due west" (159). According to the Anishnawbe, west, the direction of sunset, has always been traditionally the place of the dead. Also both Fleur and Pauline "skated on...bark shoes, floated the iced pathway." To the Anishnawbe (of course this varies from region to region) death also means floating on a great river up towards the stars to a 'pure' land as it was before the coming of the whiteman. Thus in Pauline's description of "vast seas of moving buffalo and not one torn field, but only earth, as it was before," (159) Erdrich is drawing directly upon traditional beliefs to set the scene.

A further example of this kind of storytelling is when Nanapush guides Eli in the moose hunt. Nanapush is able not only to see Eli but actually help him with his task. Clearly, Nanapush's vision is much more than merely a product of fancy or imagination in that he is actually able to be there with Eli and actually influence events in the physical world while never leaving his cabin. That Nanapush undergoes an orderly process to attain his vision and make contact with Eli underlines the whole concept of order and harmony in a (moral) universe.

Johnston succinctly explains the idea of order as it relates to the creator's vision: "Kitchie Manitou...made The Great Laws of Nature for the well being and harmony of all things and all creatures. The Great Laws governed the place and movement of sun, moon, earth and stars; governed the powers of wind, water, fire and rock; governed the rhythm and continuity of life, birth, growth and decay. All things lived and worked by these laws. Kitchie Manitou had brought into existence his vision [18]. Likewise, through her artistic vision, Erdrich creates a scene in which order is of prime importance. Nanapush doesn't haphazardly or casually have a vision; on the contrary, we see him go through an elaborate ritual in which everything he does is of the utmost importance. On the verge of starvation, he describes what he does to attain his vision:

> That's when I lay down. In my fist I had a lump of charcoal with which I blackened my face. I placed my otter bag upon my chest, my rattle near. I began to sing slowly, calling on my helpers, until the words came from my mouth but were not mine, until the rattle started, the song sang itself, and there, in the deep bright drifts, I saw the tracks of Eli's snowshoes clearly (101).

Along with this notion of order is an elaborate array of traditional objects included as an integral part of the ritual, each object having its significance and purpose -- the charcoal for the face used to assume the status of the dead, the otter bag used as a medicine bag in which are personal power objects, a rattle used to evoke the spirits. Erdrich also makes specific reference to song; in oral tradition song has always been used (along with the drum) to speak with the spirits. When Nanapush says "the song gathered I exerted myself," he is in fact acknowledging the song's power and how important it is to his vision. Eli, in turn, upon killing the moose he's been hunting performs his own ceremony: "To gain strength for the hard work ahead he carefully removed the liver, sliced off a bit. With a strip of cloth torn from the hem of his shirt, he wrapped that piece, sprinkled it with tobacco, and buried it under a handful of snow. Half of the rest, he ate" (103). A central tenet of Anishnawbe culture is respect for all forms of life; accordingly, Eli's actions illustrate this perspective. Although half starved, he makes sure to pay homage to the spirit of the animal he has just killed prior to eating. And as tobacco is a substance traditionally used by the Anishnawbe for communicating with the spirit world, so Eli sprinkles a morsel of the moose's flesh with tobacco.

What is evident in Erdrich's use of these 'objects of power' is the varation she employs to illustrate her thematic concerns. Such an example is when Lulu freezes her feet and Nanapush says that "Eventually, my songs overcame the painful burning and you [Lulu] were suspended, my eyes open, looking into mine" (167). Here it is interesting to note that for the healing Erdrich chooses to use a combination of old time 'doctoring' and traditional medicine: "I (Nanapush) bathed those feet in water and pickling salt, fanned them with purifying smoke" (167). Why is Nanapush using old time medicine? Perhaps to show that Native culture is adaptable. Again the power of the word is at work, which perhaps is nowhere better expressed by Nanapush then when he tells Lulu of his experience of fighting off his own sickness: "When I was the last one left, I saved myself by telling a story....Death could not get a word in edgewise, grew discouraged and traveled on" (118). In another powerful scene involving vision, Nanapush visits Moses and then brings him back to help with a healing ceremony for Fleur. Again the qualities of order and process in conjunction with power objects and song are central. In seeking Moses' help, Nanapush brings him some braids of sweetgrass" (187) a plant most sacred to the Anishnawbe, which Moses puts into his drum's "tobacco box." The two drums which Moses brings over to Nanapush's make a striking contrast:

> One was no more that a tin pail, across which a rawhide was stretched and bound. The other, fancier one was strapped to his back. This instrument was never allowed to touch the ground, and was decorated with long ribbons, with beaded skirt and tabs. It was painted for the directions, with a clawed spirit figure on one side (188).

The significance of the tobacco box, ribbons, the four directions, and the clawed spirit figure cannot be overlooked in that they are all traditional signs representing power within Anishnawbe culture. The drum being unable to touch the ground indicates that it belongs to the spiritual plane. Here Erdrich juxtaposes the one elaborate drum with a plain one constructed out of a tin pail as if she were once again commenting on the adaptability of Native culture.

Included within this elaborate array of objects is the paste which Nanapush makes to help cure Fleur. Nanapush says, "When I first dreamed the method of doing this, I got rude laughter...But the person who visited my dream told me what plants to spread so that I could plunge my arms into a boiling stew kettle." This comment is particularly telling because it indicates the power of dream and foreshadows the upcoming scene between Nanapush and Pauline.

Dream, the first and simplest form of vision, is one of the greatest gifts of Kitche Manitou. This whole scene, then, leading up to the point where Pauline bursts out of the sweatlodge may be viewed as one elaborate ritual, which Erdrich has constructed by employing cultural tradition in an imaginative, personal manner. Consider, for example, Nanapush's explanation of his water drum. This type of drum is used in Anishnawbe Midewiwin ceremonies; Nanapush's drum, however, is unique in that it is made of Margaret's kettle, "covered and filled...partway with water" (189) his explanation being that "it would make a sound to attract trouble and then drown it inside" (189). Of course, both the drum and the explanation are uniquely products of Erdrich's imagination and, yet, taken within context and considering who Nanapush is -- or rather who Nanabush is -- the drum works perfectly for the purposes of the story. For just as Moses can adapt to the circumstance of cultural disruption and use a drum made from a tin pail, so too can Nanapush use one made from a kettle. Again, the recurring concepts of order and process are emphasized by Nanapush who says, "We worked quickly. Not long and had everything prepared the proper way" (189).

Thus, what is evident from the points of view of the novel's two narrators, Nanapush and Pauline, there is a commingling of the spiritual and physical worlds posited as a given. Integral to this given is the all- embracing notion of power, which may simply be defined as force or the ability to act and effect change. And because *Tracks* is grounded in Anishnawbe culture, this "access" to power functions in ways outside the normal realm of western experience. For example, Nanapush, through ordered ceremony and the application of his special paste, attains vision and, in doing so, plunges his hands into boiling water without burning them. And although Pauline does burn herself -- because she tries to gain power from her own brand of religion -- nevertheless, as part of Anishnawbe culture, and thus part of its belief system, she too has access to this system of power; a prime example is when she obtains some of Moses' "medicine powder" (80) and uses it to draw Eli over to Sophie. Here, again, Erdrich employs imagination to give a vivid description of the medicine powder. "The dust Moses had concocted was crushed fine of certain roots, crane's bill, something else and slivers of Sophie's fingernails. I would bake it in Eli's lunch" (80). Again, what is important here is not so much what the love medicine consists of -- as this is a work of fiction -- but the fact that the power of such a concoction is readily accepted by the characters involved and becomes instrumental in shaping their lives. Because of this cultural homogeneity, Pauline seeks Moses' help to seduce Eli and accepts the power of his powder without further thought. Only when Eli hesitates and 'shakes his head as if to clear it,' does she have a momentary doubt and feel a "thin panic" (83) however, this quickly subsides as Eli soon makes his move for Sophie. This again reinforces the notion that individuals are able to have power, or control, over others beyond what western cultural normally accepts as possible. Clearly, it is not Sophie who is in control or even really feels what is going on between herself and Eli. As Pauline tells it, "She (Sophie) shivered and I dug my fingers through the tough claws of sumac, through the wood-sod, clutched bark, shrank backward into pleasure" (83). To Pauline both Eli and Sophie become "mechanical things, toys, dolls wound past their limits" (84). So even though Pauline turns her back on her culture, she continues to draw upon it for her own benefit up until the time she begins to see visions of Christ. In renouncing her Native traditions, Pauline says that "It was clear that Indians were not protected by the thing in the lake (referring to Misshepeshu) or by the other Manitous who lived in trees, the bush, or spirits of the animals that were hunted so scarce they became discouraged and did not mate" (139). Ironically, in seeing Native culture on the verge of destruction, Pauline joins the agressors believing that Christianity is the only way to salvation and as a result aids in the destruction.

It is describing Fleur's power, Pauline goes so far as to say that "She got herself into some half-forgotten medicine, studied ways we shouldn't talk about" (12). Here the implications are clear; Pauline appears to be referring to Fleur as a "Bear-walker," one who controls a powerful 'evil medicine.' This comment, however, is from Pauline's point of view and must be taken with no small amount of skepticism, considering that she is an unreliable narrator, someone determined at all costs to become "Christ's champion" (195). Another interpretation for the bear that barges into Fleur's cabin is that it is her bear-clan spirit. Even Nanapush says "it could have been a spirit bear" (60) although he's uncertain. The fact remains that Fleur has power -- which those familiar with Anishnawbe culture could interpret as coming from Mother Earth -- and appears to be able to harness the life-force in nature. As such, Fleur lives near Misshepeshu, and even draws Eli towards her when she wants. As Nanapush tells it, "I said this to Eli Kashpaw, 'I understand Fleur. I know that was no ordinary doe'"(42). In fact both Nanapush and Pauline remark that the Pillagers are a powerful family. Nanapush himself says, "The Pillagers were as stubborn as the Nanapush clan and would not leave my thoughts. I think they followed me home" (6). This is a telling comment in consideration of who the Nanapush (or Nanabush) clan is. Pauline's own comment is that "Power travels in the bloodlines, handed out before birth. It comes down through the hands, which in the Pillagers are strong and knotted, big, spidery and rough... sensitive." (31) And although the connection is not specifically stated, it is Fleur who appears to summon the tornado while in Argus, which literally destroys all those who have done her harm. This is not to say that Fleur maintains her powerful ability throughout the novel; on the contrary, as the lumber company encroaches upon Anishnawbe land, like the trees, her power begins to wane and recede. An indication of her diminishing power first appears when she tells Eli of the path that had appeared in her sleep, where the deer tracks began. But he comes back empty-handed (171). The relationship here between Fleur's power and nature is both inextricable and integral to the novel as is the relationship of Native people to the land. In the end, Fleur is left with the ability to create merely a "shifting wind," and she must resort to cutting and hacking down her own trees by hand in her attempt to thwart the ever approaching lumber company, a telling comment on the contemporary situation of both Mother Earth and Native people.

Beginning in the oral tradition, words and stories have always meant power in Native culture, and it is through this sacred power that Native people have always expressed their sense of identity and place on the land. In Louise Erdrich's *Tracks*, it is clear that the values and beliefs that underpin the work are fundamentally different from those of western culture in that Erdrich posits a wealth of cultural knowledge arising from Anishnawbe tradition. And, yet, *Tracks* as literature is an act of the imagination, and so the novel arises from a way of seeing, feeling and understanding Mother Earth that is uniquely the author's. For the outsider, then, attempting to come to terms with Native people and their literature, the problem is not one to be solved by merely attaining the necessary background, reading all the anthropological data that one can get one's hands on. Rather, for those who are serious, it is more a question of cultural initiation, of involvement and commitment, so that the culture and literature itself becomes more than a mere museum piece, dusty pages, something lifeless. Think of Eli, after his kill, wrapped in moose meat; in Nanapush's words "the moose is transformed into the mold of Eli, an armor that would fit no other" (104). That is how Native culture should fit if one is truly to understand its literature and people.

End Notes

[1] Paula Gunn Allen, ed.,
   Studies in American Indian Literature, Critical Essays and Course Designs (New York: The Modern Language Association of America, 1983), p. x.

[2] *Ibid.* p. 222.

[3] Elaine A. Jahner,
   "A Critical Approach to American Indian Literature," in *Studies in American Indian Literature*, ed., Paula Gunn Allen, p.222.

[4] John Fiske,
   Introduction to Communication Studies, 2nd ed., (London: Routledge: 1990), p. 65.

[5] Robert Siberman,
   "Opening The Text: Love Medicine & the Return of the Native American Woman," in Narrative Chance: Post Modern Discourse on Native American Indian Literatures, ed., Gerald Vizenor (Albuquerque: U of New Mexico: 1989), p.112.

[6] Elaine A. Jahner,
   "Metalanguages," in *Narrative Chance*, ed., Gerald Vizenor, p. 160.

[7] Paula Gunn Allen,
   "Bringing Home the Facts: Tradition and Continuity in the Imagination," *Recovering the Word, Essays on Native American Literature*, eds., Brian Swann & Arnold Krupat (Los Angeles: U. of California Press, 1987), p. 565.

[8] Louise Erdrich,
   Tracks (New York: Harper & Row, Publishers, 1989), p. 14. All further references to this work appear in the text.

[9] Basil Johnston,
   Ojibway Heritage (Toronto: McClelland and Steward Ltd., 1981), p 12.

[10] *Ibid.*, p. 23.

[11] Johnston, p. 17.

[12] Ibid., p. 20.

[13] Solomon,
   Songs For The People: Teaching On The Natural Way (Toronto: NC Press, 1990), p. 65.

[14] Johnston,
   Ojibway Heritage, p.119.

[15] Ibid, p. 122.

[16] *The Random House College Dictionary*,

The Unabridged Edition, ed. in chief, Jess Stein , revised edition, (Random House: New York, 1975), p. 1471.

[17] Johnston,
Ojibway Heritage, p.120.

[18] Ibid, p. 13.

Bibliography

Allen Gunn, Paula, ed.
Studies In American Indian Literature, Critical Essays and Course Designs. New York: The Modern Language Ass.,1983.

Erdrich, Louise.
Tracks. New York: Harper and Row,1989.

Fiske, John.
Introduction to Communication Studies. 2nd ed. London: Routledge, 1990.

Johnston, Basil.
Ojibway Heritage. McCelland and Steward. reprint. Toronto: McClelland and Stewart, 1981.

Solomon, Arthur.
Songs For The People: Teachings On The Natural Way. NC Press Ltd.: Toronto, 1990.

Swann, Brian and Krupat, Arnold, eds.
Recovering The Word, Essays On Native American Literature. Univ. of California Press: Los Angeles, 1987.

The Random House College Dictionary,
The Unabridged Edition. New York: Random House, 1975.

Vizenor, Gerald, ed.
Narrative Chance: Post-Modern Discourse on North American Indian Literatures. Univ. of New Mexico: Albuquerque, 1989.

Aboriginal Peoples' Estrangement

MARGINALIZATION IN THE PUBLISHING INDUSTRY

by

Greg Young-Ing

Greg Young-Ing

Greg is a Cree from The Pas, Manitoba, who holds a Masters Degree from the Institute of Canadian Studies, Carleton University. He is currently the Manager of Theytus Books, an Instructor at the En'owkin International School of Writing in Penticton, British Columbia, and a member of the BC Arts Board. He recently published his first collection of poetry through DisOrientation Chapbooks entitled *"The Random Flow of Blood and Flowers."*

Traditional Aboriginal Voice

Traditionally, Aboriginal cultural knowledge has been transmitted and documented primarily through the Oral Tradition, but also through dramatic productions, dance performances, petroglyphs and artifacts such as birch bark scrolls, totem poles, wampum belts and masks. This is the Aboriginal way of transmitting knowledge and recording information and history. If publishing is understood to be the documentation and dissemination of information on a wide scale, this was the method of "publishing" employed in North America for thousands of years before colonization.

Not only are traditional Aboriginal methods of information transmission and documentation in sharp contrast to European methods, but the content of the information is also radically different. The vast pools of knowledge encompassed in the Oral Tradition comprise unique bodies of knowledge with distinct Aboriginal content. The expression of this cultural material by Aboriginal people constitutes what can be referred to as "the Aboriginal Voice."

One of the key aspects of the Oral Tradition is that words are substantiated through the act of being spoken or stated. This aspect of Aboriginal philosophy is referred to by Okanagan author Jeannette Armstrong in the book *The Native Creative Process* wherein she states:

"One of the central instructions to my people is to practise quietness, to listen, and speak only if you know the full meaning of what you say. It is said that you cannot call your words back once they are uttered, and so you are responsible for all which results from your words. It is said that, for those reasons, it is best to prepare very seriously and carefully to make public contributions" (The Native Creative Process, Douglas Cardinal and Jeannette Armstrong, Theytus Books Ltd., 1991, Page 90).

The value of Aboriginal storytelling is well appreciated by anyone, Aboriginal or non-Aboriginal alike, who has witnessed the poetry and wisdom in the words of the Elders even when spoken in the English language. Although much of it remains unwritten, the Oral Tradition contains highly meaningful and symbolic "worlds" populated with fantastic, inanimate, animal, human and spirit characters who act out some of the most fascinating tales in world literature today. Similarly, the intense drama and intricate costume in traditional and/or ceremonial dance performances done by Aboriginal peoples easily rivals that of any production done in a Canadian theatre.

Perhaps most importantly, the body of knowledge encompassed in the Aboriginal Voice contains valuable paradigms, teachings and information that can benefit all of the World Family of Nations. Indeed, sectors of the scientific and academic establishment have recently come to the realization that Aboriginal knowledge is an integral part of the key to human survival.

Residential Schools

The devastating impact the Canadian residential school system has had and continues to have on First Nations and Aboriginal people cannot be understated, nor can the scope of ongoing problems that it has created. As part of the federal government's vigorous strategy to indoctrinate and subjugate First Nations, generations of children were removed from their homes, families and communities, punished for speaking their language or practising their religious ceremonies, forced to pray to the Christian God, forced to wear uniforms; subjected to rigid and culturally alien daily routines; separated by gender and subjected to physical and sexual abuse, among other things.

At these schools, children were also exposed to a culturally alien curriculum and taught that their ancestors' ways were "pagan" and "uncivilized," and that the world view that they had developed in their earlier formative years was "illegitimate" and "wrong." The Aboriginal body of knowledge and traditions of the First Nations were not contained whatsoever in the curriculum. Instead, children were indoctrinated with alien traditions and historical events based in Europe. It has also frequently been noted that the standards of education were considerably lower in the residential schools than Canadian public schools.

This schooling system was hardly a training ground or a vehicle for promoting Aboriginal literature. One impact of the residential school system was to effectively stifle the Aboriginal Voice by denying generations of children access to their cultural knowledge while instilling in them negative perceptions of their cultural identities. Even if exceptional children were able to miraculously overcome these impositions, as well as the other racial, social and economic barriers, they were not given adequate skills enabling them to write. According to the renowned First Nations author Lee Maracle the residential school system produced "languageless generations" as it "forbade them to speak their own language and impeded their mastery of English, creating an entire population, with few exceptions, who were unfamiliar with language in general" (*Gatherings: The En'owkin Journal of First North American Peoples - Volume II*, "*Skyros Bruce: First Voice of Contemporary Native Poetry*", Lee Maracle, Theytus Books Ltd., 1991, Page 85).

The deep rooted psychological effects the residential school experience had on the First Nations and Aboriginal children were not only carried through to adult life, but imbedded through generations in ways that may never be fully documented or understood. However, these were the conditions that the vast majority of Aboriginal people were enduring in the era when the publishing industry and literature were developing in Canada.

The Publishing Industry

The unique contribution the Aboriginal Voice could make to world literature is in many ways potentially more valuable and unique than the contribution of Canadian literature. In spite of this (as is the case with most sectors of Canadian industry, economy, and society) Aboriginal peoples have historically been blocked from equitable participation in the publishing industry.

In some regards, this has been more damaging than marginalization in other sectors because it has had the effect of silencing the Aboriginal Voice paving the way for a rash of non-Aboriginal writers to profit from the creation of a body of literature focusing on Aboriginal peoples that is based on ethnocentric, racist and largely incorrect presumptions. This has led to a situation where incorrect images, ridiculous stereotypes and highly problematic academic paradigms have created perceptions of Aboriginal peoples that are entirely based outside any reality or truth.

Non-Aboriginal Literature

Early writings about Aboriginal peoples were done by missionaries like John McDougal in the 1800s, anthropologists like Diamond Jeness around the turn of the century, and literary writers like James Fenimore Cooper and Steven Leacock in the early to mid 1900s -- all of whom spoke frankly of Aboriginal peoples as an inferior vanishing race. The level of insight that the majority of these writings provided into the cultures of Aboriginal peoples is comparable to that provided by the portrayal of "Indians" in the Hollywood Western movies which were to follow in the early to mid 1900s. Later, charlatans such as Grey Owl and Long Lance came to considerable notoriety lecturing, writing, and publishing while masquerading as Indians. Although displaying a less overtly condescending attitude toward Aboriginal peoples, these writers served to enforce an incorrect stereotypical image of Aboriginal peoples as glorified remnants of the past.

The Canadian and American public would have been far better off knowing nothing at all of Aboriginal peoples than to be exposed to such kitsch literature. Even today the patterns set by Cooper and Leacock are continued by Canadian writers like W.P Kinsella and Anne Cameron, and the ghosts of Grey Owl and Long Lance live on through "plastic shaman" writers like Lynn Andrews and Adolf Hungry Wolf.

A more recent development has been a wave of writing by non-Aboriginal academics, such as Frank Cassidy, Boyce Richardson, Thomas Berger, Michael Ashe, Sally Weaver, Menno Bolt and Anthony Long. Many of these authors are involved with higher level academic institutions, and have established themselves in the Canadian public mindset as authoritative "Native studies experts." The majority of these writers are knowledgeable and supportive of Aboriginal peoples political aspirations, and they must also be credited with some of the increased public awareness in recent years. However, these academics do not promote Aboriginal Voice nor do they speak for Aboriginal peoples' unique perspective on the issues.

Albeit well intentioned, this body of work tends to reduce the emotionally, historically and culturally-charged issues to dry information-laden legalise and/or academic jargon. Furthermore, by creating a recognized school of experts who are a relatively "low risk" to publishers, and by saturating the market with a wave of books about Aboriginal peoples, this wave of academic writing has the effect of ultimately blocking-out the Aboriginal Voice.

Contemporary Aboriginal Literature

Aboriginal literature has had to struggle through a number of impeding factors including cultural and language barriers, residential schools, ethnocentrism in the academic establishment, competition from non-Aboriginal authors, estrangement in the publishing industry, and a lack of Aboriginal controlled publishing. Under these conditions it is not surprising that in the Canadian publishing industry Aboriginal literature has gone from being virtually non-existent to currently being delegated a low profile marginal position.

The late Mohawk author Pauline Johnson was the first Aboriginal author to be published in Canada. Johnson published three books in the early 1900s and was one of the most prominent poets of her time. To this day, she still holds the distinction of being the Aboriginal author who gained the highest level and notoriety in the literary world and sold the most books in Canada. However, the "Pauline Johnson phenomenon" was not to be a catalyst that would open up the Canadian publishing industry to Aboriginal literature. In hindsight, her success as an Aboriginal author must be viewed as an aberration. After Pauline Johnson's untimely death in 1913, almost six decades were to pass before another Aboriginal author would be published in Canada.

In the late 1960s and early 1970s an explosion of Aboriginal literature followed the upswing in Aboriginal political organization and resistance. The Cree writer Harold Cardinal stunned the publishing world with *The Unjust Society* in 1969, his unrelenting and articulate denunciation of Canadian Indian Policy. The Odawa author Wilfred Peltier seemed to come out of nowhere publishing three books in as many years: *Two Articles* in 1969, *For Every North American Indian Who Begins to Disappear, I Also Begin to Disappear* in 1971 and his classic *No Foreign Land* in 1973. *The Only Good Indian* an anthology of essays by Aboriginal people edited by Waubageshig, and Lee Maracle's autobiographical *Bobbi Lee: Indian Rebel* both came out in 1970. *Red on White*, Marty Dunn's biography of another Aboriginal author Duke Redbird, was released in 1971. A number of important books by Aboriginal authors followed, including *Chiefly Indian* by Henry Pennier in 1972, *The Fourth World* by George Manuel in 1974, *My Heart Soars* by Chief Dan George in 1974, *Prison of Grass* by Howard Adams in 1975, and Maria Campbell's classic autobiography *Halfbreed* in 1973.

Most of these books tended to be characteristic of protest literature; political in content and angry in tone. This first rash of Aboriginal literature seemed to be lashing out in the face of the Canadian establishment, after years of oppression and the silencing of the Aboriginal Voice. The quantity of writing by Aboriginal authors in this period can be attributed not only to the political activism of the day, but also to the related fact that this was the first generation of Aboriginal people not to be subjected to residential schools, many of whom were able to learn to write by attending College and University. This tended to have the effect on some of the work of presenting Aboriginal ideas in a European-based literary style.

In retrospect, in terms of the number of books published, this era can be seen as somewhat of a heyday in publishing by Aboriginal authors. As with the writings of Pauline Johnson, this rash of books did not manage to carve a respectable, ongoing niche for Aboriginal literature in the Canadian publishing industry. Indeed, much of the interest from the publishing industry in this era can probably be attributed to the novelty value of the first wave of books written by Aboriginal people.

In the late seventies and early eighties the frequency of books published by Aboriginal people tapered off dramatically. Some of the more notable books of this period were Beatrice Culleton's *In Search of April Raintree*, Basil Johnson's *Moose Meat and Wild Rice*, Chief John Snow's *These Mountains Are Sacred Places*, *Poems of Rita Joe* and Daniel David Moses' *Delicate Bodies*. However, this period was important because a uniquely Aboriginal form of literature began to take hold. Aspects of traditional storytelling were present in the earlier writing of Wilf Peltier and in books like George Manuel's *The Fourth World* and Maria Campbell's *Halfbreed*; but in the 1980s writers like Beatrice Culleton and Basil Johnson began to develop styles of writing that would carry the unique Aboriginal Voice into contemporary literature.

Throughout the 1980s and early 1990s writers like Lee Maracle, Jeannette Armstrong, Ruby Slipperjack, Beth Cuthand and Tomson Highway have further developed Aboriginal literature to the point that it now stands alone as a distinct body of literature. The Ojibway author Kim Blaeser has pointed out several characteristics of contemporary Aboriginal literature: it gives authority to the voices of all people involved in the story, instead of a monological voice speaking out as if it had ultimate authority; it gives authority to the voices of animals and messages given by spirits and natural phenomenon; it stretches across large spaces in time, ranging from ancient times to present to the future, displaying the Aboriginal concept that all time is closely connected and that actions can transcend time (Akwe:kon Journal, Volume X, # 1, Kim Blaeser, Papers from Returning the Gift: North American Native Writers Festival).

Lee Maracle's novel *Sundogs* is written in a style that she calls "Contemporary Aboriginal Voice." It is written cover to cover with no chapter breaks and often jumps out of the storyline on a tangent, the relevance of which does not necessarily become immediately apparent. This is similar to the oratory style of an Elder speaking in a storytelling or ceremonial setting. Jeannette Armstrong shocked some of those preoccupied with gender politics by writing *Slash*, the first novel by a First Nations women in Canada, from a first person male perspective. This, she later explained, was based partly on Aboriginal cultural beliefs that each gender is capable of assuming the characteristics of the other (Contemporary Challenges: Conversations with Canadian Native Authors, Fifth House Publishers, 1991). Tomson Highway's plays have astounded the drama establishment with their ability to go from the metaphysical domain to the domain of reality — and even feature characters transcending domains. These examples all illustrate how Aboriginal philosophy and traditions are being brought into contemporary literature, thus contributing to the ongoing development of the contemporary Aboriginal Voice. There are many more examples.

Continuing Discrimination

Despite all it has to offer, Aboriginal literature continues to be discriminated against in the Canadian publishing industry. Larger Canadian publishing houses will publish a novel by a recognized author like W.P. Kinsella, which mocks life on the Hobema Reserve, before they will publish books by Aboriginal authors. Lee Maracle, the most highly published Aboriginal author in Canada today, has published all her books through small independent presses, or the Aboriginal and feminist small presses. At the same time, the largest publishing house in Western Canada, and one of the largest in Canada, comes out with a Fall 1992 catalogue that lists five titles about Aboriginal peoples written by non-Aboriginal authors in its front list -- and no books written by Aboriginal authors. Perhaps it should come as no suprise but, regarding Aboriginal subject material, publishers and booksellers are more concerned with low-risk profit making ventures than with the nature and authenticity of the material.

In the 1990s, all books by Aboriginal peoples have been published through small and independent presses. Not one Aboriginal author has been published by a large Canadian publishing house; while over a hundred books about Aboriginal peoples have been published by large Canadian houses already in the 1900s. Typically, a so-called Native studies section in a high volume bookstore in Canada will have books by non-Aboriginal authors prominently displayed. If they are lucky, Aboriginal authors will have their books on the bottom shelves of the display. Furthermore, books by Lee Maracle and Jeannette Armstrong will almost always be on the bottom of the Native studies section and not in the literature section, as if they are not legitimate literature. Kim Blaeser has sarcastically commented on this particular phenomenon saying, "No, I'm not a poet, I just write Indian stuff" (Akwe:kon Journal, Volume X, # 1, Kim Blaeser, Papers from Returning the Gift: North American Native Writers Festival).

These examples are evidence of ongoing discrimination and a form of colonization against Aboriginal people in the publishing industry which amounts to nothing less than racism. It is perhaps an even higher and more sinister level of racism which not only discriminates against the race, but blocks out the voice of the race while putting others in place to speak about the race and profit from doing so.

Aboriginal Publishing

Realizing that little can be done to change the attitudes and practices of executives who run large publishing houses in Canada, and being aware that Aboriginal authors have had difficulties with a lack of cultural sensitivity even among small presses, some Aboriginal peoples have undertaken to start their own publishing ventures. Pemmican Publications and Theytus Books were both founded in 1980.

Based in Winnipeg, Pemmican is a Metis publishing house committed to publishing books that depict Metis and Native cultures in a positive manner. The purpose of the press is to "provide opportunities for Metis and Native people to tell their own stories from their own perspective". However, Pemmican do publish non-Native writers whose works are related to Native issues. The company has published about thirty titles to date.

In 1980, Theytus Books established itself as the first publisher in Canada to be under First Nation ownership and control. The company is entirely staffed by Aboriginal people and has published over forty titles. Similar to Pemmican, the company continues to carry out its mandate of producing quality literature presented from a First Nations' perspective; however, Theytus publishes only Aboriginal authors. Theytus' general philosophy has remained intact since its inception and is contained in the company's name. "Theytus" is a Salishian word which means "preserving for the sake of handing down." The name "Theytus" was chosen to symbolize the goal of documenting First Nation cultures and worldviews through books.

Theytus Books is a division of The En'owkin Centre in Penticton, British Columbia, which also houses the En'owkin International School of Writing (EISW), the only First Nations writing school in North America founded by the School's Director Jeannette Armstrong. Each year at EISW, First Nation students from across Canada and the U.S. study the Aboriginal process of literary creativity under the instruction of Armstrong and other First Nation authors. While developing their writing skills through this unique program, students also receive accreditation from the University of Victoria. Several prestigious Canadian authors sit on the EISW Board of Directors including: **Michael Ondaatje, Margaret Atwood, Ruby Wiebe, Joy Kogawa, Thomas King and Maria Campbell**.

In 1990, Theytus Books and EISW began publishing *Gatherings: The En'owkin Journal of First North American Peoples*. Gatherings is the only journal of writing by First Nations people in North America. Published annually, the Journal features a wide array of poetry, stories, essays, songs and oratory from authors across North America - ranging from some of the most highly acclaimed First Nation authors, to young aspiring authors studying at EISW and being published for the first time.

There are also numerous Aboriginal organizations and schools that have formed publishing operations to produce materials primarily for their own use; such as the Yinka Dene Language Institute, the Gabriel Dumont Institute and the Grand Council of the Cree's (of Quebec). However, Theytus and Pemmican remain the only Aboriginal controlled publishers who participate primarily in the book trade in Canada. Over the years both companies have experienced extreme difficulties and have remained relatively small in scale. In recent years, Theytus has slowly begun to expand, but still remains well within the parameters of a small press struggling to compete in the industry.

Conclusion:

Self-controlled publishing is the best solution to all the problems which have held back and continue to hold back Aboriginal people in the publishing industry. It eliminates editorial discrimination. It incorporates cultural sensitivity. It makes writing and publishing a cohesive and fluid process under the control of Aboriginal people, so that the writer does not have to step into an alienating situation to get published. Most of all, it produces material in which the highest possible level and most authentic expression of the Aboriginal Voice is attained in the contemporary publishing world. Indeed, the majority of the problems that have been mentioned above can be overcome through Aboriginal controlled publishing.

Every effort should be made within Canadian arts and industry funding agencies to support existing Aboriginal publishing ventures and encourage the establishment of others. This can be partly achieved by providing additional funding sources for existing Aboriginal publishers to help them grow and to offset the inequity they face competing within the larger Canadian publishing industry. Further, additional programs should be available for Aboriginal groups to begin publishing ventures. Such programs should also be complemented with increased access to publishing training for Aboriginal people, which would be best carried out through the establishment of publishing training programs geared specifically toward the concerns of Aboriginal people. If initiatives such as these were put in place the Aboriginal publishing would soon reach a more equitable status within the Canadian publishing industry and the Aboriginal Voice would once again flourish and assume its rightful place in contemporary literature.

In and Around the Forum

by

D. L. Birchfield

D. L. Birchfield

D. L. Birchfield, a Chickasaw/Choctaw and member of the Choctaw Nation of Oklahoma, is a graduate of the University of Oklahoma College of Law and a former editor of *Camp Crier*, published by the Oklahoma City Native American Center. He is presently serving on the National Advisory Caucus for Wordcraft Circle of Native American Mentor and Apprentice Writers. He is also the co-editor of the Winter 1994 Native American special issue of *Callaloo*. His work has appeared in *Bishinik, Gatherings III, Wicazo Sa Review* and the *Native Press Research Journal*.

You surely would think the Forum is underground once you have entered it, had you not had to ascend staircases or take the elevator up to its entrances. These entrances bring you to the room's highest level, where you may look down into the nearly circular chamber, or you may proceed down one of the aisles until you find a seat, where you discover that all seats are chairs which place you at roomy, continuous desk tops, upon which you may rest your elbows, or set a cup of coffee, or spread out your papers, or pour yourself a glass of water, and relax.

Into this arena on the campus of the University of Oklahoma were cast, largely by invitation, a rich mixture of well established native literary voices, predominantly Native poets, storytellers, and fiction writers, from Canada and Alaska to Central America and Hawaii, supplemented by emerging Native voices at various stages of their careers, with a healthy admixture of Native writers who specialize in others kinds of writing, an informal, structured, four-day gathering that would see a total of 368 Native writers registered for the conference, and dozens of others who were able only to attend the readings in the evenings or to drop by for a few hours to visit, a place of name tags and first names, a gathering of some of the best and most promising literary minds which the Native world of the upper Western Hemisphere has published, emphasis on published.

Many of the people here have long track records. They are known entities. They are the names you see in the tables of contents of the best known anthologies of Native American writing, especially poetry Voices of the Rainbow; Carriers of the Dream Wheel; The Remembered Earth; Songs From This Earth On Turtle's Back; That's What She Said; Harper's Anthology of 20th Century Native American Poetry; Spider Woman's Granddaughters; Dancing On The Rim Of The World; Gatherings, and others. Or their short fictions and novel excerpts have appeared in such anthologies as The Man To Send Rain Clouds; The Clouds Threw This Light; Earth Power Coming; Words In The Blood; All My Relations; Talking Leaves, and others, or will appear in such forthcoming anthologies as Earth Song, Sky Spirit, or Tales From The Great Turtle.

Present are most of the ones who shared the stories of their lives and of their work in Survival This Way: Interviews with American Indian Poets, and in Winged Words—American Indian Writers speak, and in I Tell You Now. Most of them, along with others, will give plenary session speeches or conduct workshops or participate in panel discussions. Best of all, in the evenings, they, and others, will read from their works. Many of the other people here could be known if you happen to have read the often limited-circulation publications in which most of them have published.

As a group they are fantastically prolific and versatile, contributing not only poetry and fiction but many different kinds of writing to or editing, many different kinds of publications, including scholarly journals, literary quarterlies, commercial magazines, association and fraternal publications, tribal publications, newsletters, governmental documents, plays, screen plays, television scripts, video scripts, radio scripts, audio cassette scripts, documentaries, speeches, textbooks, book reviews, brochures, comedy, grant proposals, environmental codes, encyclopedia articles, legal research, tribal histories, and lectures. Collectively it is the most talent laden collection of Native literary writers ever assembled. Above all else, the thread that ties them together, in one way or another, other than their Nativeness, is poetry, Native poetry.

It is not a political gathering. They have been brought together to share with one another, to learn from one another, to meet and know and network with one another. It is a literary festival.

They have been brought together through the efforts of people like Steering Committee Chair Joseph Bruchac, indefatigable Abenaki publisher and networker, whose vision for a gathering such as this lasted the twenty years it took to bring it about, and Barbara Hobson, of the University of Oklahoma, a Comanche who will receive a standing ovation at the closing night banquet of such intensity and duration as to leave no doubt about the affection in which she is held for her work as Project Coordinator; all of it made possible by the generosity of numerous private foundations and public and private institutions which contributed more than a quarter of a million dollars to pay all the expenses for 220 invited writers, give scholarships to 47 students, and provide fee waivers for 101 other Native writers, so they might be part of a gruelling week of literary interchange, to see what might happen.

What happened was a severely reduced amount of sleep, day after day, night after night. One might weigh sleep against the opportunity to visit, as we Okies call it, with multiple nominees for the Pulitzer Prize in poetry, a Pulitzer Prize—winning novelist, National Book Award and American Book Award and Critics Circle Award poets, a recipient of the Spur Award, directors of Native American studies programs, former directors of Native American studies programs, alumni and members of the steering committee of the En'owkin Centre International School of Writing, enough alumni of the Institute of American Indian Arts to hold a serious alumni meeting, recipients of the North American Indian Prose Award, the Five Civilized Tribes Museum playwriting award, the National Public Radio Broadcasting Award, the Hodson Award, the Nilon Minority Fiction Award, the Cherokee Nation Prose Award, the National Endowment for the Arts Discovery Award, the National Endowment for the Arts

Creative Writing Fellowship, the National Endowment for the Humanities Creative Writing Fellowship, the Wallace Stegner Creative Writing Fellowship, the PEN Syndicated Fiction Award, the Native American Prize for Literature, the Susan Koppleman Award, foundation fellows such as Kellogg, Ford, Rockefeller, and Fullbright, Rhodes Scholars, publishers, editors, exiled poets on death lists...

At the opening ceremonies for the first plenary session of Returning The Gift: A Festival of North American Native Writers, early in the mid-morning of Tuesday, July 7, 1992, at the Oklahoma Center for Continuing Education in Norman, Oklahoma, two-hundred and fifty-six people were seated in the peculiar spaciousness of the Forum, give or take a few who came and went as I sketched the room. Dozens of others were still downstairs, scurrying about, registering, still arriving.

The Forum is a sunken, terraced chamber, almost a theatre in the round (the room misses being perfectly round only in that it is six-sided), with seating in six sections, there being six aisles leading down to a spacious, thirty-foot wide, nearly circular arena at the bottom, where the speakers are provided with a microphone podium facing a video camera at near ground level across the way.

The nature of the room is such that one can come and go without causing a distraction. Best of all you can see and hear. You can see every person in the room, and you can hear the speaker at the microphone.

At many times during the week all of the people in this room will be engaged in casual conversation in a long, wide, ground-level circular walkway, directly beneath the outer rim of the Forum, or in three corridors that radiate out from the circular walkway like spokes. The core of the building, on the ground floor, is taken up with administrative offices, restrooms, and storage rooms. Most of the ground floor, however, is circular walkway, wide enough and long enough to hold hundreds of people. Along the circular walkway, at intervals, are unpartitioned lounges, three large identical staircases (and one elevator) which lead up to the Forum, and two other identical staircases which lead down to snack machines in the basement, and, one also finds, at intervals, the open entrances to the three corridors, and between them, three separate banks of multiple, double glass door exits.

The corridors, labelled A, B, and C, are identical in design, until you reach the end of a corridor. At the end of one corridor (A) is a terraced-chamber room identical to the Forum, only on a smaller scale. At the end of another corridor (B) is a large, flat-surfaced room the same size as the scaled-down version of the Forum. These two rooms, and the Forum upstairs, will be the three principal concurrent sites for the readings in the evenings, though one evening a bookstore in Norman will also serve as a venue for readings, as will the lawn of the Jacobsen House, a Native American Art Gallery near the campus. At the end of the other corridor (C) is a cable television studio, where many interviews with conference participants will be filmed.

The corridors have crooked walls. They narrow at points to about ten feet wide, and they spread out at points to more than twenty-five feet wide, alternately narrowing and widening as their length snakes away into the distance. The walls are crooked because lining each side of each corridor are classroom-size, six-sided, circular rooms identical in shape and size to the arena at the lowest level in the center of the Forum. The roomy alcoves in the corridors, where the corridors widen, provided excellent space for setting up tables for publishing houses to display their books.

For nearly everyone, for at least two days, and for the entire conference for many people, the distinctive architectural design of the Thurman J. White Forum Building of the Oklahoma Center For Continuing Education (OCCE) had conference participants in a state of continual disorientation. One set of double-glass doors led to the Sooner House where many participants were lodged, further along the circular walkway another set of doors led to the Commons Cafeteria where all-you-can-eat cafeteria style breakfasts, lunches, and dinners were served in two serving lines, and where the Wednesday night awards banquet was held, while another set of doors let to the parking lot where bleachers were assembled and 161 people showed up for the group photo at 5 P.M. on Tuesday afternoon, and where shuttle buses loaded to take participants to the Sac & Fox Powwow at the Sac & Fox tribal complex in Stroud, Oklahoma, on Saturday afternoon, the day after the conference ended. But which set of doors led to what? For the longest time one could never be sure where one was in this nearly round, six-sided building, with its look-alike staircases, corridors, lounges, exits, and with its big, terraced chamber up above that seemed to be underground. Leaving the building late at night, few could quickly find where they had parked, ascending a staircase, one could never be sure at which portion of the Forum one might arrive, and, after learning the location of the restroom, many engaged in long circular walks trying to find it again. It was a perfect complement, a perfect ambience, to the disorienting effect of meeting many people of differing orientations of one sort or another. It takes awhile to notice that the corridors are color coded, each being a different color, or that the lounges that open off the circular walkway do not have identical arrangements of furniture, or that there are small signs here and there labelling practically everything, especially when the place is filled with hundreds of people.

At the informal reception for conference participants on Monday evening, the evening before the conference began, one group of twenty-two Native poets reacted to the dizzying, disorienting effect of the facilities by retreating to a popular watering hole nearby where they collectively composed "A Really Big, Group Indian Poem," 189 lines appropriate to the occasion.

In the central circular walkway, directly beneath the Forum, one could get lost. Around and around you might walk amid hundreds of people, most of whom are meeting one another for the first time, talking, agreeing, disagreeing, qualifying, questioning, laughing, in clusters of two and three and four and more, making it easy to miss signs and landmarks that might have told you where in the walkway you were.

Around you go, overhearing snatches of conversations, reading name tags, noting particularly some of the people who, though most of them poets themselves, add a breadth and diversity of other specialties to this gathering of poets, seeing -- near the entrance to a corridor, beside a countertop filled with free material (Native newspapers, fliers, calls for submissions of manuscripts, sample copies of literary publications) -- Bobbie Bush, a Chehalis, of SPIPA Intertribal News of the South Puget Sound Intertribal Planning Agency, who attended the Native American Journalists Association Conference in Green Bay, WI, in April; and, a few feet away, Robert Warrior (Osage), who recently completed his Ph.D. at Union Theological Seminary in New York City, author of scholarly articles in Wicazo Sa Review, who had a book review in the premier issue of the new international watchdog for Native rights The Indigenous Eye, published in Tahlequah, OK; and, not far away, Julie Moss (Cherokee), who recently travelled throughout remote Native sections of Mexico as a Kellogg Fellow, who is editor of The Indigenous Eye.

At the foot of a stairway leading up to the Forum is Tom Radko, former Submissions Editor of the University of Oklahoma Press, now Director of the University of Nevada Press, with two members of the Western Writers of America: Robert J. Conley (Cherokee), novelist, poet, author of Cherokee viewpoint westerns, such as Back To Malachi and Ned Christies's War, winner of the Spur Award for "Yellow Bird: An Imaginary Autobiography" (in The Witch of Goingsnake and Other Stories, with a foreword by Wilma P. Mankiller, Principal Chief of the Cherokee Nation); in 1993 Robert J. Conley will win his second Spur Award; and Ronald Burns Querry (Choctaw), ethnic studies scholar, professional farrier (horseshoer), former editor of horse industry magazines, who writes book reviews for Bishinik, the Choctaw Nation of Oklahoma newspaper, editor of Growing Old at Willie Nelson's Picnic and Other Sketches of Life in the Southwest, author of the "unauthorized" autobiography I See By

My Get-Up, whose first novel The Death of Bernadette Lefthand will be released in June, 1993 by Red Crane Books in Sante Fe, NM.

Next we see historian Jack D. Forbes (Renape-Lenape) and Carter Revard (Osage), who teaches the Navajo creation story in a university great books course, which surely must be a surprise for students anticipating only the Eurocentric book selections of people like Mortimer J. Adler and Robert Hutchins of the Encyclopedia Britannica great books series.

Jack Forbes and Carter Revard have something in common. They each found their Native voice at age twenty-six. Jack Forbes found his Native voice in Apache, Navajo and Spaniard, revisionist history, a tiny pinpoint of light in a great darkness, Native viewpoint history that the world and the history profession were not quite ready for in 1960. He has consistently done violence to the rock of entrenched Eurocentric historical dogma ever since then, chipping away, leading the way for a generation of Native historians who now chip away side by side with him, confident that the rock will crack.

Carter Revard, having been a Rhodes Scholar at Oxford, having passed through the graduate school at Yale, woke up one morning in an historic house in Amherst, a house in which Emily Dickenson's poems had lain in an old camphor chest for years, woke up hearing the rain on the roof, and the "second rain" dripping from the roof, and contemplated the osteosclerosis that, as a young man, was stealing his sense of sound.

He recalled another thunderstorm on the bluestem Osage prairie where, as a teenager, he had taken refuge in a shallow cavern beneath large boulders in the Buck Creek Valley. There had been coyote sign there, he remembered now, and he began to wonder what such a thunderstorm might sound like to coyote pups, new to the world, new to thunderstorms, and how they might give it voice -- and in those moments he found his Native voice.

On the other side of Forbes and Revard, past double glass-door exits, banks of telephones, postage machines, a water fountain, we see three key members of Cornell University's American Indian Studies program, Jose Barriero, a Guajiro Native of Cuba and editor of Cornell's Akwe:kon Journal ("All of us;" formerly Northeast Indian Quarterly), whose account of what it was like to be inside the archives in Spain, with the archival assistants bringing you the five-hundred year-old documents, holding those documents in your hands, would transport a roomful of festival workshop participants out of that workshop and into the archives of Spain; and Michael Wilson (Oklahoma Choctaw), doctoral candidate at Cornell, who, as literature editor of Akwe:kon convinced Jose Barriero that the time had come to begin publishing Native fiction; and Skarionate (Ron LaFrance, Mohawk), Director of Native American Studies at Cornell, whose vision became Cornell's new AKWE:KON Native-architecture multi-cultural housing and office complex, and who, descended from a distinguished line of high rise Ironworkers, one day got into a daring game of one-upsmanship, hundreds of feet above a city, not learning until later that the man he was partnered with was the legendary Roger Horn.

Past an unpartitioned lounge filled with sofas and chairs and with people standing, sitting, talking, in which we see -- Geary Hobson (Cherokee/Quapaw/Chickasaw), editor of The Remembered Earth, who is the former Director of Native American Studies at the University of New Mexico, with Marie Frawley-Henry, of Ontario, whose job takes her all over Canada, and Choctaw short story writer and playwright LeAnn Howe, co-author of, with Scott Morrison (Choctaw attorney), "Sewage of Foreigners" in the Federal Bar News & Journal, and Victoria Bomberry (Creek), on her way to doctoral studies at Stanford, on the editorial board of High Country News, the most respected environmental journal in the Inter-Mountain West, and who will participate in a Native delegation to Bolivia in the fall, and Vi Hilbert (Upper Skagit), who tells traditional stories bi-lingually, and short story writer Annie Hansen (Lenape), who has published her stories in Carolina Quarterly, and has had multiple publishings of her stories in The Duckbush Journal and in Kenyan Review, and who will become a fiction editor for The Raven Chronicles within the coming year, and Erica Sanger, of the New York Historical Society, and Elise Paschen, Executive Director of the Poetry Society of America.

And everywhere you look, poets--near the foot of another stairway leading up to the Forum, Lance Henson (Southern Cheyenne), a Cheyenne Dog Soldier, who has published some of his work in Italy, in Germany, in the Netherlands; with him is Sherman Alexie (Spokane/ Coer d'Alene) and Jose Garza (Coahuilateca/Apache) and Nita Pahdopny (Comanche): near the complimentary coffee and tea dispensers, Charlotte DeClue (Osage) and Victor Blanchard-Singing Eagle (Potawatomi) and Janice Gould (Maidu); in the entryway to yet to another corridor, Beth Brant (Bay of Quinte Mohawk), editor of A Gathering of Spirit: A Collection by North American Indian Women, and Jim Northrup, prolific Native American short story writer and syndicated columnist, who will publish his first collection of short stories during the coming year, and Ramson Lomatewama (Hopi); and around another unpartitioned lounge, with many other writers Earle Thompson (Yakima), Laura Tohe (Navajo), Duane Niatum (Klallam), editor of Carriers of the Dream Wheel and Harper's Anthology of 20th Century Native American Poetry, with Maurice Kenny (Mohawk), of Strawberry Press, and Mary Goose (Mesquakie/ Chippewa), Cheryl Savageau (Abenaki), globe-trotting Joy Harjo (Creek), fresh from a tour of poetry readings in Europe, and Simon J.

Ortiz (Acoma Pueblo), editor of Earth Power Coming, and editor of, two decades ago, Americans Before Columbus, the newspaper of the National Indian Youth Council, who will be quoted more often by other poets and writers at this festival than any other person; and Linda Hogan (Chickasaw), whose grandmother studied classical violin at the Bloomfield Chickasaw Girls School, and who became an accomplished pianist too, and then spent the rest of her life living in small rural places, choosing to remain Chickasaw and to leave the Western world to others, watching with quiet dignity as her land-swindled allotment became the Ardmore Airport.

Past the Men's room, the Women's Room, the registration tables, the Conference Services office, seeing Rayna Green (Cherokee), prolific scholar and Director of the American Indian Program at the National Museum of the American Indian at the Smithsonian Institution, editor of That's What She Said: Contemporary Fiction and Poetry by American Indian Women, and, nearby, Alaskan Inupeaq storyteller Mary Jane Lockwood, and Daniel Littlefield (Creek), former editor of the Native Press Research Journal, and Victor Montejo (Maya), exiled anthropologist and poet of Mayan traditional stories, with someone asking him about his interview in the current issue of Curbstone Ink, and Greg Young-Ing (Cree), from the En'owkin Centre in Penticton, British Columbia, Canada, editor of Gatherings, and Humberto Ak'abal (K'iche-Maya), of Guatemala.

Past the elevator leading up to the Forum, past wall racks filled with literature, past dramatist Diane Benson (Tlingit), of Alaska, past Michael Edmonds (Caddo), on his way to California to film an Indian documentary for Turner Broadcasting, past Robert F. Gish (Cherokee/Choctaw), contributing editor to Bloomsbury Review, whose short story collection, First Horses will be published within the year by the University of Nevada Press; past more poets—Duane Big Eagle (Osage), Ed Edmo (Shoshone-Bannock), Barney Bush (Shawnee), Chrystos (Menominee), Luci Tapahonso (Navajo), Lorenzo Baca (Isleta Pueblo/Mescalero Apache), past Alex Jacobs (Akwesasne Mohawk), who twenty years ago while still in his teens became poetry editor of Akwesasne Notes, past Ron Welburn, former poetry editor of Eagle Wing Press.

Past another corridor entrance filled with people; past another stairway leading up to the Forum, past another lounge filled to overflowing with poets and editors, among them Elizabeth Cook-Lynn (Crow Creek Sioux), editor of Wicazo Sa Review, with Diane Burns (Anishinabe/Chemehuevi), Gladys Cardiff (Eastern Band Cherokee), Anita Endreze (Yaqui), Roxy Gordon (Choctaw), Basil H. Johnson (Ojibway), of the Department of Ethnology of the Royal Ontario Museum, and many others, including Joel Monture, Mohawk essayist and short story writer, on his way to teach at the Institute of

American Indian Arts.

Past a table where the group picture was sold, past Duane Hale (Creek), author of <u>Researching and Writing Tribal Histories</u> (Michigan Indian Press, 1991), who knows as much mining history of the southwest as anyone is ever likely to know, past Anishinabe poet Kimberly Blaeser, whose forthcoming book from the University of Oklahoma Press is based on her Notre Dame doctoral dissertation on the work of prolific fellow Anishinabe writer Gerald Vizenor, past Rennard Strickland (Osage/Cherokee), author of <u>The Indians In Oklahoma,</u> who is Director of the Center for the Study of American Indian Law and Policy at OU law school, past historian Blue Clark (Creek), who is a vice-president of Oklahoma City University, past Oneida Nation poets Diane Schenandoah and Shirlee Winder, past Lenni Lenape poet Jeannetta Calhoun, past Jeannette Armstrong (Okanagan), who is Director of the En'owkin International School of Writing in British Columbia, Canada, and Gail Tremblay (Onondaga/Micmac), past Darlene Speidel (Lakota), who works with people of five different languages out of Saskatoon, Saskatchewan, Canada.

Past stairwells leading down to soft drink and snack machines, past a 4'x4' glassed-in scale model of the buildings and grounds of the Oklahoma Center for Continuing Education. Past scores and scores of other people, some of whom have waited half their lives to meet the person they are talking to, people who are so absorbed in what they are saying and hearing that they are oblivious to their immediate surroundings, people giving off an energy that is tangible, people who are mostly contemporary Native poets, despite the fact that many of them are specialists in other areas as well.

Question: Who reads contemporary Native poetry?
Answer: Other contemporary Native poets (and some Eurocentric academicians, trying to make sense of it).

Question: Anybody else?
Answer: No. People watch T.V. They don't read poetry.

Maybe ordinary Native people read contemporary Native poetry.

No, they don't. They might read popular fiction, but not poetry. No one but other contemporary poets reads contemporary poetry. Navajos, for example, can tell you much more about the Navajo Tribal Police mysteries of the German/American Tony Hillerman than they can tell you about the work of Luci Tapahonso or Laura Tohe, fine Navajo poets. When Ernie Bulow was operating his book store in Gallup, NM, he couldn't keep Hillerman's books in stock. No Native poet has that desirable problem.

In order to appreciate the intensity of this gathering of Native poets one must understand that they are people who are accustomed to doing readings from their work to audiences who are being exposed to it for the first time. The people who really know their work are the other contemporary Native poets who are scattered all over the continent; that is, they were scattered all over the continent until they were brought together at this place.

There are few Native poets the equal of Mohawk poet Maurice Kenny, author of more than twenty books of poetry, winner of the American Book Award, the National Public Radio Broadcasting Award, who has been twice nominated for the Pulitzer Prize in poetry. Kenny is fond of telling about the time a college paid him $1500 to come read some of his poems. The faculty sponsor escorted him to the site for the readings, a room in the college library. After they had waited for an hour and no one had showed up, the man gave Kenny the check for $1500 and he left.

I went to Oklahoma City University one evening some years ago to hear Kenny give a public reading from his work. I was not the only one there. The other dozen or so people, huddled together at the far end of that cavernous banquet hall in the student union, were all enrolled in Blue Clark's Indian literature class, and their attendance at Kenny's reading was a requirement for the class.

I have heard Kenny read his poetry to something of a crowd. Several years ago, at the dedication ceremonies for the Multi-Cultural Center at OU, which is mostly a housing unit for Indian students, and is the refurnished structure of the oldest fraternity house in Oklahoma, there was a respectable crowd of more than fifty people. They had received invitations to a free banquet of buffalo, garden salad, potatoes, and peach cobbler.

At the Oklahoma City Native American Center, a few years before it went broke and then burned down, Kenny drew a crowd that overflowed the Intertribal Council Chambers, which was not a small room. His poetry reading was the only item on the program. People came to see him, to meet him, to hear him read his poetry.

The elders had gotten behind the program, to give him gifts and to honour this man who had brought honour to Native peoples everywhere. The Oklahoma County Metropolitan Library system co-sponsored it. It was advertised within the Native community by word of mouth by the right people, which is what counts.

Kenny was magnificent. There was not a dry eye anywhere in the room when he got to those portions of the Mama Poems that he cannot read without nearly weeping. People were moved. Native people who had never before experienced contemporary Native poetry experienced it that night. There was also free food.

Contemporary Native poetry can be a powerful thing in the hands of a poet such as Maurice Kenny in a setting such as the one described above. But its ordinary shelf life is something else.

The publication of contemporary poetry of any kind in the United States is not a profitable venture. The poetry that is published is subsidized in some way, with only the very few exceptions of a very few small presses, and even there the publishing process is most likely to be a labour of love on the part of a handful of people, or one person, for whom profit is not the chief motivation force behind the enterprise. Poetry is subsidized either by university presses, or by endowments of one sort or another, or by arts councils, or by someone. It must be subsidized because people don't buy it. They don't buy it because they don't read it. They don't read it because they don't write it.

Almost alone among written art forms, in a class by itself, really, is contemporary poetry. The people who write it are the ones, almost the only ones, who read it. There are, of course, some exceptions, some people who don't write it who do buy it and read it, but statistically they don't amount to much of a commercial market. Contemporary Native poetry differs from contemporary Eurocentric poetry, in this regard, only in that mainstream contemporary poets are not read at all by practitioners of other forms of creative writing within the mainstream culture. Mainstream novelists and short story writers, unless they happen also to consider themselves to be poets, know nothing about contemporary poetry and couldn't possibly care less about it.

Contemporary Native poetry, however, enjoys a wider audience among Native intellectuals because there is a war on, a war to save Native cultures from extinction. Native intellectuals want to know what their brothers and sisters are doing in this war on fronts other than their own academic or creative specialty. That's one reason; by far the most important reason, however, is that Native intellectuals refuse to specialize. Yes, one might be primarily an historian, or primarily a short story writer, or primarily a novelist, or an accountant, or an administrator, or an editor, or what have you, but look closely and you will find that the Native lawyer is writing a novel, the accountant writes short stories, the novelist writes essays, the short story writer writes history, etc., and almost all of them write poetry. Because they write it, they read it; because they read it, contemporary Native poetry is fast becoming a universal language between Native intellectuals of highly diversified educational and professional training. It is the new sign language, even though it remains, at present, largely an exercise, and a means of communication, that has not reached out into the rural, bookless world from which most of us come.

The truth is that contemporary Native poetry does not reach very many Native people, except other contemporary Native poets, who know where to look for it, where to find it. You'll not find much of it in tribal newspapers, and the tribal newspaper is often about the only Native literature that many Native people read. It's about the only Native publication that comes free in the mail.

Why there isn't more publishing in tribal newspapers by contemporary Native poets is not difficult to understand. Most tribal newspapers exist as public relations vehicles for the chief, and they are edited so as to insure the reelection of the chief by absentee voters who have virtually no contact with their tribe except to receive the tribal newspaper free in the mail. The power of this tool is not to be taken lightly. In 1988, when the late Claude Cox sought his fifth four-year term as chief of the Muscogee Nation, he was soundly defeated by voters within the boundaries of the Muscogee Nation (in East-Central Oklahoma), but he pulled out the election with a landslide from the absentee voters. Space devoted to poetry in a tribal newspaper doesn't do much to make the chief look good, and poets who boldly, and sometimes not so subtly, speak their mind have always been viewed as a potentially dangerous thing by upholders of the status quo. It's a rare tribal newspaper that projects anything but a picture of bright promise and sound management under the guidance of a courageous chief, no matter how bitterly the nation may be engaged in turmoil.

Much of the contemporary Native poetry is highly accessible to people without much formal education, as long as they are Indians. It is the cultural messages that are baffling to Eurocentrics, who, for example, think a 49er was a miner in a gold rush. This presents no barrier to ordinary Native people. This is not to imply that contemporary Native poetry is being written largely by people without much formal education.

Scratch a contemporary Native poet or fiction writer and quite often you will find a professor. It might be Luci Tapahonso at the University of Kansas; Paula Gunn Allen at the University of California at Berkeley; Joy Harjo at the University of Arizona; Elizabeth Cook-Lynn, who only recently left the faculty at Eastern Washington University; Kimberly Blaeser at the University of Wisconsin at Milwaukee; Haunani Kay-Trask at the University of Hawai'i; Maurice Kenny at the University of Oklahoma; Geary Hobson at the University of Oklahoma; Jack D. Forbes at the University of California at Davis; Gerald Vizenor, at the University of California at Berkely; N. Scott Momaday at the University of Arizona, and before that Stanford; James Welch, sometimes at the University of Washington, sometimes at Cornell; Linda Hogan at the University of Colorado; Simon J. Ortiz at California State University at San Diego or at the University of New Mexico or at Sente Gleska College or wherever you might happen to catch up with him; Wendy Rose at California State College, Fresno; Leslie Marman Silko at the Universities of New Mexico or Arizona, depending upon where she happens to be; Diane Glancy at Macalester College in St. Paul, Minnesota; Thomas King at the University of Minnesota; Judith Minty at Humbold State University; Carter Revard at Washington University in St. Louis; Robert F. Gish at California Polytechnic State University, San Luis Obispo; Rodney Simard at California State University, San Berardino; Clifford Trafzer, at the University of California at Riverside, Roberta Hill Whiteman at the University of Wisconsin, Eau Claire; Robert Warrior at Stanford University; Louis Owens at the University of California at Santa Cruz; Daniel Littlefield at the University of Arkansas at Little Rock. This list could go on.

Or they may be former professors, such as novelist Michael Dorris, former professor at Dartmouth; or those two members of the Western Writers of America, Robert J. Conley, former Director of Indian Studies at Morningside College, and Ronald Burns Querry, former English professor at the University of Oklahoma.

Joseph Bruchac, Steering Committee Chair for Returning The Gift, got his Ph.D. in 1975; Barbara Hobson, Project Coordinator, passed her doctoral general examination recently enough for the achievement to be announced at the closing night banquet.

These Native people know how to read. They know how to write. There is no upper strata of the English language that is beyond their grasp. Many of the highly educated Native poets spent years toying with the mechanics of Eurocentric notions of prosody, of syllabics and metric feet and trochees and spondees and such. N. Scott Momaday studied those very things for one year on a Wallace Stegner Creative Scholarship at Stanford, under Yvor Winters, and then stayed on at Stanford to get a Ph.D.

Louis Littlecoon Oliver knew nothing but Western notions of poetry until very late in life. Past the age of seventy he was still writing in iambic pentameter and the like. When he discovered the idiom of contemporary Native poetic expression, and switched to it, the rest, as they say, is history.

At least it is history for an exceedingly thin strip of Native life, a minutiae of the Native world in which the name Louis Littlecoon Oliver brings something other than a blank stare.

Some contemporary Native poets have worked hard to get Native poetry to the people. Duane Big Eagle, Ed Edmo, Cheryl Savageau, and Lance Henson have, between them, been poets in residence in, or have worked actively in, hundreds of schools. Lance Henson has been poet in residence in more than two hundred schools. And there are others like them who have worked just as hard.

Just because much of this poetry has not yet reached very many Native people does not mean that it is not written in their behalf. It is, in fact, a vibrant expression of Native life. It is a celebration of the survival and dignity of our cultures. It serves many useful purposes, not the least of which is helping the people who write it and who read it to maintain their sanity.

"I wouldn't be writing now," Paula Gunn Allen has said, in a published interview, "if Momaday hadn't done that book (House Made of Dawn). I would have died."

And therein lies the story of an entire group of people, and the story of how contemporary Native poetry came about, at least one thread in the story of how it came about, so long as the explanation is not examined too closely. To understand Allen's statement, as representative of a group of Native people who now write contemporary Native poetry (overlooking the fact that she was referring to a novel rather than poetry), one must realize that many university-educated Indians went through a difficult period of estrangement. Many were teaching at colleges far from home, where they were often the only (token) Indian on the faculty. Others were off working in the Western world where their circumstances were often very similar. It took them some time to discover that there were other Indians, scattered throughout the continent, who were very much like them.

Estranged from the home folks by distance and by multiple layerings of education, estranged from their colleagues by their Nativeness, the second half of the 20th century has produced few crueler, more lonely paths to privileged agony. Their spirits were dying. Imagine their joy when they discovered they were not alone. As they began discovering one another, mostly by reading one another's published poetry, the emotional explosion of affirmation and celebration created a new literature, now still in its infancy, as literature goes, now as old as the earth, as literature goes, changing, remaining constant, alive.

With the bone marrow-embedded oral-tradition resources of The People informing their work, and with dazzlingly competent acquired skills in the language the presidents speak, and with something to say and with someone to hear it who could appreciate it, who could decipher the cultural messages, which were safely beyond the prison-for-the-mind which is the Eurocentric conception of literature and literary theory and metaphysics, a new kind of game came into being, a sort of literarily adept hand game played between distant, doctoraly-lonely Skins. When reading and writing this contemporary Native poetry they were suddenly young again, with not a care in the world. They were at the "9".

Question: How strange did this poetry and fiction strike the Eurocentrics?

Answer: Strange indeed.

In a plenary session speech at the festival, Kimberly Blaeser pointed out that as recently as 1991 when Poetry East put out an issue which included a feature highlighting the work of many of the Native poets present at the festival, the contributor's notes were divided into "Native Americans" and "The Poets," not "Native American Poets," just "Native Americans."

These Native poets, having read one another for years, could barely believe they had finally been brought together. Everywhere they looked was a name tag that meant something to them, and there that person stood. And some of the most rewarding voyages of discovery were with people, and their writings, that were new to them.

This is not to say that everyone who attended the festival was enthusiastic about it. For some, especially perhaps some of those who had been attending one sort of Native conference or another for most of their professional lives, and who had long since become acquainted with most of their colleagues, it was just another conference. One respected editor told me that the festival was "a distinct disappointment, personally. Not at all the kind of thing which would come out of a gathering of black writers from South Africa or other anti-colonial bodies." But for most of those present it was a singular experience.

The first day everything worked according to plan, except the scheduled talking circles (where each person in turn has a chance to say something). That was supposed to have happened just before lunch, after the first plenary session. But when the plenary ended, the visiting began, and if anyone made it to a talking circle that morning it happened outside my knowledge.

After lunch, however, we were hungry for the concurrent workshops. Since most people here have published in more than one category, the first of a week-long series of hard choices had to be made. The same would be true of the five concurrent panel discussions later in the afternoons, and the readings at night, from 7 p.m. to near midnight, taking place each night at three different locations, all of them open to the public. No one who attended Returning the Gift got to see it all, be a part of it all, and we will be a long time wondering, and asking questions, about the parts we missed.

Happily, we will be able to find out, because we now know one another, because even after the readings, into the wee hours of the mornings, there was no way to stop the visiting. Not even the dictates of common sense or the pull of exhaustion could stop the talking, the networking, the exchanging of manuscripts, of ideas, of addresses.

The structure of the conference was such that each morning began with a plenary session in the Forum during which from three to six people gave speeches on that day's plenary session topic. These speeches, eighteen in all, are available on one eight-hour video cassette tape titled "Returning The Gift Video Tape" for $50, plus $1.50 for shipping and handling, from: Native American Writers Distribution Project, The Greenfield Review Literary Center, 2 Middle Grove Road, P.O. Box 308, Greenfield Center, New York 12833 (phone: 518-584-1728). Day #1, Tuesday, July 7th, Welcome by Jerry Bread of the University of Oklahoma, and by Eddie Wilson, Chairman of the Cheyenne-Arapaho Nation. Plenary Session #1, "Writing for Ourselves, Writing for Our Children—Native Writing and Native Identity," moderated by Roberta Hill Whiteman, with presentations by Virginia Driving Hawk Sneve, Ofelia Zepeda, and Harold Littlebird.

Day #2, Wednesday, July 8th, Opening by Ted C. Williams of the Tuscarora Nation. Plenary Session #2, "Emerging Native Images—Natives in the Media, Books and Texts," moderated by Doris Seale, with presentations by Jack Forbes, Greg Young-Ing, Simon Ortiz, Leslie Silko, Beth Brant, and Alex Jacobs.

Day #3, Thursday, July 9, Plenary Session #3, "Entering the Canons—Our Place in World Literature," moderated by Jeannette Armstrong, with presentations by Lincoln Tritt, David Daniel Moses, Duane Niatum, Lance Henson, Kimberly Blaeser, and Kelly Morgan.

Day #4, Friday, July 10, Opening by Roland Haig, of the Cheyenne Nation. Plenary Session #4, "Earth and the Circle of Life—Native Writers and the Environment," moderated by Linda Hogan, with presentations by Elizabeth Woody, Barney Bush, and Eleanor Sioui.

In the Spring, 1993 issue of Cornell University's Awe:kon Journal one may find extracts of the plenary session speeches of Kimberly Blaeser, Simon Ortiz, and Virginia Driving Hawk Sneve.

For one hour before lunch each day, Talking Circles were scheduled, which enabled conference participants who were not making presentations in a plenary session or a workshop or a panel discussion to have an opportunity to express themselves.

On Day #1 the afternoon concurrent workshop topics were: Writing the Essay, with Martin F. Dunn, Maurice Kenny, Marie Baker, and Rayna Green; Poetry Writing, with Cheryl Savageau, Eleanor Sioui, and Jean Starr; Short Story Writing, with Lee Maracle, Beth Brant, and Jim Northrup; Storytelling, with Vi Hilbert, Salli Benedict, and Sister Goodwin; and Using Computers for Writing, a workshop for high school students, with Jackie Crow-Hiendlmayr. The late afternoon concurrent panel discussion topics were: Writing for Our Children, with Doris Seale, Salli Benedict, Marilou Awiakta, Bernelda Wheeler, Laura Tohe, Lincoln Tritt, and Duane Big Eagle; Writing in Native Languages, with Ofelia Zepeda, Vi Hilbert, Jacinto Arias Perez, Rex Jim, and Rita Joe; Native Writing in the Classrooms, with Wendy Rose, Vee F. Browne, Ron Welburn, and Sylvester Brito; Using History in Native Writing, with Maurice Kenny, Raven Hail, Jose Barriero, Rayna Green, and Lincoln Tritt; and Native Literature and Education, with Janice Gould, Emma Lee Warrior, Ramona C. Wilson, and Eleanor Sioui.

On Day #2 the afternoon concurrent workshop topics were; Native Publishing and Getting Published, with Anna Lee Walters, Greg Young-Ing, William Oandasan, Andrew Hope, and Jose Barriero; Craft Workshop for Beginning Poets, with Roberta Hill Whiteman, Linda Noel, and Carol Lee Sanchez; Getting Started, a Workshop for Beginning Writers with Joel Monture and Anita Endrezze; Novel Writing, with LeAnn Howe and Beatrice Culleton; and Resources for Native Writers, with Jeanetta Calhoun, Elise Paschen, and Basil Johnson. The late afternoon concurrent panel discussion topics were: Telling Our Own Stories, Native Writing and Autobiography, with Maria Campbell, Nora Dauenhauer, Robert L. Perea, and A.C. Ross; Bringing Native Writing to the Schools, with Chrystos, Duane Big Eagle, and Lance Henson; Teaching Native Literature in Colleges and Universities, with Carrol Arnett, Gloria Bird, Carter Revard, and Denise Sweet; Native Images in Non-Native Writing, with Beth Brant and Joel Monture; and Native Images and Native Identity, with Jacinto Arias Perez, Jack D. Forbes, Robert A. Warrior, Gladys Cardiff, Mary Lockwood, and Jose Barriero.

On Day #3 the afternoon concurrent workshop topics were: Forming an Organization for North American Native Writers, with Fred Bigjim, Alice Sadongei, Victor Montejo, Elizabeth Woody, and Geary Hobson; Script-Writing, with Russell Bates and Jordan Wheeler; Presenting Yourself as a Professional, with Rayna Green; Poetry Workshop, with Wendy Rose, Gloria Bird, Marie Baker, and Sherman Alexie; and Novel Writing, with Robert J. Conley and Anna L. Walters. The late afternoon panel discussion topics were: Native Writing in Mexico and Guatemala, with Victor Montejo; Native Writing in French, with Eleanor Sioui and Bernard Assiniwi; Spiderwoman Theatre, with Lisa Mayo, Gloria Miguel, and Muriel Miguel; European Views on Native Writing, with Jeannette Armstrong; and Native Writing and Contemporary Native Issues, with Haunani Kay Trask, Charlotte DeClue, Elizabeth Woody, Annette Arkeketa, and Tracey Kim Bonneau.

On Day #4 there were no concurrent workshops so that an Open Forum plenary session might be held in the late afternoon. In the early afternoon the concurrent panel discussion topics were: Native Writing, the Environment and Politics, with Elizabeth Cook-Lynn, Ssipsis, and Gail Tremblay; Sacred Circles, with Ted C. Williams, Carol L. Sanchez, Ramson Lomatewama, and Laura Tohe; Native Writers and the New Age, Deep Ecology, the Men's Movement, with Mary Goose, LeAnn Howe, and Alex Jacobs; Contemporary Native Writing and the Oral Tradition, with Diane Burns, Sister Goodwin, and Melissa Fawcett Sayet; and Native Gay and Lesbian Writing, Part of the Circle, with Beth Brant, Chrystos, Janice Gould, Vickie L. Sears, Craig Womack, and Kelly Morgan.

There was a lot of anger expressed at the festival, anger at the way non-Natives have portrayed Native peoples in works of history, anger at the way Native literature, poetry and fiction is evaluated by Eurocentric literary conceptions, anger that abysmally ignorant people such as television's Andy Rooney of 60 Minutes can have the platform of a newspaper column to proclaim the senselessness of Native values in the contemporary world, anger at New Age, non-Native commercial exploitation of sweat baths and sacred ceremonials, anger at the contemptuous attitude of prison officials for the cultural and religious rights of incarcerated Native peoples, anger at appalling rates of suicide and its aftermath, anger at the callous indifference of governmental institutions to the needs of urban Indians, anger at the seemingly unopposable plans to dump nuclear waste on Indian reservations, anger at stereotyping, anger at the well-meaning, unintentionally destructive activities of friends, anger at the murder of an employee of a Native publishing house in Canada, anger that Native writers from portions of Central America cannot share the places of their youth with their own children because they are on a death list, anger at the intimidation and racial slurs and threats of physical violence of bigots against Native voices, including those of poets who refuse to be cowed into submission, but who do not relish the thought of becoming martyrs.

In workshops and in panel discussions and in plenary session speeches and in casual conversation and in readings, these angers were voiced in an environment that made networking a natural thing—the joining together in common cause, the offering of support and knowledge and resources, one to another.

Where there were angers, there were also joys, joy in the appreciation of the literary work of others, joy in hearing a poet read a poem that some people listening knew by heart, joy in the insuppressible humour of Native peoples, joy in being brought together to share with one another, to draw strength from one another.

When poets and other literary writers are filled with angers and joys the predictable result is writing and publishing. Much publishing will result from the energies generated at the festival. Joseph Bruchac will edit an anthology of the work of festival participants, to be published by Studies In American Indian Literatures and the University of Arizona Press.

Periodicals and publishing houses throughout the continent will receive manuscripts and book proposals from festival participants, many of the ideas for which were conceived during the festival, many of them a direct result of vigorously discussed topics in workshops and panel discussions and plenary session speeches, and casual conversation.

An immediate result of the festival was the formation of a Native Writer's Circle of the Americas, with a quarterly newsletter, edited by Joseph Bruchac, and available for a $24 subscription from the Greenfield Review Literary Center. Bruchac is serving as Acting Chair, and the Interim Board consists of Ann Acco, Jeannette Armstrong, Joseph Bruchac, Jack Forbes, Lee Frances, Geary Hobson, Andrew Hope, Victor Montejo, Sandra Orie, Jacineto Arias Perez, Suzanne Rancourt, Philip H. Red Eagle, and Dorothy Thorsen,

Plans were made to have another large, international Returning the Gift conference every fourth year, with smaller regional conferences during the intervening years. In furtherance of this plan a southwest regional Returning the Gift conference was scheduled at the University of Oklahoma for July 9 and 10, 1993, sponsored by the Bay Foundation and the College of Arts and Sciences of the University of Oklahoma.

The Bay Foundation also provided a supplemental grant to retire the $20,000 deficit incurred at the 1992 festival. Sponsors for the 1992 festival included the Geraldine R. Dodge Foundation, the W.K. Kellogg Foundation, the State Arts Council of Oklahoma, the Bay Foundation, the New York Times Foundation, the College of Arts and Sciences of the University of Oklahoma, the Josephine Bay Paul and Michael Paul Foundation, the Poetry Society of America, the Wingspread Foundation, and the Winner Byner Foundation.

The festival steering committee met in Wisconsin, New York and New Mexico as early as 1989. It consisted of: Joseph Bruchac, Chairperson, Phillip Lujan and Dorscine Spigner-Littles, University Liaison, Mary Jo Watson, Community Liaison, Barbara Hobson, Project Coordinator, Gloria Sly, Assistant Project Coordinator, Geary Hobson, Project Historian, and steering committee members Jeannette Armstrong, Nora Daauenhauer, Rayna Green, Ted Jojola, Maurice Kenny, Gail Tremblay, Lisa Mayo, Victor Montejo, Carter Revard, Alyce Sadongei, Virginia Driving Hawk Sneve, and Lucy Tapahonso. The festival advisory board consisted of N. Scott Momaday, Peter McDonald, Paula Gunn Allen, A. LaVonne Brown Ruoff, Jose

Barriero, Tim Troy, Larry Evers, Gerald Vizenor, Joy Harjo, and James Welch. The festival staff included Susan Shannon Gray, Secretary, Jeannetta Calhoun, Publicity Coordinator, Kelly Morgan and Craig Womack, graduate student assistants, and Sean Oberly and Michael Bread, student assistants. The facilities staff was led by Dr. Linda Norton, Director, and Phyllis Walls, coordinator. Twenty-seven festival volunteers assisted the festival staff, and thirty local Native writers served as hosts to assist festival participants in answering questions about the area.

To help increase the amount of Native writing being published, a new organization was formed, the Wordcraft Circle of Native American Mentor & Apprentice Writers, which has paired eighty Native mentor writers with eighty apprentice writers in a one-on-one, year-long mentoring relationship, exchanging manuscripts and critiques through the mail. Under the direction of Lee Francis, National Director/ Editor, the 1993-1994 national advisory caucus consists of D.L.Birchfield, Beth Brant, Joseph Bruchac, Blue Clark, Robert J. Conley, Karl Gilmont, Janice Gould, Rayna Green, Clara Sue Kidwell, Paulette Fairbanks Molin, Nita Pahdopony, Bill Penn, A.C. Ross, Laura Tohe, and Anna Lee Walters. Newsletters for Wordcraft Circle include the Wordcraft Circle Forum and the Moccasin Telegraph. A literary quarterly is being planned, as well as an anthology to showcase the best writing of each apprentice, along with the critique of the mentor. Four regional Wordcraft Circle writing workshops are being conducted throughout the United States in 1993. The first one took place in New York City on July 1 and 2, which was attended by twenty-five Native writers. Anyone desiring information about Wordcraft Circle programs may write: Wordcraft Circle, 2951 Ellenwood Drive, Fairfax, VA 22031-2038 or call (703)280-1028.

Native theatre was an important part of the festival. A Native theatre production was presented by Spiderwoman Theatre, which also presented a workshop, another play was presented by Ed Edmo (Through Coyote's Eyes, written by Ed Edmo), another one was presented by Gloria Miguel (Grandma, written by Hanay Geiogamah), and Returning the Gift featured the debut performance of Grandpa, written by Hanay Geiogamah, and directed and performed by Joe Cross. The festival inspired a proposal for a newsletter for Native playwrights, and in the spring of 1993 the Native Playwrights' Newsletter made its debut, edited by Paul Rathbun. Three issues per year are planned, at an annual subscription rate of $10 from: Native Playwrights' Newsletter. P.O. Box 1364, Madison, WI 53701-1364. The premiere issue is available for $5 (608) 277-0097.

Other publishing projects have resulted from the festival. One of them is the 1993 Directory of the Native Writer's Circle of the Americas, listing more than 200 Native writers, including tribal affiliation, address, phone, and a bibliography of selected works, available from the American Indian Program, National Museum of

American History/5119, Smithsonian Institution, Washington, DC 20560.

Another reference book, edited by Kelly Morgan (Lakota) and Kay Juricek Lyons, will consist of biographies of Native American authors of North America who have published their work between 1961 and 1991, containing answers to questions that many authors would love to have a chance to answer, including major influences on one's life, whether you had a mentor, whose work influenced you the most, where you grew up—to be published by North American Press, a subsidiary of Fulcrum Press, Golden, Colorado.

Several books will be published as a direct result of manuscripts submitted to the festival competition for the First Book Awards. At the festival awards banquet, the second night of the festival, where N. Scott Momaday was presented a life-time achievement award, The Returning The Gift Native Writer's Festival First Book Awards were presented: The Diane Decorah Memorial Award for Poetry was shared by Joe Dale Tate Nevaquaya (Comanche) for Leaving Holes and by Gloria Byrd for Moon Over The Reservation: the Louis Littlecoon Oliver Memorial Award for Short Fiction was presented to Robert Perea (Oglala Sioux) for Stacey's Story: the Richard Margolis Memorial Award for Creative Non-Fiction was presented to Melissa Fawcett Sayett for The Lasting of the Mohegans: and the Drama Award was presented to William S. Yellow Robe, Jr. (Assiniboine) for The Star Quilter. These books will be published by Contact II Press, Snowbird Publishing Co., and the Greenfield Review Press.

The first two days of the festival were by invitation only, an opportunity for the Native writers to get acquainted in a relaxed environment without distractions. On the third day of the festival, non-Native people and Native people who have a special relationship with Native literature were invited to attend. One corridor was filled with the promotional tables of university presses, to augment another corridor which had been filled from the first day with the displays of Native publishing houses. Editors and publishers and university press representatives added a new rhythm to the pace of things. Ben Carnes (Choctaw) was there, who, to the embarrassment of the Oklahoma Department of Corrections, for his assertion of the religious rights of incarcerated Native peoples, received the Oklahoma Human Rights Award while still incarcerated. Professors from the University of Oklahoma and other universities came to visit, some of them deeply involved in publishing Native voices, such as Alan Velie, editor of The Lightning Within.

Also on the third day, the Returning the Gift 1992 group photo (11x14 inches, colour) was distributed by Cole Studio, 2600 Acacia Ct, Norman, OK 73072. One hundred and sixty-one people showed up for the group photo, which was taken at 5 P.M. on Tuesday. It was

211

windy the moment the photo was snapped, as Betty Louise Bell can testify. Those who are pictured, in seven rows of bleachers assembled for the occasion, are:

First row: Gail Tremblay, Vee F. Browne, Rosa Jean Howling Buffalo, Vickie L. Sears, Beth Brant, Anne Anderson, LeAnne Howe, Philip Red-Eagle, Lisa Mayo, Rudy Martin, Elizabeth Cook-Lynn, Vi Hilbert, A.C. Ross, Basil H. Johnston, Russell M. Peters, Wendy Rose, Catron Grieves, Rayna Green, Joel Monture, Joy Harjo, Krista Chico, Bernelda Wheeler, E.K. Kim Caldwell, Helen Slwooko Carius, and Lana Grant.

Second row: Carol Lee Sanchez, Jeannette Armstrong, Camela Pappan, Geary Hobson, Barbara Hobson, Gloria E. Sly, Melissa Fawcett Sayet, Gayle Ross, Janice Gould, Linda Hogan, Ellen White, Lee Maracle, Jo Ann Trujillo, Grace Slwooko, Tina Villalobos, Carter Revard, Gary McLain, Beatrice Harrell, Bernice Armstrong, Susan Arkeketa, Barney Bush, Bobbie Bush, Jean Starr, Boyd E. Pinto, Mario Perfecto Tema, and Shelley Montalvo.

Third row: Robert Gish, Lance Henson, Mary Goose, Laura Tohe, Marilou Awiakta, Gloria Miguel, Lee Frances, Dorothy Thorsen, William Oandasan, Ron Welburn, Jack D. Forbes, Simon J. Ortiz, Robert L. Perea, Richard G. Green, Annette Arkeketa, Ofelia Zepeda, Carroll Arnett, Helen Chalakee Burgess, Ssipisi, Linda Poolaw, Ed Edmo, Phyliss Walls, Joe Dale Nevaquaya, Cody Chalakee.

Fourth row: Linda Noel, Maurice Kenny, Ted Williams, Theresa Palmer, Jose Camposeco, Russell L. Bates, Miryam Yataco, Duane Niatum, Sherman Alexie, Gloria Bird, Elizabeth Woody, Diane E. Benson, Brian Maracle, Armand Garnet Ruffo, Raven Hail, Leta Rector, Michael Edmonds, Marie Frawley-Henry, Vincent Wannasay, Ann Brady, Anne Acco, Bob Perry, and Harold Littlebird.

Fifth row: Glen Simpson, Alex Jacobs, Robert Warrior, Hortensia Colorado, Elvira Colorado, Betty Louise Bell, Nora Dauenhauer, Dick Dauenhauer, Ramona Wilson, Duane Big Eagle, Joe Bruchac, Carol Bruchac, Ramson Lomatewama, Rex Jim, Cheryl Savageau, Judith Volborth, Doris Seale, Shirley Brozzo, Lincoln Tritt, Diane Schenandoah and Victor Garcia.

Sixth row: Sean Oberly, Michael G. Bread, (staff), Susan Shannan, (staff), Kimberly M. Blaeser, Greg Young-Ing, Cora Weber-Pillwax, Roberta Hill Whiteman, Darlene Speidel, Emma Lee Warrior, Lorenzo Baca, Eric Gansworth, Barry Milliken, Fredy Roncolla, Ronald Burns Querry, Jose Garza, Louis Gray, Charles Redcorn, Yancey Redcorn, Shirlee Winder and D.L. Birchfield.

Seventh row: Moses Jumper, Jr., Nila Northsun, Denise Sweet, Al Hunter, Jordan Wheeler, Alootook Ipellie, Earle Thompson, Michael Simpson, Margaret Sisk, Robert Sisk, Jim Northrup, Jose Barreiro, Alyce Sadongei, Richard Whiteman, Dewayne Mathews,

Robin Coffee, Robert J. Conley, Eddie Webb, Mary Lockwood, Murv Jacob, Duane K. Hale, and V. Blanchard Singing Eagle.

On the fourth day the general public was invited to register and participate in the festival. New faces appeared in the workshops and other festival sessions. Elders from the community also came to visit, among them John Aunko (Kiowa), former member of the board of directors of the Oklahoma City Native American Center, who would be invited to give a welcome at the 1993 conference. By the fourth day people who shared deep knowledge in some specialized field had discovered one another. Many sat in awe of the intense discussions of theories of literary criticism between Michael Wilson (who was writing his doctoral dissertation at Cornell) and Betty Louise Bell, of Berkeley, on her way to teach at Harvard, and then to the University of Michigan (who would shortly be elected vice-president of ASAIL, the Association for the Study of American Indian Literature).

There were poignant moments at the festival. No one present at one afternoon panel discussion could fail to be moved by the spontaneous outburst of warmth and feeling from an audience that overflowed the room when Annette Arkeketa (Otoe-Missouria/Creek) introduced her parents, who had travelled to Norman to hear her presentation.

There were hilarious moments at the festival. Vincent Wannasay had an entire roomful of people in tears, the big kind that roll down the cheeks when you cannot stop laughing, at one evening reading as he detailed the life of a porcupine with an ingrown quill.

There were unforgettable moments at the festival. One occurred at 11:10 P.M., when a weary audience had already listened to the readings of fifteen poets that evening, and not for the first night either, when Haunani Kay-Trask, Hawai'ian, Director of Hawai'ian Studies at the University of Hawai'i, sister of Mililani, stepped to the microphone and electrified her suddenly attentive listeners, chronicling the struggles of native Hawai'ians to establish some vestige of sovereignty in their militarily conquered native land. It started the moment she began speaking, and by the time she began reading her poetry we would have collapsed before we would have stopped listening.

And that's how many who attended the festival will remember it—a time when there was too much to be doing to be bothered by sleep. A special time. A rare time. A time of receiving a gift to be returned.

Nearly everyone present would report, in the following months, an infusion of energy. Manuscripts poured forth from these Native writers, and they are pouring out of them still. Philip Red-Eagle, a founder and a co-editor of The Raven Chronicles, would be inspired to return home and set down some of his most deeply wrenching emotional experiences in the form of short stories. The result, his first short story collection, <u>Red Earth: Native American Experiences In Vietnam,</u> would win the Louis Littlecoon Oliver Memorial Prose Award at the 1993 regional conference of Returning the Gift: Southwest Native American Voices, again at the Forum, on the campus of the University of Oklahoma, July 9 and 10, 1993, where approximately sixty Native literary writers gathered, most of them at their own expense, from Oklahoma, and from Canada, Washington, Oregon, California, Arizona, New Mexico, Texas, Arkansas, Missouri, Iowa, South Dakota, Wisconsin, Michigan, Virginia, Massachusetts, New York, and Florida, to honour Simon J. Ortiz, who, by vote open to the entire membership of the Native Writers Circle of the Americas, received the 1993 Lifetime Achievement Award. At this conference tentative plans were made to hold the 1994 Returning the Gift regional conference in the Pacific Northwest, in the early summer of 1994, at a site yet to be determined.

Kimberly M. Blaeser said, shortly after the 1992 festival, "...not until I was back home and still experiencing day after day, wave after wave of the incredible feelings of the conference did I realize it would ever after affect my work and how I view it, did I come to a better understanding of what you all intuited about 'Returning the Gift'. It seems that it will always go on, just like gift-giving always does in Indian Country, where people keep giving back and forth and back and forth in love and repayment for love received." She would return home from the 1992 festival to write a volume of poetry entitled <u>Trailing You,</u> which would win the Diane Decorah Memorial Poetry Award at the 1993 Returning the Gift conference.

There is a plaque on the outside wall of the Thurman J. White Forum Building at the Oklahoma Center for Continuing Education. The plaque tells of a time capsule enclosed behind the bricks in the wall. It tells about the ceremony, long ago, when the capsule was buried, and it tells about all the distinguished members of the university community, most of them now deceased, who wrote papers for the occasion, papers which are contained in the time capsule, and it gives a date, far in the future, when the capsule, with proper ceremony, is to be opened. Something like that happened at Returning the Gift in 1992, both the planting of something like a time capsule, and the opening of one, too.